POISON PILL

a novel

M.A. GRANOVSKY

Swimming Otter Press

Poison Pill
All Rights Reserved.
Copyright © 2012 M. A. Granovsky
v3.0

Cover Design by Christine Van Bree, copyright © 2012 M. A. Granovsky.

Cover art work (composite): running woman © Andy and Michelle Kerry/Trevillion Images; capsule © Steffan L. Jones/Arcangel Images; Istanbul skyline © Peeter Viisimaa/istockphoto.com <http://istockphoto.com>

Swimming Otter Press

ISBN: 978-0-578-11138-4

Library of Congress Control Number: 2012947919

PRINTED IN THE UNITED STATES OF AMERICA

To my parents
Thank you for teaching me to love books and travel,
and for not thinking it at all strange
to want to write a novel.

Peter Gardiner's suicide merited a Breaking News bulletin on CNN. His body was found by a couple of hikers coming back from an afternoon trek. He was slumped on a park bench near the exit from the Palisades State Park, on the New Jersey side of the Hudson River, his right hand still gripping the gun with which he'd shot himself. His Baltic Black Maybach 57-S was in the parking lot, and his suicide note, addressed to his wife and handwritten, was found inside a manila envelope on the driver's seat.

Of course, most of these details were not communicated in CNN's bulletin. Instead, the news channel concentrated on Gardiner's achievements. He was a renowned economist who created and managed a family of well-regarded and highly profitable venture and hedge funds. He was on the Economic Advisory Panel for the current president as well as his two immediate predecessors. His status as a fixture of New York society and his patronage of the arts was also duly noted.

Benedict Vickers caught the last few seconds of the bulletin as he walked into the living room from the kitchen, wiping his hands after washing his coffee mug. The news made him stop. He slung the dish towel over his shoulder and quickly grabbed the remote to see whether other channels were also discussing this development. None were.

Benedict returned to CNN, increased the volume and dropped the remote onto the leather armchair next to him.

They'll return to the story soon enough, he assured himself, and walked back into the kitchen. His phone rang just then and he picked up on the first ring.

"Did you see the news?"

"Just caught the tail end of it on CNN. That was unexpected."

"Are you being sarcastic?"

"No. I really am surprised."

"Are you okay?"

"I didn't think he'd off himself. Poor Jennie. She doesn't deserve this."

"Does it change our plans?"

"I don't think so. Although I'd rather leave the country today instead of waiting until Friday. Come with, won't you?"

There was a long pause on the other end of the line.

"Please?" Benedict prompted gently.

"I'll meet you at Grand Central and decide there."

Benedict sighed with relief. "Right. By the information booth in the middle? In an hour?"

"See you there."

Benedict hung up and headed to the third floor of his townhouse, taking two steps at a time. In his bedroom, he took a small suitcase out of the closet and checked its contents. It was nearly fully packed, and he decided it only required the addition of toiletries, a pair of socks, and a pair of cuff links.

After quickly showering and changing, he went downstairs and scanned his suitcase and himself for tracking devices with a hand-held wand, silently cursing his paranoia, but not willing to take a chance. Satisfied that he wasn't a walking beacon, he armed the state-of-the-art alarm system he'd recently installed and left the house.

PART I

Chapter 1

October 14, 2010 (eight months earlier)

Terminal 1 at John F. Kennedy International Airport wasn't busy when the chauffeured Lincoln Town Car dropped Benedict off. Having ascertained that he had all necessary documents, he grabbed the handle of his suitcase, hoisted his carry-on bag onto his shoulder, and proceeded to the Turkish Airlines business class check-in counter.

As the ticketing agent was printing his boarding pass, Benedict's attention was drawn to the tall woman standing next to him, talking to an agent designated for coach passengers. The woman seemed excited, clapping her hands and beaming widely. Benedict, finding the behavior childish, raised an eyebrow and gave her a frosty, questioning stare.

"Upgrade to business class," the woman informed him, still beaming and looking up at him with startlingly light blue eyes. At least she'd stopped clapping. "Sorry about the seal imitation," she said, not looking sorry at all. Benedict sighed and said a silent prayer that his seat would be as far away from the woman's as possible. Despite finding her attractive, she struck him as a talker, and he was in no mood for that.

———◦((◦))◦———

Olga Mueller was thrilled to learn she'd be able to upgrade to business class on her flight to Istanbul. She took it as a sign that the rest of her airport and flight experiences would be just as easy, and indeed, she breezed through security in five minutes, leaving her with almost three hours to wander around the dingy corridors or sit in the worn out chairs near the gate.

Neither the shabbiness of the airport nor the ridiculousness of its ever-changing security regulations could dampen her mood at that moment. She had time to herself, a rarity in Olga's world. The fact that she wasn't at work and couldn't reasonably be expected to cater to every whim of whatever stray partner who wanted something from her felt like an exotic luxury. She was giddy with possibilities. She could read a book; she could sit and do nothing; she could drink coffee and eat a donut without the crumbs littering a work document.

Olga was an attorney at Kress, Rubinoff & Twist PLLC. With a web of eight offices spanning six continents, 612 attorneys, 1058 support staff, and $2.8 M in average annual profits per partner, Kress Rubinoff was at the top of the global legal food chain. As an associate, Olga was expected to be available 24/7, carry her firm-issued BlackBerry at all times, and check it at least once an hour. There were few acceptable exceptions to this rule but an international flight still qualified as one such *bona fide* reason to disconnect.

The BlackBerry vibrated and blinked its red eye from the outside pocket of her handbag, reminding Olga that the international flight exception unfortunately didn't encompass the time in the airport prior to embarkation. Her jaw clenched as she debated whether she could get away with ignoring the incoming messages. But reflex won out and, instead of shutting her BlackBerry off, she began scrolling through the twenty-seven new messages that had queued up while she was checking in and going through security.

Ignoring all firm-wide messages not directed at her specifically, Olga concentrated on the eight that were sent only to her. One was from her friend Cindy, asking if she had time to go to dinner that evening, and seven were from Eric McIvor, the partner she worked with most. Olga chose to read and answer Cindy's message first.

"Would love to go to dinner," she typed, "but am at JFK, flying to Istanbul, where will be pulling ten-hour days sorting boring, dusty & useless docs for pending litigation. Will be in Istanbul and will have no chance to see any sights. Can you tell I'm bitter?"

While waiting for Cindy's reply, in which Cindy would be duty-bound as a friend and fellow attorney to offer unqualified commiseration, Olga began reviewing McIvor's messages, by now numbering twelve, with the last four carrying a red exclamation mark denoting high priority.

Honestly, he's like a child, she thought. When McIvor wanted something it had to be done that instant. She moved to the nearest seat, dropped the laptop case onto it, then sat on the edge of the adjacent seat. Chewing on a nail absent-mindedly, she started reading McIvor's messages.

They made no sense to her. They concerned some case she wasn't involved in, one in which the parties had apparently finally settled. He was directing her to drop everything, review and mark up the draft settlement agreement attached to his first e-mail, and send him the marked-up version with whatever changes she thought were needed. The rest of the messages were iterations of the same thing, each more hysterical in tone than the last.

The man has some kind of chemical imbalance, Olga thought, not for the first time. Here she was, at the airport, ready to fly to Turkey on another of McIvor's cases and she was supposed to review a 64-page settlement agreement negotiated in a case she knew nothing about, then opine on the suitability of its provisions in a neatly typed, well-reasoned e-mail, suitable for forwarding to the client.

Giving McIvor the benefit of the doubt, Olga decided he must have forgotten which of his associates worked on which of his cases. Therefore, she responded to his last e-mail by explaining that it wasn't her case, that it was Robert's. McIvor replied almost instantly. "I know. I want you to look at the settlement agreement. Do you have a problem with that?"

Olga did have a problem with that. Or several. She debated whether to elaborate by e-mail or chance a tongue lashing from the increasingly irate McIvor by calling him. Her fear of McIvor's temper won. She spent the next several minutes explaining where she was and why she couldn't do what he was asking of her. Then she changed the settings of her BlackBerry to "quiet," so it only blinked but no longer vibrated with each new incoming message, and dropped it into the depths of her handbag. She knew that her refusal to further engage with McIvor was an act of grand disobedience and that her chances of continuing employment with Kress Rubinoff were diminishing with each such display of attitude, but she no longer cared. She was tired.

Olga tried to get back the sense of exhilaration she had before becoming aware of McIvor's e-mails, but to no avail. She couldn't rid herself of the mounting mixture of stress and anger that was by now shaking her physically. She decided to find a bar and down a double vodka to calm her nerves. Normally, she would have rejected this option for fear of slowly descending into the attorney alcoholic cliché she never wanted to become. But this time her state was unusually acute, coming as it did on the tail of a period in which she had worked thirty-eight fifteen-hour days in a row. She gathered her belongings and walked to the nearest saloon.

Climbing onto a bar stool, Olga reflexively fished out her blinking BlackBerry but willed herself to leave it on the bar rather than read the incoming messages. She rotated it so its evil red eye faced away from her and ordered her double shot of Smirnoff.

While waiting for her vodka to be poured, Olga swiveled around to survey her fellow patrons. The man sitting one seat over from her looked familiar. She noticed he was reading a book titled *Advances in Turkish Metallurgy, Twelfth Century B.C. to the Present*, and that helped place him as the man who had glared at her so disapprovingly while checking in at the business class counter. By his looks, she didn't peg him to be Turkish.

As friendly a person as Olga was generally, she tended to keep to herself with strangers, especially the good-looking ones, like her fellow barfly. She'd already noticed his height and his athletic build and admired his easy gait as he walked away from the check-in counter, but now she had an opportunity to observe him in greater detail. By the lines forming on his face and his tan, she guessed he was in his mid-thirties and loved the outdoors. His hands were finely shaped, with long fingers, and no wedding ring or indentation or tan line where one would have been. Just then, the man turned to speak with the bartender and Olga was struck anew by the unusually dark grey color of his eyes, and by their coldness.

But the grey-eyed man was her only viable option for a conversation partner. She weighed her discomfort at speaking to someone that striking and unfriendly against her discomfort at drinking alone, and the latter won. *What doesn't kill me makes me stronger*, she thought, while downing her double shot in one gulp. Taking a deep breath, she turned back to face her target.

"Hi!" she began brightly, only to earn a scowl and a withering flash of the man's eyes, leading her to finish in a much quieter tone. "We're on the same flight."

"So are hundreds of other passengers," the man responded and turned back to his book. Olga blushed and was mortified to feel her eyes smarting as she hurried to turn away. She hadn't expected her opening to go that badly.

The man glanced over at her, taking in the empty shot glass standing in front of her just as it was making friends with a fresh, full one, and appeared to soften. "I apologize.

That was rude even by my standards. Rough day?" he asked, indicating the shot glasses with his chin.

"You could say that. And apology accepted. For the record, I don't make it a habit to speak to strangers in bars. Chatting with you was supposed to provide the illusion that this is a social drink and not an I-will-crawl-out-of-my-skin-with-stress-unless-I-have-a-shot drink."

The man hesitated a moment, deciding between brushing Olga off and continuing their interaction. With a sigh, he marked the page where he stopped reading with a bar napkin and turned back to Olga. A hint of a smile lit his face as he extended his hand. "I'm Benedict. If nothing else, you do have a novel approach to conversations."

"If you chat with me long enough, you'll experience all sorts of nonsensical and non-linear discussions, I promise. I'm Olga." They shook hands and Olga was surprised by the calluses on his palm. She didn't guess him to be a man who earned his living by hard physical labor.

"Isn't your BlackBerry company enough for you? It's been blinking nonstop since you sat down."

"The BlackBerry is not company, or at least not friendly company." She picked up the device and scrolled through the new messages. "In fact, it's the source of the trauma that has led me to drink this afternoon. I'm communicating with my deranged boss. Or to be more accurate, he's communicating with me. Now in all capitals. Bolded."

"What about?" asked Benedict, appearing genuinely interested in her answer. Olga obliged with a short description of her back and forth with McIvor. She heard her cell phone ring, but by the time she fished it out of her bag, the call had gone to voicemail. She recognized the number as McIvor's and vacillated about whether to listen to the message.

"Was that him?" Benedict asked, then took a sip of his martini.

Olga nodded in response.

"Go on then, put him on speaker. I'd love to hear what this ogre sounds like."

"If you insist." Olga accessed her voicemail without much enthusiasm.

"Olga, this is Eric. I'm sick of the fucking attitude you're giving me here. I don't give a shit where you are, what you're doing, how you're feeling, or what else you've got going on. You're my associate, and you do what I tell you to do. If I tell you to wipe my goddamned ass you ask what brand of toilet paper you should use. Now go find a fucking printer, mark up the proposed settlement agreement and get it back to me before your flight leaves. We're talking about hundreds of millions of dollars of the client's money here. For once, just show a little dedication to your job. Please."

Olga felt rage welling up, but was distracted by Benedict's laughter. She glared at him only to feel her anger dissolve as she realized just how absurd it all must sound to any sane listener. She couldn't help but laugh then, too.

"I don't know why it's funny," she said. "I could lose my job over this. It doesn't matter how irrational his demands are. He owns me."

"You must admit that the toilet paper brand comment is an interesting update on the 'I say jump and you ask how high' adage," answered Benedict. "And he does not own you. As a lawyer you of all people should know that slavery was outlawed here a while back."

"Sorry, I need to deal with this right now before it spirals out of control any further. When the bartender comes back this way, can you please order me another double shot and a Cobb salad?" She slid off the stool and headed to an empty corner with her cell phone, noticing with satisfaction that Benedict swiveled to watch her depart.

———◦❖◦———

Olga returned a few minutes later looking much happier. "All handled then?" asked Benedict.

"Yep. I found Robert, the associate who's actually on this case and who didn't know anything about the settlement. He contacted another partner on the case, who contacted my insane boss and pretended that he'd already instructed Robert to mark up the agreement. So I'm off the hook. Part of me is sad that we calmed McIvor down. He's less likely to develop an aneurism or a fatal heart attack."

"And these byzantine machinations are normal in your world?"

"Normal? That's an interesting term. Frequent, certainly. But I hope not to stay at that place long enough for them to appear normal to me." Olga drank from the water glass the bartender had placed on the bar along with her ordered shot.

"What kind of lawyer are you?" asked Benedict

"A litigatrix. I still love saying the word even though I loathe what being one entails. I litigate patent-related matters."

"Your firm sounds like a modern-day torture chamber."

"It's not just my firm. Most big law firms are similar. Come to think of it, though, this firm does have an unusually high asshole quotient."

"My brother used to say that every situation is either a good situation or a good story. I'll bet you have some good stories."

Olga sighed. "I have thousands."

"Tell me a few."

Olga stared at the liquor bottles behind the bar unseeingly, trying to come up with a particularly illustrative example.

"Okay," she said, turning back to Benedict and again becoming disconcerted by his looks. "My best friend was marrying a Marine who served three tours in Afghanistan and two in Iraq. He was given short leave just to get married before being sent back. There was no way I was missing this wedding, but because of work I planned to fly out on Friday evening and come back on Sunday afternoon. Except that McIvor had other ideas. He went ballistic when I reminded him that I was taking part of that weekend off. Turned out he'd screwed up and had forgotten to give me an assignment the client was expecting on the following Monday, an assignment that had sat on his desk for over a month by then.

"I really thought that the mention of Marines and Afghanistan would shut him up, but I was wrong. He said, 'I don't care if it's your own sister coming back from Mars to get married.' The choice was clear, either cancel the trip or face the possibility of losing the job."

"And did you? Cancel the trip, I mean?"

"I didn't. But I did work at the airport, and at the hotel,

and through the night after the reception."

"Let me guess. McIvor met you with flowers and chocolates when you returned."

Olga laughed. "No, he met me with deafening silence on this matter for the next couple of weeks. When I finally asked about the client's reaction to my memo, he said 'Didn't I tell you? The client called me on the Friday before the deadline and said he wasn't going forward with the project. So I never sent him your memo. It was a real bitch convincing Kress,' that's our managing partner, 'to write off your time. Why did you spend so many hours on it anyway?'"

Benedict shook his head. "Brilliant!"

"Oh, and here's a doozy!" Olga continued. "It's Christmas Eve two years ago. A male partner and a female associate leave a deposition together. He's 6'3", 350 pounds easy. She's 5'1", 100 pounds soaking wet. Leaving aside the fact that she's schlepping all the deposition materials in a heavy box while he is carrying just a dainty Hermès leather briefcase, he spots a homeless man sprawled on the sidewalk and wants to do something good because it's Christmas. So he fishes a twenty out of his wallet, gives it to the associate, and tells her to give it to the homeless man. He actually says, 'I'm too disgusted to touch the guy myself, so you go give it to him.'" Olga stopped and took a deep breath. "Okay, that's plenty. There's a fine line between telling stories and devolving into a psychotic rant."

Benedict picked an olive out of his martini glass and chewed reflectively. "Why don't you leave?" he asked eventually.

"I plan to. Just as soon as I figure out what I want to be

when I grow up." Olga passed her finger along the rim of her shot glass, seeing if she could make it sing. She was growing bored with the conversation. It was far too similar to the reel that was constantly playing in her mind. "Can we please change the subject? If I spend so much of my discretionary time speaking about Kress Rubinoff then they win, and I'm determined not to let them."

Benedict raised an eyebrow. "Do they even know you're at war with them?"

"Probably not, which is even more frustrating. Seriously, new topic, please. Impotent rage is not an attractive emotion."

Benedict looked down into his martini glass. "I'm very familiar with impotent rage," he said quietly, but didn't elaborate.

Olga unilaterally decided to switch directions before the conversation descended into even greater gloom. "Why are you going to Istanbul?" she asked.

"Research." Benedict brightened in response to the new topic. "I'm a historian specializing in the Ottoman Empire. I go over at least twice a year because much of what I need is in the Imperial archives."

"I'd have thought these papers would be digitized by now to minimize human contact with the originals."

"Many have been, but thankfully not all. Life's going to be awful once everything is available online and there's no good excuse to travel for work."

"That would be a bleak world, indeed. So you're an academic? Tenured?"

Benedict smiled. "And by 'tenured' you're implying old," he teased Olga, who shook her head vehemently at his remark. "No, I'm still working on my Ph.D.," he explained. "And yes, I am well over thirty."

"You're a grad student?" Olga's eyes widened in surprise. "How does a grad student afford business class?" she asked, and immediately regretted her intrusion into his finances even though Benedict didn't seem to take offense.

"Trust fund. Mine's not sufficient to make working for a living unnecessary, but it does help to make life more civilized. You do ask a lot of questions, don't you," he said when Olga looked like she was about to speak again, but his smile neutralized some of the sting his words carried.

"Yes," she said, biting off the question she actually wanted to ask. Then she suddenly gasped. "Rock climbing!"

"Sorry, what?" Benedict appeared confused.

"Your hand. I've been racking my brain trying to remember what those calluses reminded me of, and I finally got it. My friend climbs and his hand feels like yours. Sorry, got us completely off topic, but I did warn you of my tendency to do so."

"Quite all right. What else can you deduce, Sherlock?"

"Alas, not much. You spent your formative years in England but you've been living in the U.S. for a while now. At some point in the last few years you lost between twenty and thirty pounds. You're a smoker who's trying to quit, hence the nicotine gum in your bag's pocket."

Olga paused to drink her vodka. "I scare my father when I say vodka tastes sweet to me," she said. "In Russia, that was considered the sign of a true alcoholic."

"So your name fits. You are Russian."

"Not ethnically. I was born in Russia, but my parents are

— 15 —

German on the one side and Jewish on the other. Queue long argument about whether Judaism is only a religion or an ethnicity, but in the Soviet Union it was considered an ethnicity so that's how I define it, too. And my father is a descendant of those Germans who came over during the reign of Catherine the Great and settled on the Volga about 250 years ago. All were shipped off to Siberia by Stalin during the war and allowed back only much, much later. Anyhow, my parents couldn't agree on a name from either of their heritages so they went with Olga." She waved her hand. "But we're off topic again. I was telling you you're trying to quit smoking. Except I might have that wrong. You might be an unreformed smoker who's facing a 10-hour flight on which smoking isn't allowed. And here's something I got completely wrong: before knowing you were a historian with a trust fund, I pegged you as one of those guys who builds algorithms for hedge funds."

Benedict laughed. "A quant? Whatever gave you that idea?"

"I don't know," admitted Olga. "Perhaps because I've been spending far too much time with some of them for one of my cases. Now tell me everything else I got wrong."

"The weight. It's held steady for the past fifteen years or so. What made you think I'd lost?"

"The band on your watch. You used to use the second notch and now you're on the fourth."

"Impressive observation skills."

"Impressive but entirely wrong. Fill in the blanks for me. English public school education?"

"Yes. I was born in England. We moved around quite a

bit when I was growing up because of Dad's job, but I was sent back to England to boarding school. The family was going to be in Albania for a while, and my parents thought that my brother and I would do better, academically speaking, back home. I continued a fairly peripatetic existence into adulthood, except that now home base is New York and has been for over ten years."

"Albania?"

"Dad was a diplomat. As you might imagine, Albania wasn't a prize posting. For a diplomat, my father had a remarkable talent for pissing powerful people off."

"And the watch mystery?"

"It belonged to my brother, who inherited it from Dad. He has no use for it anymore so I wear it."

Olga took Benedict's tone for dismay at his brother's disregard for a family heirloom. "He prefers to tell time by his smartphone?"

"No. He's dead," said Benedict curtly. Olga was taken aback and fell silent. She didn't know what to say but sensed that a trite "I'm so sorry" would land badly. Benedict stared distractedly at the stem of his martini glass, occasionally turning it a quarter of a turn. He was entirely tuned out, and when their food came, it took the bartender a couple of excuse me's to get his attention.

Benedict pointed at his glass. "I'll have another of those." Then he returned to the conversation with Olga. "Thank you for the silence. You've no idea how I despise people murmuring 'I'm sorry' or 'oh, how awful.' What do they know." He ran a hand through his hair, then collected himself. "There must be something about airport bars that invites confessional conversations like these. I vote we speak of the weather from now on."

Olga agreed, and they spent the next half hour discussing safe and banal topics. Benedict glanced over at the clock above the bar. "We should get ourselves to the gate. It's nearly time to board," he said, pulling out his wallet and signaling to the bartender for the bill. Olga followed suit. "Glad you managed to upgrade to business."

He picked up his travel bag and offered to carry Olga's computer bag too. She hesitated a moment before accepting his offer. Chivalry wasn't common in her world and she'd forgotten the appropriate response to it. Benedict was growing on her by the minute.

Chapter 2
October 14-15

"Why are you going to Istanbul?" asked Benedict once they boarded and he switched his seat with Olga's neighbor.

Olga gave him a synopsis of what she'd be doing—spending hours at a client's plant on the outskirts of Istanbul, interviewing people about where their physical and electronic documents were stored, and roughly sorting through hundreds of thousands of documents to see which ones needed to be sent back to New York for the pharmaceutical patent litigation in which their client was now embroiled.

"Sounds perfectly dreadful," Benedict said when she concluded.

"It is that." Olga yawned. "Sorry, need sleep. I've done these trips before, and if it weren't for the pilot banking the plane to show us the pyramids on my last trip, I'd never have known that I was in Egypt. It's airport, generic luxury business hotel, stuffy internal storage room with mountains of paper. And repeat."

"How'd you become specialized in patent litigation?"

"I was a molecular biologist before going to law school and therefore I'm a valuable commodity in the legal world. Patent litigation is very lucrative, and it requires a scientific background."

"My brother was a scientist, too." Benedict looked out the window, but Olga saw in his reflection his narrowed eyes and creased brow.

"What kind of scientist?" she asked.

"He was a physician specializing in obesity. He then got his doctorate in biomedical science doing research into molecular pathways of brown fat cells. Mean anything to you?"

Olga nodded and tried to suppress another yawn. "It certainly does." She hoped the conversation wasn't going to veer toward the seriously scientific because her brain was rapidly shutting down and she was making heroic efforts just to stay awake out of politeness.

"You really do look done in," Benedict said, "but when you're in better shape, could I ask for your professional opinion on something?" He seemed to regret his request right after stating it. "I'm sorry. You must get this all the time and it's probably awfully irritating."

"Not at all." Olga shook her head emphatically. "I like it when people think of me as an expert."

"Well, you are one."

"Oh, right. I'm not just a document mule."

Two hours from landing, Olga woke up to the smell of dark coffee and freshly baked pastries. Breakfast was being served.

"I hope you'll be able to stay for a few days after your work is done. It would be a pity to be in Istanbul, especially in the early fall, without having a chance to explore it," said Benedict when he noticed that Olga had opened her eyes. She was still groggy. Benedict, on the other hand, appeared to be a morning person, and continued talking until Olga raised her hand to stop him.

"I can't process information without coffee. So unless you want to repeat everything you just said, let me have the first cup, then we can converse."

Benedict chuckled. "This is fantastic. Our relationship is progressing by leaps and bounds. We've already slept together and are now finding out about each other's morning personalities."

Olga smiled and sipped her coffee before replying. "All potential relationships should start on intercontinental flights."

"If you do swing it so that you have free time, I'll be happy to play tour guide." Benedict said.

"Thank you. I'll definitely take you up on the offer if I can." As the coffee kicked in, a vague memory formed in Olga's mind. "Did I dream it or did you want to ask me about something to do with patent law?"

Benedict shrugged. "It'll keep. We'll talk about it later."

"But what if I don't free up on this trip?"

"Then I'll catch up with you back in New York. It's really nothing urgent, but it might take more than the time we have before we land." Benedict pulled out his wallet and took out a business card. He wrote a phone number and an e-mail address on the back of it and handed it to Olga.

"My cell phone and private e-mail." Olga flipped the card over and whipped her head up to stare at Benedict in surprise. "Gardiner Funds? So you do work for a hedge fund after all!"

"Venture capital, not hedge. Different beast. And I don't work for the fund but for the family. We're issued the same business cards for anonymity's sake."

Olga got her own card out and, after adding her private information to it, handed it to Benedict, who put it in his wallet without glancing at it.

Chapter 3
October 23

Olga's first eight days in Istanbul went exactly as she had predicted. She got up at 6 each morning, breakfasted in her room, got into a company car at 7, and was in a windowless room filled with Turkish, German, and English documents by 7:30. She was sent on this assignment because she read German and because her scientific background enabled her to make sense of Turkish lab books at the superficial level at which she was triaging the documents on the current pass-through.

Her allergy to dust caused her sinuses to be completely blocked by 7:45, and the combination of decongestant and strong tea never failed to have her hands shaking by 8:30. Afternoons were spent talking to individuals who could have additional relevant documents, and most such conversations yielded more boxes of papers to sort through. Her work day at the client's site usually ended around 6 p.m. She was then driven back to her hotel, where she worked on other matters until midnight, then dropped into bed for six hours of dreamless sleep. This process was repeated on the weekend as well.

Through it all, Olga hoped she'd find some free time. She entertained herself with a self-devised attempt at the dark magic of manifesting. She drew a stick figure picture of herself sightseeing, and spent a couple of minutes every morning visualizing this scenario. While she didn't expect this ritual to actually work, it never failed to make her smile.

On the ninth day of her document collection trip, a Wednesday, Olga's attempts as a budding occultist bore fruit, and she learned that she would, indeed, have a free long weekend in Istanbul. There was one more key employee whom she needed to interview, but he would be away until the following week. Because she was finished with everything else she had to do on the case, four full days were now hers. It took all Olga's professionalism not to burst into her happy dance right there at the client's offices, and she vowed to give New Age self-help methods more credence from that day forward.

Olga debated calling Benedict that evening. She wasn't sure he'd meant his offer to squire her around Istanbul especially as he hadn't bothered contacting since they went into their separate lines at Turkish immigration at the Ataturk Airport. After mulling over the pros and cons, she finally got up her nerve and dialed.

"Vickers." Benedict said tersely.

"Mueller." Olga matched his tone.

Benedict's voice softened immediately. "Oh, hello. I'd nearly given up hope of hearing from you."

"It's not a generally well-known fact, but it has been

scientifically proven that phones work just as well to call people as to receive their calls."

"I'm bowled over that you noticed I hadn't called."

Olga grimaced and banged her head lightly against the wall of her hotel room. "I'm detail oriented like that. Sorry, this is the wrong way to start a conversation. Let's start over."

"I'm feeling magnanimous this evening so I'll save you from yourself. You're calling because you've got a few days off and you'd like to spend them with me."

"Now that's an interesting way of putting things."

Benedict laughed. "When?"

"I have four days starting tomorrow. So whenever you can spare a few hours."

"I can spare the whole day tomorrow. I could really use a day away from the archives, frankly."

"Great! Where and when shall we meet?"

"Let's meet at 10 at the entrance to the Hagia Sofia. Actually, you'll get lost. Let me be a gentleman and pick you at your hotel."

"I never get lost." Olga took umbrage at Benedict's assumption. A snort of disbelief on the other end of the line greeted her statement. "Seriously. Well, except that one time in Barcelona when I ended up going in precisely the wrong direction, but I was jetlagged, and I ended up in a wonderful little seaside restaurant with great cava."

"I'm going to hang up now. This is your last chance to ask me over to your hotel."

"I'll see you at 10 at the Hagia Sofia," said Olga defiantly and clicked her phone shut.

Chapter 4
October 24

Olga woke up the next morning in a panic. It dawned on her to start worrying about what, exactly, she knew about the man she was going to spend a day with in a strange city. Years of watching American news stories about women coming to bad ends through chance encounters with charming men had taken their toll on her trust. She powered up her laptop and Googled Benedict Vickers.

She quickly found academic papers that he'd written and notices of talks he'd given in which he was identified as a Ph.D. candidate in the Department of History at Columbia University. Older items showed that he'd worked at Christie's, the auction house, first in London, then in New York.

The search also brought up several news stories from the previous summer about the accidental death of a Dr. Jonathan Vickers on a climb in the Himalayas. One of them yielded a photograph of two men in climbing kit identified in the caption as Jonathan and Benedict Vickers. Olga exhaled with relief and stretched, somewhat embarrassed by her fears. The man she was about to meet that morning was indeed who he said he was.

She ran another search, this time on Jonathan Vickers. He left a wide electronic trail in his wake, and Olga was quickly able to piece together the general contours of his career: Oxford medical degree, Harvard-Massachusetts General Hospital internal medicine residency, Harvard Ph.D., a brief stint as an attending at New York's Rockefeller School of Medicine, where he also had a grant to do research in obesity remediation, then his own independent biomedical startup called Sliema Pharmaceuticals.

The startup information sent Olga to the U.S. Patent and Trademark Office Web site, where she searched for patents on which Jonathan was named as an inventor. Sure enough, eleven patents and patent applications popped up, all relating to obesity and all assigned to Sliema.

Olga Googled Sliema next, and learned that Sliema had a very promising drug in advanced-stage human trials. Vickers was poised to become a billionaire.

"My, my," Olga murmured. "You were a real go-getter, weren't you." A picture of an ambitious, driven, and proud man crystalized in her mind. Men like Jonathan Vickers were well-known to her from her days in science.

Curiosity propelled her further. A couple of searches later, she sat back in surprise. Sliema Pharmaceuticals was funded by a major investment from the Gardiner New Horizons Fund. Olga promised herself that she wouldn't ambush Benedict the minute she saw him about the coincidence of his working for the man who was funding his brother's startup.

The weather on Thursday morning was glorious—warm and sunny with just enough of a breeze to make long sleeves comfortable. Olga had originally intended to walk the two miles from her hotel in the New District to her meeting with Benedict, but she got lost in her online research and was forced to take a cab to make it there on time. She wanted to spend the ride considering how or even whether to bring up what she'd learned about Jonathan's work with Benedict, but the scenery before her made thinking of anything else impossible.

Crossing the bridge from the New District into the Sultanahmet neighborhood of the city transported Olga from the present to a curious mélange of ages in which an ancient city had made room for tram tracks and parking lots. Giant, multidomed mosques were everywhere, their tall, graceful minarets providing a perfect balance to the vastness of their footprint.

Olga expected to see streets teeming with pedestrians attempting to negotiate the narrow roads while avoiding peddler carts and merchants standing outside their shops, inviting all who walk by to come in and browse their wares. That is, she expected the old part of town in Cairo. Instead, although the sound of the muezzins' calls to prayer firmly grounded her in the Middle East, the orderly, Western-garbed and purpose-driven foot traffic made her think of Florence.

The cab deposited Olga at the gate to the Hagia Sofia complex a few minutes early. She was hoping to be there before Benedict so she could cheat and crow that she'd walked over without getting lost, and was a touch irked to see him already there, leaning against the wall, smoking a cigarette and observing her pay her cab fare. Olga waved and Benedict acknowledged her with a nod, taking a last drag of his cigarette before extinguishing it and throwing the butt into a trash can.

Olga said hello as she walked up to him.

"I bought the tickets already," he said, handing her one.

"Thank you." Worry about splitting entrance fees and the other costs associated with their tour now sprang to her mind. "Um, an awkward question."

"No!" exclaimed Benedict turning to look at her in mock surprise. "From you? Never would have expected that."

Olga blushed and reconsidered. "Forget it, it doesn't matter," she muttered as she covered her hair with a scarf prior to following Benedict inside.

No amount of reading or film-watching could prepare Olga for the grandeur of the Hagia Sofia in real life. She walked to the center of the main hall and spun around slowly, taking in the delicate carving work on the balustrades, the stylized Arabic inscriptions, and the perfection of the dome above her.

"You'll get dizzy," Benedict cautioned.

Olga stopped, immediately feeling the truth of his words but not willing to admit it. "I've seen some impressive places before, but this…"

Benedict smiled. "Welcome to my world. Now, as I'm sure you know, the Hagia Sofia was originally consecrated as a Byzantine church, and there are still Greek Orthodox icons gracing its walls, as you'll see shortly." He turned out to be a knowledgeable and entertaining guide, and his love for the history of the famous mosque was obvious. When they left, Olga was surprised that more than two hours had gone by so quickly.

——— ⫸《◉》⫷ ———

Next, they decided to visit the Byzantine Cistern, situated cattycorner from the Hagia Sofia. They bought a couple of sesame-encrusted bagels called *simits* from a street cart and walked over. Having lived in New York long enough to acquire its inhabitants' obnoxious habits, neither Olga nor Benedict thought anything of jaywalking across the intersection that separated them from their destination.

Benedict saw the tram round the corner just as he heard Olga cry out. She'd fallen on the tracks, dropping her bag and her *simit*. He helped her to her feet, picked up her bag, and walked her out of the street. They stepped onto the sidewalk just as the tram rushed past them, its brakes squealing. A small crowd gathered around Olga, murmuring their concern. She assured everyone that she was more embarrassed than hurt and they soon dispersed.

Looking down at her dirty pant leg, Olga smiled ruefully. "At least I decided not to wear my white skirt today. That would have been quite a sight."

"Dirty knees are totally in fashion now," Benedict assured her.

Olga touched his sleeve. "Thank you."

Benedict handed Olga her purse and shrugged. "No worries. The paperwork would have been unending had you been hit. Would have totally ruined my day."

Olga looked down at the flattened and shredded *simit* on the tracks and wiped tears from her eyes. Benedict put his arm around her shoulders, and pulled her close.

"Sorry," she mumbled.

"It's all right. You just had a really bad fright. Or perhaps you're regretting the passing of the *simit*, in which case I'll buy you another."

"And now I also look like a raccoon."

"More like Cleopatra. The heavily rimmed eye is in right now, just look around you. Along with the scraped knee, I'd say you're right on trend."

Olga laughed. "I'm tired of thanking you," she managed to say finally.

"Then I'll find a way to play damsel in distress next time, and you'll get a chance to rescue me."

"You have a deal." Olga disengaged from his embrace. "I'm over the cistern now. Let's go to the Topkapi Palace instead. There are no tram tracks there."

"Yes, but to get there, we'll need to cross back over the tracks that were such formidable foes just minutes ago."

"I'm not afraid of them. Knowing the enemy is the first step toward victory."

***

Olga and Benedict stopped at a large map near the

entrance to the palace complex, mapping out their route through that vast, fortified compound. The Topkapi Palace was the home of the Ottoman rulers for centuries, and its history is displayed in the buildings dotting its expansive grounds through exhibits that include original furnishings, artisanal works, and costumes. Olga immediately focused on the building that interested her most—the treasury—but she asked that it be left for dessert.

Here, as in the Hagia Sofia, Benedict's expertise and enthusiasm shone. He edited the tour to the highlights—the harem, the Sultan's bedchamber, the ministers' meeting room—making sure the tour didn't tip from interesting to tiring. When he noticed that Olga's jaw stopped dropping, it was time for the treasury.

Standing in front of an inch-thick glass behind which lay a bowl filled with emerald beads the size of robin eggs, Olga sighed, "I think I've watched too many movies. Every time I see a treasure like this, my first thought is how exciting it'd be to steal it in some elegant fashion—not a smash and grab job, but employing an intricate ruse."

"Fascinating. I would have never ascribed criminal tendencies to you. Especially as you're a lawyer."

"We're first thieves among the lot, remember?" Olga laughed.

"You'd really steal if given an opportunity?"

"No, of course not. I'm a card-carrying bleeding heart liberal, well-schooled in the importance of respecting the cultural patrimony of peoples. So no, I wouldn't steal any of this stuff even if I could get away with it. But as an intellectual exercise, trying to come up with a clever and original plan is far more entertaining than trying to come up with, say, barely plausible patent infringement positions."

Benedict looked around the treasury, noting the multiple security features that the museum deliberately made obvious. "Go on then. How would you steal something from here? Say just one of the emeralds in this bowl."

"Don't know," replied Olga, pensively. "You have thick glass that's probably bullet-proof. It looks like there are motion sensors inside the case itself, as well as in the room. The doors are solid steel. I tapped on one as we walked by and it made a distinctly un-hollow sound. The windows are high and probably wired to an alarm." She noticed one of the heavily armed guards watching her closely and decided to be more circumspect in her inspection of the security arrangements. "I don't think the guards appreciate our intellectual exercise, no matter how innocent it is. Perhaps we should move on." Benedict agreed.

When they walked out into the central courtyard, Benedict continued Olga's speculation. "Some exhibits, like that bowl, are likely placed on pressure pads," he mused.

Olga looked around them. "Of course, even if you somehow breached the treasury room, you'd still have to traverse the palace grounds. Makes sense that they placed the treasury far from the perimeter."

"I think we can safely conclude that one will need inside help to burgle this particular treasury."

"I'll stipulate to that. I wonder if all the electronic surveillance is on the same grid. And what kind of backup there is for when the electricity cuts out. I wouldn't be surprised if they had several generators backing up the main electricity line, followed by a third line of defense in the form of batteries."

Benedict looked at her with unconcealed amusement. "Care to ask the museum management what their security arrangements are? I could introduce you to one of the curators here, if you'd like."

"Are you suggesting that he could be the inside help we need?"

"Absolutely not! *She* is a totally straight arrow. But it's not like this type of corruption would be unheard of, especially in Turkey."

"Let's talk about something else," Olga said, shivering theatrically. "I'll feel guilty if I open my morning paper tomorrow morning and read that something went missing from here. How about some tea? Let's pretend to be regular tourists and not budding con artists." They followed the signs to the Palace's restaurant and cafeteria.

Taking advantage of the balmy October day, they had tea and sandwiches on the restaurant's terrace overlooking the Bosporus Strait. Despite an effort to censor herself, Olga blurted out the question that was bound to ruin a so-far perfect day.

"Speaking of grand theft," she began, "Sliema Pharmaceuticals and Gardiner New Horizons Fund."

Benedict nearly dropped his tea glass. He put it down with an angry clink and faced her with the coldness she'd seen on first meeting him at the airport. An uncomfortable silence stretched between them as Olga waited for him to speak while he, apparently, waited for her to do the same. She gave in.

"I'm sorry. I'm a curious person, and Google makes it

easy to be nosey these days." Olga saw a vein stand out on Benedict's temple. Playing cute wasn't going to salvage the situation. She changed her tone.

"Here's what I know," she said in the clipped diction that marked her professional conversations. "Your brother invented a compound and a method of using that compound to treat obesity. It's now in Phase II human trials as an injectable. The buzz is that the results are amazing. People lose between 75 and 100 percent of their excess weight with minimal side effects. Apparently, the worst side effect is increased sweating. Oh, and an increased desire to exercise—that's an adverse side effect in my personal opinion. I saw one financial article touting Sliema as the next Google and Facebook combined in terms of its earning potential. That's probably hyperbolic, but maybe not. Obesity is huge, so to speak.

"Your brother assigned his patents to Sliema Pharmaceuticals. That makes sense. That's how it's usually done. Gardiner New Horizons are the first big money guys in this venture." She locked her gaze onto Benedict's eyes. "What happened next? And how come you're working for Gardiner, too?"

The breeze picked up and blew Olga's hair into her face, momentarily enveloping her in a honey brown curtain. She turned away to put her mane into a ponytail. When she pivoted back to Benedict, he was smiling. It wasn't a wildly joyous smile, but it was there nonetheless. "You really are rather forward, aren't you," he said.

"Why waste effort on a superficial conversation?"

When Benedict didn't respond, Olga persisted. "Well?" she asked.

"I'd prefer to be a lot less sober than I am now when I talk about it. I'll tell you the story over dinner." He got up, but Olga remained seated.

"I can't do dinner this evening. Clients. And you may remember that I had a traumatic experience this morning. I think you should humor me and tell me your story now."

"You're seriously trying to use a scraped knee to get your way? How old are you?"

"Thirty-four going on three. Four when I try to be very mature."

Benedict sat back down. "Fine. You want the story? Here it is. Jon started Sliema with his own money and with loans. I'm not a biologist, so I'm not going to tell you exactly how it all worked, but the gist of it is that he figured out a way to convert regular fat cells into brown fat cells, the energy furnaces of the body. He had a chemical company synthesize a series of compounds to his specifications. Then he tested it in the lab and demonstrated the conversion in a Petri dish. Those results were sufficient to file the initial patent applications."

"He provided all the specs to the chemical company? They didn't do any independent research?" asked Olga.

"Yes, the specs were all his. Bottom line, once some of the patent applications were filed and the compound's action was demonstrated in mice, Jon began looking for investors. He'd heard that a new venture fund was being formed by Peter Gardiner, and he approached Peter. Jon had crossed paths with him at Harvard; Peter spent a year teaching at the business school there." Benedict sneered. "Peter is rather big on prestige. Anyway, he jumped at the chance to invest because it was exactly the type of project the New Horizons Fund was created for—high risk, high reward."

Olga nodded. "I can see that. Obesity is the holy grail of biomedical research right now, but so many pharmaceutical companies have gotten burned, the big multinationals and the small startups." She played with her ponytail. "What share did Gardiner initially get in exchange for his investment and what is it now?"

Benedict chuckled and shook his head. "You are clever."

Olga wrinkled her nose. "Yeah, I know. But truth be told, I'd much rather be pretty than clever."

"I think you're both."

"Thank you," Olga mumbled, dropping her hand away from the ponytail. "Flattery will get you everywhere with me. But back to my question."

"The initial split was 55% Gardiner, 45% Jon. Now, even though Gardiner still has 50%, Jon's share has been diluted out and his estate owns a mere half percent."

Olga whistled. "I thought it was going to be something along these lines, but I didn't expect highway robbery. And you continue to work for the man who swindled your brother?"

"Yes, Olga. I continue to work for him. I need the money." Benedict got up and stretched. "I'm tired of talking about this. Let's either get back to what this day was supposed to be about, the splendors of the Ottoman Empire, or call it quits."

"Okay. You're the guide. Where to next?" Olga began piling their tea glasses and saucers on a tray.

Benedict stared at her in amazement. "That's it? You just

fold? No reliance on your morning trauma to pester me with more questions?"

"First, please note I'm giving you a free pass on your choice of language with respect to the term 'pester.' Second, part of being a good negotiator is knowing the best and worst alternatives to negotiation for each of the participants. Right now, I know that if I push any harder, you're likely to walk away and I'll never get what I want from you. We're not really friends; nothing holds us together except some mutual curiosity and a certain compatibility. In short, I have a weak hand and no leverage so I might as well fold."

"What's it like living in your world?" Benedict asked. "Do you always compute every move and countermove in advance of saying something?"

Olga laughed. "You're kidding, right? Most of the stuff I say just comes out, then I spend many useless hours trying to gauge the damage and war game the alternatives I didn't take."

They started toward the exit of the Imperial compound and Olga's muscles let her know that a whole day of walking was a burden to which they were not accustomed. After months during which the sum total of her exercise consisted of shifting binders on her desk, her hip joints felt like they were grinding to a halt, prompting her to propose a visit to a Turkish bath known locally as a *hammam*.

She was puzzled by the odd expression on Benedict's face until she remembered that Istanbul now boasted *hammams* in which women and men bathed in the same room. Blushing crimson, she hastened to suggest *Cemberlitas*, a historic *hammam* she had read about in her guidebook, where propriety ruled and the women's section occupied a wholly separate wing.

"A chaste and safe choice," Benedict observed dryly, causing Olga's blush to deepen further. "Been there, done that, and have a firsthand understanding that lying on a marble slab surrounded by other naked men, being scrubbed to within an inch of my life isn't really my scene. Do enjoy yourself, though."

"Sorry I can't have dinner with you—I was invited to the home of one of the client's employees. Do you have time for more sightseeing tomorrow? Maybe take the ferry up the Bosporus to the Black Sea?"

"I can take another day off, especially as you're leaving me all alone this evening and I'll have nothing to do but work." He leaned over and kissed her cheek. "Let's meet at the ferry terminal at 8:30 tomorrow."

Chapter 5
October 25

Olga woke up the next morning, at the insistence of her alarm, much worse for wear. Her unsettled stomach and her pulsing head reminded her that she was too old to drink immoderately and assume no consequences would follow. She tried to remember the previous night's dinner and couldn't come up with the last couple of hours of it. It was a raucous affair, and her host made sure that her glass was never empty.

When she roused herself, she saw that heavy rain, falling almost horizontally because of the whipping winds, was obscuring the view of the buildings and the river.

Benedict called a few minutes after she got out of the shower, asking if she'd be amenable to a change of plans. She enthusiastically agreed to spend the day in indoor spaces, such as the Grand Bazaar and the Archaeology Museum. They made plans to meet at the Blue House Hotel, where Benedict was staying.

An hour later, and fifteen minutes after she promised, Olga walked into the lobby of the hotel, dripping water on the polished marble floor. Benedict looked up from his newspaper at the sound of her squeaky shoes and acknowledged her with a smile.

"Sorry I'm late. I was feeling a bit delicate this morning. It appears that I'm out of practice in the drinking department," Olga apologized, continuing to stand for fear that her wet clothes would soak the armchair were she to sit in it.

"I would have never guessed it from how well you did back at JFK," Benedict observed, dropping the paper on the table and getting up.

"Red wine is a totally different story. Impurities." Olga twisted her ponytail to wring water from it.

"Haven't you got an umbrella?" Benedict asked.

Olga pulled one from her bag. "Strong wind. There was no point in even trying to open it. Oh, and I've found the one way in which Istanbul is exactly like New York. There are no free cabs to be had for love or money when it's pouring outside."

Benedict frowned. "That will make our modified plans something of a challenge."

"I agree. A modification to the modification is in order. Can we stay here for a while?" she asked enthusiastically. "With copious amounts of coffee? Perhaps the weather will clear." She sneezed and shivered.

"You're welcome to go up to my room to dry off," Benedict offered. "I'll stay here," he hastened to add. She nodded and Benedict handed her his room key.

———— ⇒»((◐))«⇐ ————

Olga came back much drier and happier. The table in front of Benedict was set with a thermos, baklava, coffee cups, and dessert plates.

"Thank you, I feel human again." Olga said as she returned the key to him. She poured coffee for them both. "I want to hear the rest of Jon's story," she said, wondering whether his temper would flare again.

But Benedict merely sighed and folded the newspaper. "Peter invested heavily in Jon's company. It operated leanly, less than ten employees in all. Everything was outsourced, and Jon was the hub to whom all data returned. There was also a board of directors consisting of four of Peter's people and Jon."

Olga interjected, "He who has the majority of shares owns the board. Didn't your brother know this when he was raising capital and agreed to hand over 55% of Sliema to Gardiner?"

"Olga, I don't know." Benedict's frustration spilled over into his voice. "I don't know a lot of things about how this all went down. But I do know that while Jon and I were on the Gasherbrum II expedition, you know about that, right? I'm sure your Googling revealed the story of Jon's fall on the climb?" Olga nodded to indicate that she knew. "Well, right around that time, the company issued a massive number of new shares. Gardiner New Horizons bought enough to keep itself at 50% and Correx Pharma bought the remaining new shares. Jon, who didn't know how much new stock was issued and didn't have an opportunity to buy in, was left with half a percent. True, it was a colossal infusion of cash, but that wasn't the deal Jon thought he was getting when he signed on with Peter."

"Correx Pharma fits. The Europeans just pulled its diet drug, Qugenon, off the market for inducing psychotic episodes. We hear the FDA isn't too far behind."

"You amaze me. Why would you know that?"

"I work at Kress Rubinoff, remember? No transgression is too vile and no corporate defendant is too dirty for us. We represent one of their competitors. Our client's own diet drug is pretty toxic, but all indications are that it'll be at least a year before any regulatory action is taken against it. If Qugenon is pulled in the U.S., our client will have a virtual monopoly for a while, which would net it an extra billion or so."

"You say it like it's a bad thing."

"Now you're channeling some of the partners I work with just to spite me." Her smile disappeared. "I can't tell you how difficult it is sometimes to remember my ethical obligations as a lawyer to help my clients to the best of my ability. Just because they own patents doesn't make it easy to squelch my moral indignation about helping them profit from the harm their products are doing."

Benedict regarded Olga with an expression that she couldn't read. It was as if he was assessing her anew, and his scrutiny made her uncomfortable.

He finally spoke up. "I'm Jon's sole heir and the executor of his estate. He was defrauded and I want his patents back. I know it sounds like I want to take my ball and go home, but there are good reasons for this.

"Jon was preoccupied with the direction Sliema was taking. He had some preliminary data that made him worry about the safety of his drug—one experiment resulted in several monkeys coming down with aggressive liver cancer a couple of years after they were injected with the drug. It was only one experiment, but it was alarming and he wanted to test it further. He was especially concerned about a big pharma company like Correx taking over and having accountants drive the schedule of the drug's human trials, and even their design, rather than heeding his warnings about possible safety concerns. I figured owning the patents would give me control and say over how Sliema goes forward." Benedict seemed to notice his untouched coffee. He took a sip, grimaced, and asked a passing waiter to bring him a fresh cup.

Olga gnawed on a nail. She would have loved to give Benedict the answer he was hoping for, but she knew that this wasn't possible. "Where do you fit in? You work for the Gardiner family. That's quite a coincidence."

"To make a long story short, Jon introduced me to Peter, who then hired me into the family's private staff. As you probably also saw on the Web, I used to work at Christie's. I specialized in Near and Middle Eastern antiquities, but had a pretty wide training in the fine and decorative arts. I was becoming bored with the auctioneering world, and I tend to be self-destructive when bored." He looked up at Olga and smiled. "I suspect you and I are alike in that regard. I noticed, for example, that you appear to have misplaced your BlackBerry these past two days."

Olga sighed. "I didn't realize it was so obvious."

"Jon suggested I quit and go to grad school," Benedict

continued. "But I needed money to do that. Enter Peter. At first, I evaluated and catalogued his art and antiquities collection. Peter is obsessed with amassing an important collection that he plans to lend to a renowned museum, *a la* Carnegie or Rockefeller. As I may have mentioned before, he desperately craves prestige, which of course he already has by the bucketful but it's still not enough.

"Anyway, before I joined his staff, his buying was uninformed and haphazard, not to say naïve. I found a few fakes among his acquisitions and that discovery elevated me in his esteem, even though the fakes were so obvious a first-year archaeology student would have spotted them. I also helped Jennie, Peter's wife, plan a couple of charity events. Within months, I grew to be their trusted factotum and when the chief of staff position became vacant they gave it to me.

"The pay is reasonable and the Gardiners are decent employers. They're liberal with leave when I need to travel for my research, and they lent me the money to cover Jon's debts during the period between his death and the payout on his life insurance policy."

Olga noticed that Benedict had taken out his lighter and was fidgeting with it. "Do you want to smoke?"

"Bloody hell, yes." Benedict got up. "Coming?"

"No. I'm going to stay indoors and drink more coffee. You have your method of self-medicating, and I have mine."

When Benedict left, Olga took out the notebook she always kept in her handbag. She found the page on which she had written short notes summarizing what Benedict had told her the day before and added the information she'd just learned.

A toxic mixture of helplessness and anger was starting to mar her mood. No matter how many times she was faced with a similar situation, it didn't get any easier to tell someone that the law didn't have an adequate remedy for a given injustice. She smelled cigarette smoke and Benedict dropped into his armchair a moment later. "What's the matter?" he asked, seeing that she was upset.

"I get disgusted when I hear stories like yours. It's unfair, but the dismal truth is that in a lot of these situations, there's nothing the wronged party can do."

"That's reassuring."

"I can tell you right now that the chances of getting your brother's patents back are nil. Unless you can demonstrate some purely mechanical error in the original assignments, say the patent number or Sliema's name was mistyped, the assignment will stand. More important, even if you find these types of errors, the current management of Sliema will ask for an injunction and the court will likely grant it."

"Why?"

"Because too much water has gone under the bridge. You have a functioning company, with real employees and third-party investors, and taking the patents away will effectively shut it down. How is it fair to Correx to kill its investment in Sliema, or even to the New Horizons Fund, when it provided the first round of financing on the basis of a fair valuation of Sliema's IP? Courts don't like unscrambling eggs, so to speak. It's too complicated. If you win, you'll win money damages, or at most some of your shares back."

Benedict didn't look happy. "But they committed fraud," he said. "Jon never intended for those patents to belong to a big pharma subsidiary, which is what Sliema has effectively become. He even said so in an e-mail he sent to Peter before the board voted to increase the number of shares and invite Correx to buy in."

Olga illustrated her point. "My own father was in a similar situation. It was one of the reasons I decided to become a lawyer. He developed a geophysical survey system, then formed a company with a geophysicist and assigned his patents to it. The company went belly-up a short while later, and Dad's partner bought all the patents for a pittance. Years later, well past the statute of limitations, we learned he'd deliberately let the original company fail and had since formed a new company that was raking in hundreds of millions of dollars, exploiting Dad's invention and not paying a dime for it. Gut-wrenchingly unfair? Sure. Legal recourse? Not even a shadow of one."

"There has to be a way," Benedict insisted.

"Well, you know where all Peter's bodies are buried. You could always try to blackmail him into aligning his fifty percent with your half a percent to create a majority voting bloc, then vote the bloc to reassign the patents to you." Olga smiled to make it obvious she meant her remark as a joke. Still, Benedict shot her a dark look. "Sorry," she apologized.

"That's that then." He stabbed his baklava.

"There's still value in retrieving the shares that rightfully belong to the estate, especially if you do it through litigation," Olga pointed out. "A significant bloc of stock will give you a voice in the future of the company. And litigation affords you the right to ask for all kinds of information and documents that will show you just how off course Sliema is."

"How many years of my life and how many millions of dollars that I don't have will this legal battle cost me?" Benedict asked.

"I couldn't tell you without having something concrete to go on. You wouldn't happen to have any of the agreements that Jon signed? His original agreement with Gardiner would be key. Also, his communications with Gardiner while they were negotiating Gardiner's investment in Sliema might provide helpful information about the deal Jon thought he was getting."

"I have them all in my e-mail. I sent the documents I've found among his papers to a lawyer. He told me exactly what you've just told me, by the way." Benedict took out his smartphone and searched his e-mail. "Here they are. I'll find a printer," he said, getting up.

He returned twenty minutes later with a thick stack of papers, which he handed to Olga. She settled further into her armchair and got comfortable. This was going to take a while.

But the second document in the pile made her sit up straight again. It was an e-mail in which Peter Gardiner explained to Jon why it was necessary for the New Horizons Fund to have a controlling share in return for its investment. But Gardiner also assured Jon that his interests would always be protected. It wasn't the strongest of guarantees, but it was something.

Chapter 6

While Olga was reviewing his documents, Benedict's cell phone rang and he wandered off so he wouldn't disturb her. It was his friend William calling to say that he and Claire, his wife, were in a taxi, on their way to Benedict's hotel. He then proceeded to amuse Benedict with a detailed account of how awfully boring the conference he was supposed to be attending at that very moment was. Benedict leaned on a column near the window and laughed at his friend's description of the keynote speech he had to endure the night before.

Benedict and William had been in public school together. Both of them had arrived on the same day, a couple of weeks after the semester had already started. That delay led to them being treated as outsiders by their classmates, and gave rise to a natural alliance that was quickly cemented into a strong friendship. Despite their diverging lives since school, the friendship endured. Benedict was godfather to all three of William's children.

Benedict saw Olga watching him. She averted her eyes

when she noticed his gaze, but not before he registered the obvious hurt on her face. He wondered how someone who couldn't help show every passing emotion thought litigation was a good career choice.

It dawned on him that Olga didn't know who he was speaking with. *Could she be jealous?* he thought and, bemused by that possibility, decided to test it. He sauntered back to Olga, pretending he hadn't noticed a thing. "So what do all these papers tell you?" he asked.

She reverted to her professional persona and launched into a clipped explanation. "First, I think you're still within the statute of limitations. Delaware has a three-year statute, which gives you about twenty more months to bring suit. As to the merits of the case, I'm not a corporate lawyer, but it seems to me that it passes the laugh test, and an attorney won't face sanctions for filing a complaint on it."

"Now there's a ringing endorsement."

"I don't think you'll gain the entirety of your brother's share back for his estate, but the estate will probably end up with a bigger chunk of Sliema than it has today. With your permission, I'm going to consult a friend, a corporate lawyer in Delaware."

"By all means." Benedict smiled but got nothing in response. "For someone who asks so many questions, you still haven't asked the seminal one. Aren't you at all curious about what my brother's original share is worth?"

Olga traced the contour of her coffee cup with her finger and didn't look up as she answered. "I don't know the exact estimates, but from everything I read it's an obscene amount of money."

"In drug company terms, probably not. In mere mortal terms, definitely yes. A conservative back-of-the-envelope calculation gets us to between four and five hundred million dollars once Sliema goes public, which should be soon."

"That's a lot of money," Olga observed dryly.

"Quite," Benedict agreed. "Everything all right?" he added after waiting a beat. "You seem irritated."

"Must be all the coffee I drank," Olga said tersely, starting to fuss with the papers on the coffee table.

"Sure you don't want to know who I was speaking with?" he asked.

"I don't see what right I have to ask that." Olga's anger flared, and Benedict wasn't certain whether it was directed at him for toying with her or at herself for letting him see she cared. Her next sentence clarified that the anger was entirely self-centered. "And I don't see why it should be of any interest to me either," she said.

"If you were to get a call now, I'd ask," he replied, trying to help her out.

"I doubt that. You're a well-bred Englishman." Apparently Olga refused to be helped.

Benedict threw his hands up. "All right, have it your way. But I'm going to tell you anyway. It was my friend William. They're here. In Istanbul."

"I should get going then." Olga rose, looking embarrassed and relieved. "You'll want to spend time with them."

"Please stay." Benedict stood and laid a hand on Olga's arm. "I'm rather hoping that you and William's wife, Claire, will hit it off and go see the Grand Bazaar together, leaving William and me to our own devices. I really don't want to tour the Grand Bazaar ever again, especially with a woman. You all get mesmerized by the shiny gold trinkets and the tour takes forever."

Olga nodded and sat down. She picked up the stack of documents and immersed herself in reading.

Half an hour later, they heard a man's voice calling Benedict's name. It was impossible to miss Claire and William as they came into the lobby. Claire wore a brilliant red raincoat that clashed happily with a bright purple umbrella, a pair of rain boots decorated with large pink flowers and a hard-shell shiny orange suitcase. William wore nothing outstanding but was noticeable for the pronounced limp that marred his ramrod straight bearing.

After a flurry of hugs and introductions, William went to the registration desk to check in, while Claire launched into an explanation of how she and William ended up in Istanbul that day.

"'Come with me to the conference in Malta,' he says," she began, pointing at her husband's departing back. "'It'll be our second honeymoon,' at which I had to remind him that that would be quite the feat since we didn't have a first honeymoon because he got shipped to Afghanistan the day after our wedding. 'I'll just attend the morning sessions and we'll enjoy ourselves the rest of the time,' he promises. So I think, why not. I've not been to Malta in ages, and on the theory that absence makes the heart grow fonder, it would do us both good to take a short break from the kids and the dogs and the Belgians. We live in Brussels now," she explained to Olga before continuing with her general flow.

"But we get to Malta, and there are all these bloody

economists who know him and he absolutely must have a word with or a drink with or a dinner with, while I'm rapidly becoming a conference widow and cannot even enjoy the place on my own because it's been raining cats and dogs since we got there. So yesterday I told him that I'm leaving to visit Benedict, who I was sure would be gentleman enough to spend more time with me than my own husband, but, of course, one mention of your name and William's on board for traveling to the ends of the earth to see you. So here we are. And I'm glad to see the weather is no less filthy here than it is on Malta."

"Please, darling," William rejoined them and gave his wife an affectionate smile, "you must repeat your story in a slightly louder voice. I don't think the kitchen staff in the basement heard you."

"It's not my fault that this lobby boasts fabulous acoustics and that my voice, which I've kept consciously low, carries in it," said Claire with a theatrical sigh. "The abuse I put up with."

Just then a timid ray of sunshine broke into the gloom of the hotel lobby. Benedict suggested the group take advantage of the temporary reprieve to relocate to one of his favorite lunch spots nearby. On the way there, the group sorted itself out as he'd hoped, with Claire and Olga making plans to browse the Grand Bazaar.

Chapter 7

When Claire and Olga left them after lunch, Benedict and William walked two doors down to a hookah café. After ordering their choice of tobacco, they settled in and began catching up on the goings on in each other's life with the easy banter and seeming randomness that mark friendships spanning decades. Soon, however, William noticed that Benedict's mind was elsewhere.

"Girl trouble?" he asked, assuming Olga was causing Benedict's inattention to their conversation.

"No. Jon trouble," replied Benedict. William exhaled a lungful of smoke, waiting for Benedict to continue. "In fact, I'm happy you're here. Else I'd have packed up and gone to see you because I really need your advice. I told Olga about what Peter Gardiner did and she made a suggestion I'm mulling over."

"What?"

"Blackmail."

"Right. Wait, she really gave you that advice?"

"She said it in jest, but the more I think about it, the more sense it makes. She also suggested litigation, but where's the fun in that?"

William laughed.

"No, I'm serious," Benedict said emphatically. "I'm beginning to think that only a combination of legal and extra-legal means could get us to where we need to be."

William stared at Benedict. "I'll repeat what you just said and you'll nod if I heard it right. You said that it makes sense to you to engage in blackmail. Yes?"

Benedict nodded.

"Brilliant. Why don't you throw murder into your plan as well?" William added. "No point in doing things by half measures, I say."

"Either we get Jon's fair share of the profits from the drug if it's safe, or we stop it from getting approved and save some lives if it's as dangerous as Jon feared. I don't care how I achieve that."

"On the other hand there is something to be said for trying less drastic measures. If you want to stop the drug from being marketed, how about a public awareness campaign, for example."

"Bugger that! You know how desperate people are for an effective obesity drug. They were taking Phen-Fen long after reports of side effects surfaced. And there are still doctors who prescribe speed for weight loss."

William smiled indulgently. "You've been living too safely for too long. When was the last time you risked your life in some misadventure like flipping over during motocross racing or piloting your glider into a tree? Come to think of it, how did I end up in military service and you end up in academia?"

"I'm not craving adrenaline right now, William. I'm really not. I think that if the four of us put our heads together, we can come up with a safe plan to get this done."

"Four of us?"

"Yes. You, Claire, Olga, and I."

William's eyebrows shot up in astonishment. "Leaving aside the insanity of whatever blackmailing scheme you think might work, you now propose to engage in highly illegal activity, confide in a lawyer, and have her participate in it? Why are you not concerned that she'll denounce us to the authorities?"

"I just have a sense about her. I'm certain she'll help."

William snapped his fingers. "Benedict. Wake up. Perhaps the problem is that you haven't shagged her yet and therefore aren't able to think too clearly about anything that concerns her."

Benedict grinned before turning serious again. "Can we get back to the issue at hand? Leaving Olga aside, will you help?"

William sat forward and beckoned his friend to do the same. With their faces mere inches apart, William spoke quietly. "You listen to me, Benedict Philip Vickers. I'm certain that if you embark upon this course of action, you'll regret it. There is no justification for crossing the boundaries that define civilized society, and once your grief subsides you'll be horrified at the actions you're so cavalierly contemplating now."

Benedict's tone dropped into the glacial range. "I'm not driven by grief, William. I am driven by justice."

William sat back. "All right, I'm going to humor you. Go ahead, try convincing me that you're doing what's right and that it's doable. But promise you'll listen to reason once I tell you all the ways in which it's not either."

"Fair enough," said Benedict. "It'll take a lot of thinking through the details yet. But here's the general idea."

———— ⊙ ————

Despite himself, William had to admit that Benedict made sense. The more he poked and prodded at what Benedict told him, the more his objections fell away.

"I think this hookah must be laced with a hallucinogenic of some kind because you're suddenly sounding perfectly reasonable to me," he told Benedict. "But, oh good God, do you need help with the details."

"Like?" asked Benedict.

"For starters, a million dollars in gold weighs about 24 kilograms. Multiply that by five and you've got 120 kilograms weighing you down. That's over 250 pounds, in case you've forgotten the metric system. Luckily for you, planning and executing covert operations is what I do for a living."

Benedict shook his head. "On second thought, I can't let you be involved in any material manner. Admittedly, it'll be great fun at least until someone is incarcerated, but you have a family."

"And thanks to Gardiner, you no longer do. If Jon weren't so distracted, a world-class climber like him would have never had that accident. And I agree Gardiner must pay for that. But before I commit, and before you breathe a word to Olga, let me talk it over with Claire and take Olga's measure for myself this evening. Can you live with a few hours of uncertainty?"

Chapter 8

Olga was late joining the other three for dinner because she had to participate in a conference call originating from the New York office on another matter. There were seven other attorneys on that interminable call to which the sum total of her contribution was informing them how many documents had already been produced to the other side ("five hundred thousand two hundred and thirty-three," said Olga, reading from the e-mail she had sent that morning to the entire team). Luckily, there was a telephone in her hotel room's bathroom with a mute button, and she was able to shower and dress for dinner while billing the client for her time. At least she wasn't screwing her secretary, as an associate in the office down the hall from her had done on a call with the Australian office. Or so he bragged.

She took a taxi to the Flower Passage, off Istiklal Caddesi, the main pedestrian thoroughfare in the New District. The Passage was on her way to the Cumhuriyet Meyhanesi, a tavern as old as the Turkish Republic, where Turkey's founder, Ataturk, was a regular. Benedict had declared that a visit to

Istanbul wouldn't be complete without walking through the Flower Passage, or eating at the tavern.

Olga stopped at the entrance to the Passage to admire its beauty. It was a wide alley between two buildings, joined by a leaded glass roof, illuminated invitingly by the soft light of gas-lit street lamps. Their muted yellow glow highlighted the multicolored flowers, to which the passage owed its name, cascading from abundant hanging flower pots. As she strolled through, she enjoyed the view of the restaurants lining the entirety of the passage. They were fronted with large, open windows, and many set tables in the passage itself, creating a festive and inviting atmosphere with their white linens, and sparkling stemware and cutlery.

Benedict, William, and Claire were already seated at a corner table in the upstairs room of Cumhuriyet Meyhanesi. As Olga joined them, she reflected on what a luxury it was to sit at a properly set table for a meal that might take two hours or longer, with nothing to concentrate on except the food, wine, and company. She contrasted that with her standard meals over the past six months, when she ate takeout every day, three times a day, while working at her desk. The ubiquitous Styrofoam and plastic containers, the cans of soda by which she could gauge her level of stress (cola if she was at tear-her-hair-out levels, seltzer if less frantic), the food often cold before she was able to start on it. Stomach upsets and indigestion were her constant companions for those six months, too. So much for the glamorous life of a high-powered attorney.

William brought her back to the present. "If my eyes don't deceive me, you earrings are identical to Claire's, except for the center stone. I thought this was the worst thing that could happen to a woman—see another woman with the same accessory or the same dress."

"We both loved them and decided we were safe buying the same thing because we literally live oceans apart," Claire explained. "And besides, it shortened our shopping considerably and gave us time to gossip about you two."

"If your comment is meant to strike the fear of God into me then it has done so effectively. What exactly has she told you?" Benedict asked Olga.

"Just things."

"It couldn't have been very bad things because Olga still decided to join us for dinner," reasoned William. Their banter was interrupted by the waiter bringing appetizers to the table and inquiring about Olga's choice for the main course. She hastily scanned the menu and settled on grilled calamari, which turned out to be the consensus choice at their table. When the waiter departed, William turned to Olga. "Benedict says you're advising him to sue Peter Gardiner and his New Horizons Fund for his brother's shares."

"I did suggest that as a possibility, yes," Olga answered with reluctance. The last thing she wanted to talk about was the law or anything else even remotely related to her job.

But William seemed oblivious to her dislike of the topic. "Do you think your firm will take this case? On contingency, I mean?"

Olga laughed. "Martin Kress will sell his own mother, the three mothers of his seven children, and perhaps even his children too, to take this case. Even on contingency. He'll, of course, drive a hard bargain and claim that it's a difficult matter and that the firm will be taking on a lot of risk, but once Benedict agrees to a contingency fee somewhere north of forty percent, I'm certain Kress will deign to help him out.

"Benedict's chances will also improve if he lets it drop that he's shopping around and mentions a couple of other firms that tend to drive Kress into fits because he takes the competition with them personally. I don't know the story behind these rivalries, but they are an effective weapon in trying to get Kress Rubinoff to represent you."

"So you think it's a strong case?"

"I spoke with a Delaware lawyer friend, not the one I was thinking about originally. R.J. is someone I want to keep in reserve for when you might actually decide to litigate. But this guy is also good, and he said the case is doable. Not foolproof, but quite solid. It's like the Facebook case, where one of the founders was diluted out and they eventually settled by giving him a lot more shares. Only this situation is even more egregious. It's like some of the investors in Facebook squeezing Mark Zuckerberg out. But he, too, cautioned against any expectation that Benedict will regain the entirety of Jon's original share back."

"Why is American litigation so expensive?" Claire's question elicited an inward groan from Olga. There was no escaping the topic this evening. Noticing the intense interest of her three dinner companions, however, and realizing that they weren't simply making small talk, she did her best to provide a proper explanation but tried to make it as dry as possible to curb their enthusiasm for the subject.

"What distinguishes American litigation from most others is the extensive discovery process. We're not supposed to litigate by ambush. Personally, having lived through these epic discovery processes, I'm all for getting back to litigating by ambush, but I seem to be in the minority because discovery is profitable for so many people—except for the clients, of course."

"So in America you're able to get everything the other side has? How extraordinary!" Claire was visibly amused. "What if it's embarrassing and not at all helpful to my side?"

"The idea is to exchange all relevant information with the other side, and presumably nothing but relevant information. In reality, you're lucky if 10% of the avalanche that the other side produces to you is even remotely useful. The overarching idea of such extensive discovery is fairness. In more pedestrian terms, it's hoped that if both sides know all the facts, good and bad, they'll settle sooner. But that Utopian vision runs smack-dab into what most lawyers are, both in personality and in profession. The vast majority are convinced there's no such thing as an absolute truth and that it's entirely possible to win a case resting on a lawyer's ability to convince a jury that the sun is ice-cold and green with pink polka-dots."

"Where will most of the money be spent?"

"Big cases, and this will be a very big case, have several expensive stages. Large volumes of documents need to be stored, reviewed, processed, and exchanged with the opposing party. Then the opposing party's documents are received and need to be stored somewhere, either electronically or physically, and they need to be reviewed as well. We're talking millions of pages. After the document phase, there's the deposition phase, and once depositions start, on top of the massive preparation time they take, there are likely to be travel expenses and court reporter expenses.

"These cases also require the hiring of many experts, both consulting and testifying, each of whom wants to cash in. It's not uncommon for experts to charge in excess of a thousand dollars per hour. Because of the discovery requirements, each testifying expert must prepare a report that summarizes the opinions he'll offer on testimony, and each report can take tens if not hundreds of hours to write.

"And, of course, there are the lawyers themselves. Just this evening, I was late coming here because I was on a conference call with seven other lawyers. We spent ninety minutes for no reason that I can think of, and the client will pay over $8000 for our time."

Olga did not succeed in boring her audience. All three of her listeners had put down their forks to concentrate on her words.

"How much of a burden is a contingency case on a law firm?" Benedict prompted her.

"A law firm taking a case on contingency will certainly feel the pinch if it's fronting the expenses. Often, a firm won't front expenses, though. They'll ask the client to cover those as the litigation progresses and will only be eating the salaries of the timekeepers on the litigation. In a firm like Kress Rubinoff these salaries are actually a real cost."

"Why? Wouldn't they be paying the salaries in any case, regardless of what matter these people are working on?"

"Kress Rubinoff doesn't believe in keeping people around if there's no work for them to do. So the contingency matter is either keeping timekeepers from working on paying cases, or it's prolonging the employment of those who would have otherwise been let go after three months of under-billing."

"You're only as good as your last three months of billed time? What if you billed above and beyond the requirement the year before?" asked Claire.

"You got to keep your job the year before, didn't you? What have you done for Kress Rubinoff this year?"

"That's rather harsh," said William.

Benedict nodded in agreement. "Reminds me of a man who owned a quarter horse at the stables where I used to ride. That horse won 400,000 pounds in race purses over a long career, then brought several additional tens of thousands in stud fees. When he, the horse, not his owner, was too old and his arthritis was getting so bad he could no longer stand, his owner sold him to the glue factory for another 200 quid. That horse had to stand in a mobile stall all the way to the factory, a three-hour drive, without so much as a shot of painkiller. We plotted doing all sorts of dreadful things to his owner."

"And did you?" asked Claire.

"Didn't get a chance. His new horse threw him off and broke his neck the very next day."

"You just made that up!"

"Yeah, but it would have been perfect if it did happen this way, no?"

"That's quite a story," said Olga thoughtfully. "I wonder if Kress Rubinoff would sell their overripe associates if they could get away with it. They probably would. But then again, they didn't reach an average of 2.8 million dollars per partner per year by being warm and sentimental. Which brings me back to the issue we started with. Just as they're not warm and sentimental with their timekeepers, they're not generally warm and sentimental with their clients, contingency clients in particular. They want the client to have skin in the game."

"So back to what makes litigation so expensive," Benedict began.

"If you insist I keep talking about litigation costs," Olga interrupted, "I'll take this plate of the best calamari I've ever eaten and go sit at the bar and strike up a conversation with one of the gentlemen sitting there."

"Isn't that how we met?" asked Benedict.

"Touché. Then maybe I should stay here, with the devils I know."

"Gentlemen, let her eat in peace," Claire aligned herself with Olga. "Instead, let me entertain you with the true anecdote of how our oldest ended up in hospital with a foreign object implanted in his right arm."

William nearly dropped his wine glass. "Max is in hospital? Why are you sitting here so calmly? We must go home!"

"It happened three years ago, while you were in Afghanistan. That's what makes it an entertaining anecdote now and not an emergency. Do try to pay attention to the tenses of the verbs I use, dear. I take professional pride in the precise use of language."

"But you never told me about it!"

"Did you tell me about every stray mortar round that hit your camp? No. So fair's fair. And besides, if you let me, I'll tell you now." Claire took a sip of water, cleared her throat, and launched into the first tale of many that had the whole table laughing uncontrollably, to the intense annoyance of the diners seated at the tables closest to theirs.

Dinner was followed by several rounds of drinks at a nearby cafe. As the evening drew to a close, all four were a few sheets to the wind. Rather than taking a cab, Olga decided to walk back to her hotel to clear her head, and Benedict volunteered to accompany her. They said goodnight to the Ashford-Crofts, confirmed their plans to meet at 9:00 the next morning for a ferry ride up the Bosporus Strait, and set off, not too steadily, in the direction of Olga's lodgings.

On the way, Benedict put his arm around Olga's waist and broke their companionable silence.

"When we get to your hotel, you will, of course, invite me to your room under some pretext only to have your way with me."

Olga giggled. "Don't let anyone tell you you're not a wild optimist, Benedict. But the answer is no."

"I promise to put up only the most perfunctory resistance."

"Still no."

"What if I were also to assure you that I'll respect you in the morning and that the whole exercise will have been entirely physical, absolutely devoid of any emotional attachment."

"These conditions certainly sweeten the original offer, but the answer stands. No."

"It doesn't strike me that you're negotiating in good faith. You haven't moved at all from your initial position."

"True. Which should tell you this isn't a negotiation."

"Ah. I see that now and stand corrected," said Benedict

affably, dropping his arm, but otherwise betraying no trace of discomfort or disappointment at being rebuffed.

"Try again tomorrow," Olga said.

"I'll write myself a reminder to do so. I'm too drunk to be certain I'll remember our conversation tomorrow, yet sufficiently sober to know I'm too drunk." He fished out a pen from his coat pocket and wrote on his hand. "There!" He displayed his handiwork to Olga when they passed under a street lamp.

"You misspelled Olga."

Chapter 9
October 26

Benedict and William opted out of the ferry ride the next morning. Both claimed to be in no shape to hazard the pitching and swaying of a marine vessel. After tiring of taking cheap shots at their general lack of manliness, Claire left them to nurse their hangovers on dry land and joined Olga for the full day trip.

Once Claire departed, the two men holed up in William's suite to continue talking.

"What did Claire say?" Benedict wanted to know.

"You two were separated at birth," William grumbled. "She thinks it's a splendid idea and she's in. Which means that to keep peace on the home front I'm in, too."

"And Olga?"

"As I said. You and Claire must have hatched from the eggs of the same anaconda. She's just as smitten with Olga as you are."

"But you still don't trust her?"

"Actually I do. I'm not sure how much she'd be willing to help, but I'm quite certain she won't betray our confidence. Of course, there's always the question of what she'll want in return."

"She doesn't strike me as particularly mercenary."

"Payments can take many forms," William pronounced solemnly.

"You speak with the wisdom of Solomon, especially when pontificating on the obvious," Benedict teased his friend, baiting him to react. But William didn't.

"If you think you know me well enough to push my buttons, I'd like to disabuse you of that certainty. You are a mere pup, Benedict, and you're dealing with a grizzled veteran."

"Last I checked, you were nearly three weeks younger than I am. Eighteen days. Younger."

"Afghanistan is in a different space-time continuum from the posh Mayfair and Park Avenue world that you've lived in."

"Posh? Stones and glass houses, William. You're an Ashford-Croft, the son of an earl and the inheritor of an authentically drafty and uninhabitable ancestral pile."

"True. Am I laying the whole Afghanistan thing on too thick?"

"You've certainly earned the right," Benedict said, involuntarily glancing at his friend's right leg, which still contained shrapnel from the roadside bomb that ended his infantry career.

Benedict also noticed that his eyes were smarting from the smoke in the room. Despite the open windows and the open door to the balcony, a light haze hung in the air from the cigarette consumption in which they engaged, flouting the nonsmoking status of the suite. He suggested they take their discussion outside before they suffocate.

They walked out into the Sultanahmet neighborhood and were engulfed by tourists. Ambling leisurely along, Benedict and William continued to refine their plans and test them for weaknesses until William suddenly changed topics.

"So back to you and Olga."

"What about us?" asked Benedict, a note of defensiveness in his voice that only seemed to encourage William.

"What's going on there?"

"Just as I said yesterday. Nothing. What you see is exactly how it is."

"And it is precisely what I see that makes me question how it is."

"Really, there's nothing."

"Because she's just a great legal resource and you're not a lecherous swine like me who notices how she fills out her jeans or how her other bits and pieces are put together."

"Perhaps I wasn't as deprived as you were all those years in the field."

"I've been back for more than two years. Two very satisfactory years with Claire, thank you. How have your last two years been?"

"Putting aside the blackmail and extortion angle of our plan, let's try to tabulate all of the other criminal behaviors that it would entail," Benedict suggested.

"Why should we, except to get you out of answering my question?"

"Just humor me. There's the procuring of fake identification papers, including passports. There's likely to be breaking and entering. Smuggling in. Smuggling out. Possibly carrying firearms. And violation of currency regulations and securities and banking laws."

"Look, we either agree that all this is being done for a worthy cause or we call it a day. Make a decision and stop losing sleep over the lawfulness of each step. The key is not to get caught. Or if you're planning on getting caught, make sure to do so in Western Europe, where the prisons are nicest, and fight extradition to the U.S., Turkey and any of the independent Caribbean island states that might have a claim on you."

"What kind of moral upbringing are you providing to your children?"

"That's Claire's department. I was just the sperm donor. My question about you and Olga isn't just idle prurience. Although it is that too. Put boys and girls in one milieu and there will always be complications. Call me a Neanderthal, but I'm very much in favor of segregated fighting units."

"I'll keep your admonition in mind." Benedict's countenance assumed a decidedly mulish cast.

"Long years of experience have taught me," William conceded, "that there's a point at which a conversation with you starts yielding diminishing returns and I can see we've reached this point." William pointed to a sign on a nondescript single-story building. "What's the Underground Cistern, then?"

"It's a Byzantine cistern built to collect and hold water for the city. I take it you've not been inside before?"

"No. Is it worth seeing?"

"It's my favorite place in all of Istanbul."

———◈———

The Ashford-Crofts insisted on hosting dinner in their suite that evening. As their balcony afforded a panoramic view of old-town Istanbul and was large enough to accommodate a four-person table, and as the evening was warm, it was an ideal setting for a leisurely meal.

Both Olga and Claire sported sunburned noses from their ferry trip. They had taken the boat all the way to the Black Sea, returning by bus. Claire was in high spirits because her behind had been pinched by three different men. "And Olga is far too modest. Not only did her bum get pinched, but a love-struck gentleman followed her off the bus and wanted to show us the sights and introduce us to his mother," she added.

Olga blushed and mumbled something about a mistake. William was about to give her a hard time, but both Claire and Benedict spoke up as he was opening his mouth.

"William! Leave her alone!" Claire instructed and cuffed his shoulder lightly while Benedict offered Olga some advice. "The best way to survive without crying around William is to show no fear and absolutely no embarrassment. He's a bully with a bloodhound's nose for discomfort honed through years of training at elite institutions for that sort of thing—the English all-boys public school and the Royal Army. He'll keep tormenting you as long as you exhibit any reaction but a readiness to give as good as you get."

Olga smiled, "Oh yeah? Bring it on. You forget that I, too, work at an elite institution where bullying has been elevated to an art form. We have the full frontal screaming, the biting sarcasm, the silent stare that has made a couple of associates wet themselves with fear, and the bodily checking into the wall. We also have high competency in casual cruelty, such as the knife-twist of reassigning one's work to a much more junior colleague while suggesting that perhaps one isn't really cut out to be a lawyer. There are others, too, but I'm trying to be modest and not overwhelm you with our institutional superiority."

William looked impressed. "I stand properly humbled and might send a recommendation up the chain of command to have our sergeants train with your people."

Olga's cell phone rang, and she walked back into the suite to see who was calling. It was Eric McIvor. She shivered involuntarily and decided to let the call go to voice mail. When it did, she listened to McIvor's recorded voice telling her the case for which she was in Istanbul was settled and that she should return to New York on the first available flight to pick up the slack on her other cases. Deflated, Olga turned her phone off before returning to the dinner table so it wouldn't interrupt dinner again. Walking back out onto the balcony, she announced, "All good things must come to an end, and I've been summoned back to New York post haste." She then became conscious of an odd mood around the table. "Did I miss something?" she asked.

"No. Nothing as such," Benedict responded, darting a glance at William.

"Oh, for heavens' sake, it's now even more imperative to lay our cards on the table, with Olga leaving tomorrow." Claire tore a piece of bread with a show of irritation then turned to Olga. "Look at these two. They have enough bravado to jump out of airplanes and be shot at and do all sorts of other idiotic things, but they don't have the guts to ask you a simple question. So I'll do it for them. Remember how you suggested that Benedict blackmail Peter Gardiner? And litigate Jon's shares? We want to do both. Will you help?"

"Seriously?" Olga couldn't keep a smile off her face.

"Yes, seriously. Obviously we need your expertise on the legal front. We'll take as little or as much help as you're willing to give. And, regardless of whether you're willing to help, it goes without saying that we'd be grateful if you don't shop us to the brass at the first opportunity."

"This is the best offer I've had since, well, ever!"

"Please think it over. What if we get caught? What will it mean for your law license?" Benedict asked and earned an incredulous stare from William.

"What's the look for, William?" Olga asked.

"I just can't believe he's suddenly showing signs of sanity and doubt. He hasn't displayed any so far. And come to think of it, where's the concern for my military career going into the crapper?"

"I don't have to think it over. I'm in," said Olga. "It's a dream opportunity to do what's right for a change rather than what's merely technically legal. And you have no idea just how little interest I have in practicing law. I switched careers once; I can do it again. And in the worst-case scenario, they have vocational classes in prison. I'm sure I'll be able to learn a new profession there."

William shook his head. "Madness is clearly contagious around this table. But if we're going ahead with this plan, I'd much rather do it with you than without you, Olga. Welcome aboard." He raised a glass, and the others joined him.

Olga then turned to Benedict. "But I'll expect a quid pro quo arrangement."

The laugh lines around Benedict's eyes deepened as he sprawled back in his chair. "I'm certainly willing to negotiate terms. All night if need be. But I warn you that I drive a very hard bargain."

Claire picked up her iced water glass and held it against her neck. "There are decent marrieds here, Benedict. Please turn your double entendres down a notch or seven."

William alone remained serious. "Seems to me you're all thinking that this is a lark, a fun little adventure we're embarking on. It's not. It's bad enough that you're all a bunch of amateurs and haven't a clue how spectacularly and unexpectedly fucked up these things can get. I will not go into this operation without each of you giving it the respect it deserves." His words turned off the levity in a snap. Benedict straightened in his chair, Claire put her glass down, and Olga fetched her notebook and a pen.

The conversation turned technical. They bandied about alternatives, worst case scenarios, and bail out points until all four were comfortable with the general contours of what they were after and how they were going to achieve it.

"To summarize then, Benedict first sets the trap for Peter, and sees whether he'll take the bait." Claire said and the others agreed. "If he does, we'll follow our three-pronged

M. A. GRANOVSKY

plan. The only major thing left to nail down is the timing of what Olga wants us to accomplish, but that'll become clearer as we progress."

Then they got down to the details from estimating the amounts of time and money each step would take to agreeing on a communications protocol.

"I'll say it again and again and again," William insisted. "Communications should be rare and use methods available in the Stone Age."

"Like the disposable cell phones that we just agreed on," Benedict remarked, goading William into yet another lecture on the easy traceability of modern electronics, and nodding with smug satisfaction when the anticipated lecture materialized.

"Who said four type-A personalities can't work together?" Claire got up and stretched when William finished.

"And no deviations without informing me. There are far too many moving parts here to suddenly start improvising," cautioned William.

Claire saluted, trying to keep a straight face but not succeeding. "I'm sorry, darling, you're absolutely right to put the fear of God into us, but we've reached the silly hour when none of us can think straight anymore because we're too tired. We all know what needs to be done, by whom and when. I'm now going to do the most ungracious thing a hostess can do and shoo my guests away because it's time for bed."

Olga and Benedict took Claire's statement with good humor, said their goodbyes, and left. They walked to Benedict's room, conversing and laughing quietly so as not to disturb the other hotel guests.

Their easy conversation abruptly stopped. Benedict sensed Olga's sudden discomfort and excused himself to smoke on the balcony and give her space.

He watched her hesitant approach toward the bed, the only horizontal surface not strewn with papers, thankful that she could not see his expression in the darkness of the balcony. To his surprise, her ambivalence toward getting involved with him disturbed him more deeply than he let on. His experience with women has been sufficiently positive that the occasional rejection didn't even sting—until now. But Olga's opinion of him mattered.

He abruptly turned away from the room and stared at the dark panorama of Istanbul. William was right, of course. Olga was becoming a complication he couldn't afford. Benedict took a deep breath and unconsciously set his jaw.

If there was one character trait he was thankful to have, it was his ability for absolute concentration on the task at hand to the exclusion of any emotional distractions. It served him well in climbing and in his research. If he was able to set aside the trauma of Jon's death to work on polishing a paper due for publication less than two months after the accident, surely Olga's charms, considerable as they were, were not going to be a match for his powers of compartmentalization.

Olga as an object of interest would simply have to cease to exist until they achieved their goals. Then he'd get back to dealing with that aspect of her. Come to think of it, some of her hesitation must stem from her reluctance to muck things up, so they were actually on the same page. Or so he hoped.

He extinguished the butt of his cigarette and flicked it into the street below. He gripped the banister tightly for a moment, then deliberately relaxed his posture and his grinding teeth before walking back into the room.

Olga looked up from her notes, and a blush spread on her face. "Hello," she said, smiling.

"Hello." Benedict matched her tone, then swept the papers occupying an armchair onto the floor and sat on it, doing his best not to notice the flicker of disappointment in her eyes. God almighty the woman had no filter between her emotions and her facial expression. "What shall we discuss first? The documents I need to print, or the finer details of enticing Kress Rubinoff to take my case?" he asked brusquely, intending to signal that it would be all business from now on.

Olga seemed to understand him perfectly, and her voice assumed a colder tone, too. "Let's talk about the documents first."

PART II
Chapter 10
October 26 – October 28

The Ashford-Crofts went back to Brussels and Olga went back to New York the next morning. Benedict was now alone in Istanbul. He wasted no time setting the trap for Peter Gardiner, using his trusted position as the buyer for Gardiner's collection, with virtually unlimited discretion to buy whatever antiquities and works of art he deemed to be important enough.

He called one of his friends in London. He'd met Charles when they were trainees at Christie's. Charles had gone out on his own recently and was handling the sale of a perfectly preserved gold necklace found in Anatolia and dating to approximately 2450 B.C. After minimal negotiation, Benedict agreed to buy it for the Gardiner collection for £ 6.7 million and said that he'd swing by London to complete the transaction on the following Monday.

"By the way, any recent scuttlebutt about what items are available for sale on the grey market these days?" Benedict inquired casually after their main business was concluded.

"Why? Are you looking to buy?"

"'Course not. I just miss the crazy stories."

Charles laughed. "They haven't gotten any less outlandish since you've left us for the lofty heights of academia. I could spend hours regaling you with them."

"And I'll gladly listen during dinner, which I'll graciously let you buy me at Pied à Terre on Monday evening." Pied à Terre was a two Michelin star restaurant in Fitzrovia that Benedict loved and made a point of visiting whenever in London. Charles mumbled something that sounded distinctly like "up yours!," but promised to make the reservation.

After lunch, Benedict visited a goldsmith in the oldest part of the Grand Bazaar. The man greeted him with a bear hug, gave him tea in a tulip-shaped glass, along with several types of Turkish Delight, and proceeded to haggle loudly and happily over the price of the services Benedict asked him to perform. Benedict left certain he was being fleeced, but not minding one bit because he knew the quality of the man's work and contacts and his reputation for discretion.

———— ◈ ————

Benedict flew into London on Sunday night. He chose to stay at the Dorchester Hotel because of its proximity to Charles's office, which was located off Curzon Street.

At 10 on Monday morning he rang the bell at Charles's office and was greeted by a pretty young receptionist. She tried hard to present herself as sophisticated by using a pretentious accent and by wearing tortoise-shell glasses.

"Am I getting older or is your taste in assistants skewing younger?" Benedict asked as they walked into Charles's private office and shut the door.

"She's legal, and I'm taking a fatherly interest in her professional development. Shall we get down to business?" Charles tried to sound aggrieved, but his obvious pleasure at seeing his friend spoiled the effect. Benedict unbuttoned his suit jacket and sat in the visitor's armchair while his host walked to the wall safe and took out a square leather box. "The documents are all in that blue folder," he said, indicating the only folder on his pristine desk.

"Clients like the spare look, do they? Makes them feel special when all they see relates to them?"

"You're in rare form today, Benedict. Keep taking the piss out of me and I'm cancelling the dinner reservation."

Benedict reviewed the documents as he spoke. "Don't do that! Where's the Art Loss Register Certificate?" he asked, looking up.

"It's in my e-mail. I'm printing it now." Charles hit a key on his computer and the printer on a side table came to life. The Art Loss Register was the world's biggest private database of lost and stolen art and antiquities. For a fee, one could ask the researchers there to certify that a given item wasn't on the register. It was common practice to provide the certificate when selling artifacts.

Benedict took the certificate from Charles and added it to the other documents in the folder. He continued reading mostly as a *pro forma* exercise. He knew the item and its history well, and knew that no shadows clouded its provenance.

Moreover, it was one of the few Turkish antiquities with a proper export license, providing some guarantee that the Turkish authorities weren't going to come after the current owner for its return. Because Turkey had outlawed virtually all exports of its patrimony, the fact that this antiquity was legally out of the country added a great deal to its monetary value.

Once he was satisfied with the papers, Benedict turned to the necklace itself. He put on the pair of thin cotton gloves that Charles had handed him, then took it out of its container. He examined every link and hanging leaf to make sure there were no signs of tampering or restoration, and indeed there were none. Benedict's breath caught and his palms became moist as he allowed himself to appreciate its beauty. It was amazing, really. Almost five thousand years before, an artisan whose name no one knew created a necklace as sophisticated as anything Bulgari or Cartier could make. And for all these years, it continued to shine with the same yellow warmth its creator first saw. Gold was magical like that.

"The way you look at it is positively indecent." Charles said. "I'd offer to leave you two alone, but I can't do that until I have the money."

Benedict grinned. He carefully replaced the necklace in its box and fastened the velvet straps that held it in place. Then he wrote a check for the full amount and handed it to Charles, who glanced at it summarily before folding it and putting it in the inner pocket of his suit jacket.

"Must be nice to have a free hand with Gardiner's bank account."

"Not entirely free. I do have a spending limit."

"Of what? Ten million quid a day?"

"Close enough." Benedict smiled and changed the subject. "As I mentioned, I'd like to keep the necklace here until I'm on my way to the airport on Wednesday."

"Not a problem. I've continued coverage on it until noon on Wednesday. Yours will, presumably, kick in a touch before then?"

"Yes, it's all arranged."

"I do have one question, now that we're done. Why didn't you push me any harder on the price?"

"Are you saying you overpriced it?"

"No. Just that my clients were, as they say, motivated and I expected a harder fight from you."

"I thought the price was fair and I didn't want to chance it going to someone else."

"It's just not your usual buying style, is it."

Benedict had anticipated Charles's curiosity and came prepared with an explanation. "Gardiner is pushing to make his collection world class. It's a bigger problem for me to have a piece slip away than perhaps to overpay for it. But if you'd like to reopen negotiations, I'm certainly game."

"I'm satisfied with the deal as it stands, thank you very much."

Chapter 11
October 30

A silver Town Car was waiting for Benedict at 3 p.m., when he landed in one of Gardiner's private jets at the Marine Terminal at LaGuardia Airport. He settled into the back of the car, asked to be taken to the office, and rolled up the partition. Forty minutes later, the car stopped in front of a modern black glass and steel tower of about forty floors on Second Avenue and Sixty-sixth Street in Manhattan. The building was saved from looking harsh by its curious lack of corners. Instead of ninety degree angles where two external walls should have met, there was a curved glass panel. Thus, the whole building had an impression of softness that belied the materials from which it was constructed and the hard-core competitiveness of the venture funds occupying most of its floors.

Greeting the guards on duty at the atrium, Benedict pressed his thumb to a scanner and a pair of glass doors parted. He walked through and banked right to a group of elevators designated for the five top floors. He again used his thumb for identification, then pressed the button for the thirty-eighth floor.

The chief of staff's office to the right of the elevators was a bright and spacious room furnished more for function than for aesthetics. Benedict hadn't bothered to change anything about it when he took over, save for hanging a small El Greco study in a heavy gilded frame on the wall farthest from the window. Benedict's parents had given the drawing to Jon upon his completion of his Ph.D. Now that all three were no longer alive, Benedict found its presence a tenuous connection to them.

Benedict closed the door to his office. He put his briefcase, which was chained to his wrist, on the desk, and unlocked the handcuffs. He got the necklace and the folder of documents out of the briefcase and took them, along with a plastic bag containing a colorfully wrapped and beribboned package, to his employer.

Peter Gardiner's office was nearly a full city block from Benedict's. As had been his habit since finding out about Peter's scheme to swindle his brother, Benedict used the walk to squelch the simmering hatred he nursed toward Peter, and to make sure that neither his face nor his manner betrayed anything other than professionalism.

As he approached, Mary Olsson, Peter's secretary of seventeen years, beckoned him to her station. "He's in a seriously shitty mood today," she whispered, even though the door to Peter's office was closed.

Benedict smiled with gratitude. "Thank you for the warning."

"You know I'll always have your back," she said and gave his arm an affectionate squeeze.

"And by 'always' you mean as long as I bring you the Cadbury chocolates you're addicted to." Benedict handed over the plastic bag.

"I'm pretty sure I'd like you even without the chocolates, but let's not test that theory." Mary's smile widened as she unwrapped the package, a two-pound collection of her favorites. "I'd offer to share, but I'm not a good enough person to do that. I don't even bring them home with me so I won't have to share with Frank."

"We all have our little vices, Mary, so who am I to judge?"

Mary cocked her head at him. "I can't say I know any of your vices, except smoking."

"And we'll just keep it that way, shall we?" Benedict laughed. "Is our fearless leader free?"

Mary looked at her phone display to make certain that Peter wasn't on a call and told Benedict to go on in. "Good luck!" she whispered as he knocked on the door.

————)((•)((————

Peter Gardiner's scowl deepened when Benedict walked into his office, accentuating the contrast between his face and his body. He had heavy features: thick brows, a big nose, thick lips, and bulldog jowls that became more pronounced the worse Peter's mood got. His body, on the other hand, was trim and in shape. The face advertised a life of heavy responsibility and made its owner look older than his chronological age of 56 years, but the body suggested a much younger man.

"You took your sweet time getting back," Peter snapped. "Weren't you supposed to be here two days ago? Jennie is having kittens over next month's gala dinner and the florist situation, whatever that is. And when Jennie is having kittens…" Peter didn't finish the sentence, letting Benedict imagine the consequences of his second wife's anger for himself.

"I have an excellent reason for my absenteeism."

Peter's face registered the question, "What?"

"I got you the Horner necklace." Benedict placed the box and the folder on the ten-foot slab of burled Redwood that was Peter's desk. He put on the white cotton curator's gloves, opened the box, and watched with satisfaction as Peter's jaw dropped.

"How much did this beauty cost me?" Peter asked as he leaned forward to admire the ancient artifact, all irritation at Benedict forgotten.

"Six point seven million pounds."

"Sweet Jesus!" muttered Peter. He reached out to touch it, but stopped when he heard Benedict's sharp intake of air. Benedict handed him a pair of gloves but Peter shoved them away. "It's mine now. I can do whatever I want with it, and touching it once with my bare hands better not make it disintegrate." He reached for the necklace again as Benedict fought his impulse to snatch it away.

"Six point seven million pounds," Peter repeated, shaking his head. "That was the best price you could get?"

"I did my best. It's a desirable piece and competition for something this clean is fierce."

"How did the Robber Barons afford to amass their collections?"

"They collected a lot of their contemporaries, a much cheaper alternative to collecting antiquities." Benedict's explanation deliberately omitted any mention of the other reason for the skyrocketing cost of art and antiquities—the fact that financiers like Peter had turned these objects into another class of commodities ripe for speculation and for hedging against exposure in currencies, oil, or stocks.

"As I mentioned to you before, you're mostly paying for the clean provenance and export licenses of the items I've been buying," Benedict continued, deliberately emphasizing the point to elicit the hoped-for response from Peter.

"Tell me again how much this would cost without good papers?" Peter asked.

"It won't fetch more than twenty percent on the grey market, if that. The going rate is about ten."

"Didn't you tell me that some stolen pieces are melted down when the thieves can't find buyers for them?"

Benedict knew that he'd never said anything of the sort but refrained from contradicting his boss.

"Could you get your hands on some of the less than 100% clean stuff?" Peter went on, and Benedict had to suppress a sigh of relief—Peter took the bait.

"How dirty are you willing to go?" Benedict asked.

"I wouldn't want the screaming hot stuff. Like the pieces you told me about."

"The Lydian hoard."

"Yes, nothing like that. But you have said that the market is full of, shall we say, liberated pieces. I'd be interested if they are real and important enough to be in the type of collection I'm trying to build." Peter avoided Benedict's gaze as he was talking. He appeared engrossed in passing his hand back and forth along the live edge of his desk.

Benedict was grateful that Peter wasn't looking at him. He wasn't sure that his contempt was perfectly masked. For all Peter's lip-service to ethics and honesty, one scratch of the facade, and his natural covetousness oozed out. "How much money can I spend?" he asked once he could trust his tone to be non-judgmental.

"Let's balance my investment in this necklace, and bring the price per item into a reasonable range. Spend up to ten million dollars."

Benedict bit his lip in concentration. After a few moments, he nodded, as if he'd come to a decision. "Let me make inquiries. I've heard rumors about some artifacts surfacing, more than twenty-five years after they were stolen. They would be ideal, because they come from the general vicinity of where Schliemann discovered what he thought was Troy. We'll be able to run noble gas tracings on the items and compare them to the Schliemann artifacts to authenticate their age. It's very difficult to date metals otherwise, especially gold."

"I leave it all in your capable hands. There are some things I'm an expert in and some things I don't even pretend to understand, and this stuff falls squarely into the latter category."

Benedict was starting for the door when a new thought stopped him. "There is one thing, though. I'll need to be free to travel at short notice for this assignment. It's not going to be compatible with my position as your chief of staff. I think it might make sense to make me an advisor, or whatever other title you want to give me, and elevate Anastasia to the chief of staff position."

"Jennie will have my nuts on a platter if I take you away from her." The clouds were back on Peter's face.

"I'll help her with her big dinner before I transition out. But in any case, it's not going to be too long before I leave. When I complete my Ph.D., I'll be searching for an academic position. I give you my word that I'll be around to ensure that the transfer to Anastasia is orderly."

"I don't know." Peter hesitated.

"She's outstandingly capable. The ideal candidate, in fact."

"But her husband is in theater! How can we trust a woman who surrounds herself with such unreliable people?"

"His career is a plus. She needs to stay in New York and won't be looking to move anytime soon." Benedict could see Peter's opposition waver and pressed his advantage. After a few more rounds of objections and assurances, he finally convinced Peter of the soundness of his logic and extracted a promise that Peter would convince Jennie, too.

Chapter 12

Benedict closed his office door behind him and dropped into his chair. He had just set his plan to ruin Peter in motion, and the enormity of his gamble took a toll on his composure. He wiped his sweaty face with a handkerchief, then took his smartphone from his pocket and stopped the recording application. He listened to enough of the playback to make sure his conversation with Gardiner was clearly audible. Then he made two disc copies of the file, which he sealed into two separate envelopes, each addressed to a different post office box in Europe.

Benedict next called William. When William picked up, he simply said, "We're on."

"It's not too late to back out. Even now," William advised.

"You're welcome to do so," Benedict responded sharply. "I'm going ahead."

"Then we're going ahead with you."

Benedict slumped in his chair. He was jetlagged, he hadn't been sleeping well for a week, and the last few hours had generated so much adrenaline that his hands were shaking.

He was grateful it was nearly quitting time because he was in no shape to handle the daily minutia with the good humor and aplomb his job required. He swiveled to face the panoramic view of the East River and allowed himself to take it in for a few minutes.

Eventually, he dragged himself out of his trance and decided to stay at the office and work, hoping that his exhaustion would overpower his insomnia. To assess the most pressing issues on his plate, he went on a tour of the six departments under his command—housekeeping, financial/legal, medical, travel, special projects, and education.

As the chief of the Gardiners' private staff, Benedict was expected to anticipate and cater to every whim and need of the family. He was in charge of twenty-eight people. It was funny and obscene that a family comprised of seven perfectly healthy members, Peter, Jennie, Jennie's two daughters from a previous marriage, and the Gardiners' three younger children, should need such a large staff, three of whom possessed doctorates in molecular biology, sociology, and fluid dynamics.

Assured that no crises were looming, Benedict toyed with the idea of calling Olga and regaling her with the absurdities of his own job. He was reaching for his cell phone when his office line rang. It was Jennie.

"Benedict. You have no idea how happy I am to know you're back. The household is falling apart without you!"

Benedict smiled at Jennie's hyperbole. "Come, now, Jennie. We both know that it's humming along like a well-oiled machine under your capable command." It was a standard bit of banter he'd developed to bring her neediness under some semblance of control.

"I have less than a month left before the charity dinner that Mrs. van Courtland all but said could get me onto the Met Opera Gala Committee. I'm not letting this chance slip away just because my chief of staff is gallivanting around in Turkey and too busy to make finding the right florist a priority."

"I was just getting started on it when you rang."

"Do tell." Jennie's tone held an unmistakable note of disbelief.

Benedict revved up his BS motor. "I'm going to deputize four highly artistic staff members from the nice selection of MFAs that we have here. Before setting them loose to vet a great number of vendors, I'll prepare a detailed evaluation form for their use. Seeing actual flower arrangements in person is far down the list of tasks on this project. First, they'll canvass the personal staffs of prominent New York socialites to ask for recommendations, and call the Met and the Frick to inquire about their florists. Even more important, we'll identify exciting, unknown florists so you can have bragging rights for discovering new talent."

"What am I going to do when you leave us?" Jennie almost purred. "How is the thesis going, by the way?"

"I have every reason to believe I'll finish writing it in the current century," said Benedict, "but, of course, it's taking a back seat to the florist crisis."

"You always keep your priorities straight," Jennie said. Benedict wondered whether she was being facetious, then reminded himself that she genuinely believed his world revolved around the Gardiners' comfort.

Chapter 13
Brussels — November 3

William stood outside the Aux Bons Enfants restaurant finishing a cigarette. The Enfants occupied a sixteenth-century house that proudly wore every wart and wrinkle it had sustained during its 500-year history. Its exposed beams were crooked and the external walls were thick with layer upon layer of white plaster, unevenly applied. Most patrons needed to duck as they entered the premises if they valued their noggins. There was barely enough room for a tiny bar and ten tables, but the atmosphere was always welcoming, the pizza delicious, and the wine cheap. It was also a five-minute walk from the Ashford-Crofts' apartment, making it an ideal spot for a casual evening out. This evening, however, William was dining there with someone other than Claire.

"Colonel Ashford-Croft!" he heard and broke into a wide grin as he turned to shake the outstretched hand of a bear of a man with a crew cut.

"Colonel Smith," he tried to mimic the broad Minnesotan accent of his friend and failed miserably to the obvious delight of the latter.

They entered the restaurant and secured the most secluded table in the place, which meant they were about two feet away from any other table instead of just one. They ordered a carafe of the house red for William, a beer for Smith, and a couple of pizzas.

"How's the family?" asked Smith.

"They're all doing well, thank you. The children are growing like weeds, the dogs break at least one glass a week wagging their tails, and God bless Claire for holding it all together. How's yours?"

"About the same. Wife, kids, and dogs all doing just fine. Retirement is good. You should try it."

The arrival of their drinks was the signal both men were waiting for to begin their business discussion. William lowered his voice to a level that wouldn't be overheard by the other patrons and began. "First, I must thank you for flying out here on such short notice. I could use your help, Gene."

"Whatever you need."

"Complete legends, some of them American. Passports, birth certificates, prior addresses, college information, the works. I need clean bank accounts, including a couple of business accounts, some of them in the U.S. Also a couple of specialty IDs. And I'll need some backup, nothing major, just couriers, perhaps some muscle."

"Mind telling me why?"

"I cannot tell you why."

"And Her Majesty's Government won't acknowledge

this operation if any account of it sees the light of day?"

"Very much so."

"I thought your days of doing shit like this were over now that you're a gimp. Aren't you supposed to be chained to a desk pretending to be an economist?"

"That was the plan. Yet here we are."

"And some of this stuff will be happening in the U.S.? Now that's what you educated gentlemen might call a touch disconcerting," Smith spoke slowly, thoughtfully massaging at the stubble that passed for his hair.

William pretended to be wrestling with how much he could divulge. "If I tell you we're looking at a multinational entity, and the U.S. portion of the operation is tangential, would that increase your comfort level?"

"Can you swear to me there's nothing here that can remotely harm the national interests of the U.S.?"

"I absolutely swear."

Smith took a long gulp from his beer mug and thought for a while. William was desperate for another cigarette but didn't dare leave the table lest it break the American's train of thought.

"How much money do you need in the accounts?" Smith asked eventually.

"Just enough to open them. Here's another issue. It'll take me a few months to pay you."

"Your money isn't good with me." Smith said emphatically.

"I can't not pay you—you're just starting out as a private contractor. Besides, it's Her Majesty's money."

"Add that money to your slush fund to lawyer up if the shit hits the fan and your government hangs you out to dry."

The two men fell silent as the waiter set their pizzas on the table.

"I owe you," William said.

"William, we both know that I'll owe you for as long as I live, and as long as you continue to limp." Smith said, invoking the night William saved his life by pushing him away from an IED a second before it detonated. "Now, did we come here to get all weepy or to eat some of Carlo's excellent pizza and wash it down with his excellent beer?"

Chapter 14
New York – November 7

Olga shuddered as she set off toward Central Park in the early morning darkness. The temperature was above freezing, but the high humidity made the cold seep through her coat, settling an unshakable chill through her body.

As a general matter, Olga wasn't used to 7 a.m. meetings, and she grumbled about inconsiderate, uncivilized people all the way to the park. Benedict waited for her at the corner of Sixty-ninth Street and Fifth Avenue with two large paper cups of coffee.

"Good morning!" he chirped, reminding Olga that he was an insufferably alert morning person. He bent down to kiss her cheek, then handed her her coffee. "This one's yours. See? I remembered that you like to cut your cream with a little coffee."

"Thank you. This goes some way to making up for depriving me of sleep."

"Oh, come on. Look around you! Have you ever seen

Central Park at this hour before? The mist still hanging over it, and the blessed quiet interrupted only by us, the sound of joggers, and the snores of homeless people."

"I think this cloak and dagger stuff is kind of idiotic. No one is aware that we're planning something." Olga shivered again and took a sip of the hot coffee to warm up.

"We do what William says, remember? He thinks we need as much practice as possible, mostly to get us into the mindset that we're not safe. He will be truly happy only when we're both paranoid lunatics."

They began strolling in a generally northern course. After a few minutes of silence Benedict said, "We're on schedule. Maybe even a little ahead."

"Good. Because I can't wait to quit."

"Is it very horrible?"

"No more so than usual, but my reservoir of patience has run dry now that I know I'm so close to getting out. How do you cope, working for Gardiner, feeling about him the way you do?"

"Of all my considerable talents, being able to compart-mentalize is my greatest. I block out what I cannot fix at a given moment. With Gardiner, this means I don't think about what he did to my brother, and see him as merely my employer. If I dwelled on his betrayal, you'd be getting a call asking for a recommendation for a criminal attorney to represent me in my homicide trial."

"When I grow up, I want to be just like you," Olga said. "When something goes wrong at work, it reminds me of all my other failings—character, looks, career, personal life— until my whole world collapses."

"That's a hard way to live," Benedict said. "Jon was like that, too."

Olga brought the conversation back to the purpose of their meeting. She unzipped her coat and pulled out from an internal pocket several hand-written pages, which she handed to Benedict. "Your legal education, the Cliff Notes version."

Benedict squinted at the papers. "Good God, who taught you to write? It's a cross between a doctor's scrawl and ancient Egyptian hieroglyphics."

"In Claire's immortal words, 'the abuse I put up with,'" said Olga, rolling her eyes.

They were walking past high boulders, remnants of the glaciers, glistening with the morning's condensation. "Will you teach me to climb?" Olga asked impulsively. She regretted her question as soon as it was uttered, worried that it would remind Benedict of his brother's death.

Benedict cocked his head and peered at her.

"It seems like a fun thing to do," she told him.

"You think so?"

"I don't know. It's not like I've ever tried."

"Go on then, find out." Benedict indicated the boulders with his chin. "Scramble up there."

"They're wet," she said petulantly.

"Do you think mountains are dry?"

"Of course not, but gym walls are dry."

"I'm not going to teach you to climb, Olga," Benedict said sharply, then softened. "I'm not a good teacher."

They began walking back. "Moving right along, then," Benedict resumed, "William wants to know how much money you'll need to live on when you quit."

"Why?" Olga had discussed this issue with William just a day earlier, and he told her that Benedict was worried about her finances.

"So he can allocate funds to a bank account you can access. Why else?"

"Tell him thanks, but I have enough saved up for a few months."

"Please humor him. I'm sure that you're perfectly self-sufficient, but it would make him feel better if he could help you while you're taking a chance on our behalf."

Olga couldn't suppress her amusement. "It would make him, William, feel better."

"That's what I said," Benedict said curtly.

"Well, in that case, please tell William that a deposit of $50,000 would be much appreciated."

"Good. I will."

They reached the Sixty-ninth Street exit again and stopped. Olga wondered what the proper protocol was for saying goodbye to a co-conspirator to whom one was attracted. Surely a handshake was wrong. Benedict solved her dilemma by pulling her into a bone-crushing hug and kissing her cheek.

"I don't know when we'll see each other again. Promise to keep safe," he said.

"I will," Olga whispered. Her eyes welled up as the daring of their undertaking finally hit her.

Chapter 15
December 6

Olga walked into her office at Kress Rubinoff and dropped her bag on the floor by her chair. It looked like someone had opened her window and a strong wind had blown papers all over the place. In reality, this was how her office had looked day in and day out for the past few months. She surveyed her lair in dismay, then checked herself. Only a month or two more of working there; she shouldn't take the state of her office so personally. As much as she hated the mess, she hated the idea of spending time cleaning it up even more. It would have taken hours and Olga couldn't be bothered to do anything that she couldn't bill to a client.

She stood at her desk, hands on her hips and lips pursed. She willed herself to concentrate on the work day ahead of her, debating which task on her to-do list should be her first priority. Her thoughts were interrupted by the ring of the office phone.

It was Bob Moore, a junior partner. Olga wrinkled her

nose in disgust and let the call go to voice mail. She loathed Bob with a particular passion since working with him on an expedited litigation in the Rocket Docket in the Eastern District of Virginia.

The man was a slob and a disorganized thinker, and required constant babysitting. He gave her assignments that made no sense or that he'd already asked some other associate to do. He changed his mind at the last possible moment, or worse, when it was already too late. He routinely lost important papers, so often that Olga had learned to keep triplicates of everything for when his inevitable panicked calls came. His slovenliness resulted in hundreds of hours of wasted effort. Granted, all those hours were billed to the client, so at least Olga wasn't dinged in that respect, but she still had sufficient professional pride to be offended by the soaking the client took on the case. The fact that she had any professional pride left surprised her greatly.

The message light lit up on her phone, and she dialed the voice mail number to retrieve Bob's message. "Need you to do something for me right away. Can you go down to whatever floor our library is on and find McCarthy on Trademarks and bring it to me? I need volume 3. Also volume 4, and just to be on the safe side, volume 5. Right away." Shaking her head, Olga deleted the message. She and Bob weren't even working on any cases together, yet he thought it was perfectly appropriate to send her on errands his secretary should have been handling.

Olga was still fuming about Bob twenty minutes later, but now she was also fuming at herself for having wasted almost four tenths of an hour, a tenth of an hour being the increment in which all attorneys measured their lives at Kress Rubinoff. She hadn't opened one document on the system yet, and therefore couldn't plausibly bill any client for her time. Even though she would be there only a short time longer, she did not want to be fired for not billing enough hours.

The phone rang again and this time Olga picked up because it was Eric McIvor, telling her to come to his office. He and Jim Silva, the senior associate she was working on a McIvor case with, were discussing the game plan for the next month. She dutifully trooped over, carrying a notepad and a pen.

McIvor was in full flight about the problems they were experiencing with the document production they owed opposing counsel. Apparently, they had failed to collect a whole shared drive on which scientists stored hundreds of thousands of pages of data relevant to the case, and now opposing counsel was threatening to seek sanctions for their failure to turn them over.

Opposing counsel would have known nothing about this drive had the client's COO not told him about it during a recent deposition. McIvor was trying hard not to lose his temper, but he wanted to understand how Jim could have screwed up so badly.

Jim, looking ashen, was attempting to show McIvor the e-mail correspondence between him, the client's in-house counsel and the client's IT person charged with collecting the electronic documents for this litigation. The e-mail chain made clear that Jim had asked for every drive of the type in question, and that in-house counsel stated unequivocally that everything the client had had already been copied and provided to Kress Rubinoff. There was even an e-mail exchange in which Jim, half-jokingly, asked if there weren't some other forgotten drives somewhere, and was assured that none existed. That e-mail exchange rang a dim bell with Olga, but try as she might, she couldn't come up with the relevant memory.

McIvor waved the printouts away. "I don't care. This happened on your watch and you need to fix it. This isn't rocket science, Jim. If you can't handle a simple task like collecting documents properly, what are you good for?"

Olga was trying to make herself inconspicuous. She was embarrassed for Jim and grateful the e-mail exchange had taken place without her participation. There but for the grace of God and all that. Anyway, it was absurd to cower before McIvor when she was so close to leaving. She wondered if she was the poster child for what an abuse victim acts like and how long it would take her to recover after she resigned.

After a few more minutes of reaming Jim out, McIvor seemed to grow bored of that particular sport and turned his attention to Olga. "Obviously these documents need to be reviewed as soon as possible. See if you can round up some other associates. I'm sorry you guys are stuck with it, but it has to be done."

Olga reminded McIvor that she couldn't work the upcoming weekend because her parents were in town.

"So?" asked McIvor.

"I worked through Thanksgiving and have been putting in thirteen-hour days since November 15 to make sure I have this weekend off. It's their fortieth anniversary."

"I. Don't. Fucking. Care."

Olga knew better than to argue with McIvor when he was in this mood. She lowered her eyes and said nothing. McIvor calmed down almost immediately, thinking he'd won the argument. True to form, he dropped the belligerent persona to assume the magnanimous, fatherly one. "Look," he said, "I know it's a great sacrifice, and I know as well as anyone how awful it is to miss out on these kinds of family occasions, but we have to do what we have to do for the client."

Olga's memory clicked. That hard drive wasn't collected on McIvor's express orders. She now remembered the telephone conversation distinctly. In-house counsel told McIvor about the hard drive and explained that most of the documents on it were duplicative or irrelevant. McIvor made the decision not to collect it. For the first time in three years she didn't censor her thoughts. "You'll be reviewing documents along with us over the weekend?" she asked.

"No," said McIvor, drawing out the word as if he were speaking to a slow child. "I have other things I need to do."

"Like go to your cottage in Vermont? While we review this crap now as opposed to when we should have done it, months ago, because you specifically told us not to collect it then?" From the corner of her eye, Olga could see Jim's appalled face.

"I don't know what you're talking about. I never said not to collect anything."

"You did, after a call with the client about six months ago."

"Then either you or Jim gave me the wrong information about what was on that hard drive. I don't make these kinds of mistakes. You two do." McIvor's voice had started rising again. "What's the matter with you today? You're lucky I'm willing to tolerate your insubordination, but I suggest you work on your attitude. Believe me, it's been noticed."

Olga threw him a murderous look and walked out. She had come close to being fired on the spot and it scared her. She rarely felt so out of control.

Jim caught up with her as she reached her office. He walked in with her and closed the door behind him. "Holy shit, Olga. What was that?"

"I'm done. I just can't do this job, be in this firm, or work for these assholes any longer." She was shaking with the effort of suppressing her anger and speaking without crying. "How do you do it? How do you sit there and take McIvor's holier-than-thou attitude when we all know that he's the one who screwed up? He's been checked out of this case, and all of his other cases for that matter, for months!?"

"You'd be amazed at how much you'll take if you have a wife, two children, and a mortgage to support," answered Jim, and dropped into her visitor's chair. Olga felt pity for him.

"True. I'm sorry. I'm being even more ornery than usual today." She sighed. "I really thought Kevin's suicide would change things around here."

Jim laughed. "That's your problem right there, Olga. You're still a closet idealist. You still hope that there are things catastrophic enough to make a dent in the collective consciousness of the partnership, beyond worrying about their exposure to a potential lawsuit from Kevin's family."

"What can I say? I did dare to hope that when someone,

considered to be the best and the brightest in the firm, cracked under pressure, at least some of the partners would raise a couple of hard questions about how associates are being treated."

"Best and brightest? Haven't you heard history being revised lately? According to new dogma, Kevin wasn't all that. He is rapidly morphing into a serious fuckup with major psychological problems who the partnership allowed to stay on only because they felt sorry for him."

"Who's been saying that?" Olga was shocked.

"I've heard the new version, verbatim, from four different associates, all of whom got here after Kevin's jump."

"That's disgusting."

"Disgusting? Yes. Surprising? Nah."

"I saw him jump, you know." Olga swiveled away from Jim. "Well, more accurately, I saw him fly through the air."

Jim looked around, trying to orient himself with respect to the building. "I thought he jumped off the other side."

"He did. I was in Mike Tajerian's office at the time." Mike Tajerian was a new partner recently acquired from a rival firm. He was installed as the practice group leader for patent litigation, effectively becoming McIvor's boss. "I was so shocked that I didn't even scream. But I told Mike and asked him to call 911. Know what he said when I told him?"

"Can't even hazard a guess."

"'I'm sure some pedestrians will once he gets to street level.'"

Jim laughed until he snorted. "There's unshakable logic to what he said."

Olga didn't begrudge him his gallows humor but found

she couldn't join in. "I never told anyone because I was ashamed. He went on as if nothing happened, and I stayed, too. We discussed charts for a meeting with a potential client."

"There was nothing you could do."

"No. But pie charts feel like the wrong thing to talk about at a moment like that."

Jim ran his finger along the credenza that stored some of Olga's files, creating a trail in the dust covering it. He shook his head.

"Jesus. Can these sons of bitches get any cheaper? Am I imagining this, or have the cleaning ladies stopped coming as regularly as they used to?"

"You're not imagining. You can have my Swiffer pads," Olga said as she stretched to reach a drawer from which she pulled out some cleaning supplies.

"Thanks, but no. This is where I draw the line. I may die of anaphylactic shock as my dust allergies become progressively worse, but I refuse to clean my office."

"You go, Jim. Stand on principle." Olga laughed. "Anyhow, back to my original problem. I have to take this weekend off. My parents are flying in from Italy for it. As it is, I've been seeing them rarely since coming to Kress Rubinoff." Olga's parents retired to Puglia shortly before she switched firms. Her plan to fly there every couple of months turned out to be unrealistic.

"You're going to have to," Jim said apologetically. "Just try to remember that McIvor is one of the nicest partners to work for in this firm."

Olga came to a decision. "I was going to hold out for

another month or two before quitting because an extra twenty or forty thousand dollars never hurt," she told Jim, "but you have just verbalized the reason why I need to leave, either by the front door, or from the roof like Kevin did, and I don't like heights. So watch me quit. Right now."

⇒«◉»⇐

Olga knocked on the open door of McIvor's office. He told her to come in without looking up from his computer screen, on which she could see a video of a golf tournament. She sat without being invited to do so. McIvor tore himself from the screen long enough to ascertain who was in his office.

"Yes?" he asked, returning to his previous position. Olga was certain that he thought she was there to apologize.

"I came to tell you that I'm resigning. Effective immediately."

McIvor took his time answering. Olga didn't know whether he'd even heard her. But just as she was about to repeat herself he stopped the video and turned to face her.

"That's very unprofessional of you," he said.

"I know it might look that way, but it's either that or going postal."

"You just couldn't hack it here, is that what you're telling me?" Olga narrowed her eyes, thinking how predictable these conversations had become. Regardless of the question at hand, he always found a way to go on the offensive. She didn't bother responding to his current dig.

"Where are you going?" he asked.

"That's none of your business. I'm done trying to please

the likes of you."

McIvor looked impressed. "I can't say I blame you for leaving." He sighed. "The past few years couldn't have been particularly interesting, career development-wise."

"It was intellectually stimulating, to the extent that I had to use all my wits to survive the politics of this place. But in terms of being a lawyer? Let's face it, I wasn't one. I spent seventy percent of my time reviewing documents that no one would ever want, twenty percent babysitting various higher ups and catering to their ridiculous whims, and ten percent being a highly overpaid secretary."

"You're too much of a drama queen for this job. Your experience wasn't any worse than any other associate's. You just chose to be more unhappy about it."

"Yes, Eric. My misery was entirely self-induced." Olga couldn't keep the sarcasm at bay, knowing that McIvor wouldn't make a scene at this stage. It was one of the ironies of law firm life: partners were at their most civil when firing or accepting resignations. Fear of employment litigation was an excellent teacher of manners.

McIvor colored slightly but otherwise kept his temper in check. "I wish you the best of luck. I'll recommend you to clients if I think you're the right lawyer for their needs," he said formally, getting up and extending his hand.

Olga shook it and left, knowing for a fact that he would badmouth her to anyone who would listen. She'd seen him turn on others who had chosen to leave his group. Nevertheless, she had to fight the urge to skip down the corridor. She was free, and freedom felt even better than she had imagined.

PART III

Chapter 16
January 17

Andy Mertz couldn't believe his luck. The U.S. Customs and Immigration officer wondered if this was the day to buy a lottery ticket. First, a gaggle of models, real, professional ones from Sweden, passed through his inspection station at Dulles Airport. They were going to do a series of fashion shoots in DC and New York. And now a Sylvia Morrison stood before him, extending her U.S. passport for inspection. In Andy's opinion, she was just as beautiful as any of the models who came before her, despite being older and curvier.

"Wow. You're a world traveler," Andy said as he thumbed through the well-worn and multistamped visa pages of her passport. "Business or pleasure?"

"Business, alas," Sylvia replied. She had a slight accent that made Andy go back to her biographical page. Born in Mobile, Alabama.

"What do you do?"

"I'm a freelance journalist. I specialize in fashion and life-style pieces."

"Sounds like a cool gig."

"It certainly can be."

"Is that why you went to France?"

"Yes."

"Did you bring anything back?"

"Cosmetics, chocolates, and a bottle of cognac." A frown flit across her face. "I did fill out the form right?"

"Man, to be able to travel to all of these places. What's your favorite?"

"That's a tough one. Probably Barcelona."

"You're all set," Merz said, energetically stamping the passport and handing it back to her along with her customs form. "Welcome back."

"Thank you," Sylvia said, and rewarded him with a warm smile. Andy watched her walk away, admiring the way she sashayed confidently in her business suit with its tight knee-length skirt and her four-inch stiletto heels, and imagining what she would look like with her hair down, so to speak.

⸺⸺⸺◈⸺⸺⸺

The woman carrying Sylvia Morrison's passport walked around the corner where the USCIS officer could no longer see her and stopped. With shaking hands, she searched her bag for her cell phone. She'd tried to use it on the plane right after they had landed but got no reception then.

William answered on the first ring. "Why didn't you call

as you landed? Air France's Web site says the flight landed almost forty minutes ago," he asked, stressed.

"Yes, I'm fine, darling, how are you?" Claire shot back.

"I'm sorry. Are you all right? Have you passed customs yet?"

"Not yet. Through immigration just now. The lines were unbelievably long, and the immigration officer wanted to chat."

"Why? Did he suspect something?"

"No, he fancied me." Claire silently thanked God for the Southern states. It was the only American accent she could fake convincingly. "How are the children?"

"Would you prefer I tell you they miss you terribly or that they hardly noticed you've been gone?"

"No one has Category 1 burns, or broken bones, or teeth missing?"

"No, Claire, they're just fine. I've even managed to feed them without poisoning them. I gave the nanny the night off to better bond with my progeny."

Claire took a deep breath and willed herself to say good-bye. "I'll call you after I clear customs."

"I love you."

"I love you, too. Don't know why, but I do," She said, wishing she had kept her snarky comments to herself for once.

She walked on toward the baggage claim area. Her feet were in agony from being stuffed into shoes that weren't designed to accommodate the swelling engendered by an eight-hour flight, but Claire was grateful for the physical pain. It distracted her from her nerves.

She thought that her suitcase would be waiting for her, considering how long it took to clear immigration, but the carousel designated for their flight hadn't even started to whirl. "Bloody American airports," muttered Claire, willing it to get going. While she waited, she pulled out a folder with official-looking receipts and forms written in Turkish. She thumbed through the flimsy pieces of paper to make sure all were there. She'd lost count of how many times she'd done this during the flight from Paris.

The baggage carousel finally started moving, whizzing asthmatically, and her suitcase was one of the first to slide down the conveyer belt. A fellow passenger was kind enough to retrieve it for her before it had left on its epic journey around the baggage area. She arranged her luggage into a manageable caravan and headed to the door marked "Nothing to Declare."

Despite feeling certain that paranoia was written on her forehead and that the customs officers would surely stop her and ask to search her luggage, no one paid the slightest attention, and Claire passed through customs without incident. She called William to let him know. Then she changed shoes.

⸺●⸺

Once the adrenaline jolt left her, Claire realized that she could barely keep her eyes open and that she was ravenous. Her nerves had kept her awake for thirty hours and she had barely eaten a morsel since leaving Brussels. She wheeled her luggage to a Dunkin' Donuts kiosk and ordered an apple fritter and a large coffee with extra cream and sugar. If her kids could see what she was having for dinner, she thought and smiled.

While wolfing down her fritter, Claire fished out a second cell phone and dialed a New York number. Benedict came on the line.

"Hello?" he said.

"May I please speak to Hillary?" asked Claire.

"You've got the wrong number, I'm afraid."

"Oh. Sorry about that."

"Not a problem."

Hillary was their code for "all going right." Cassandra, predictably enough, was the code for trouble.

The taxi dropped Claire at a newly constructed condominium in Friendship Heights. The tony Washington DC neighborhood had changed greatly since the last time she'd visited, almost ten years before. New buildings sprouted on both sides of Wisconsin Avenue, the main artery running through the neighborhood, and the shopping had become more interesting too.

Claire got the set of keys out of her handbag, squared her shoulders and wheeled her luggage through the main entrance into a granite mausoleum designed to signal to all who enter that this is a high-end luxury building. She waved at the uniformed attendant manning the front desk, making sure he saw the keys in her hand, and strolled with a confidence she didn't feel toward the elevators. The chutzpah she exhibited did the trick, because the attendant, who clearly didn't recognize her, didn't stop her or ask who she was.

The elevator deposited Claire on the twenty-seventh floor, and she found Apartment H. She unlocked the door and walked into a furnished one-bedroom flat. Dropping her luggage in the foyer, Claire locked, bolted, and chained the apartment door behind her, then surveyed her surroundings. The place was fully stocked—toiletries and towels in the bathroom, a made-up bed, and food in the refrigerator and the pantry. There were even some books on a shelf in the living room.

Claire looked out the windows. No buildings obscured her view of the suburban landscape stretching to the north and west, which also meant that there were no buildings from which others could look in. She wondered if privacy had been a consideration in choosing this particular apartment.

She called William again. It was approaching 1 a.m. in Brussels but she knew he'd be awake, waiting for her call. "We've done quite well in the real estate department," she told him. "Is there any way that we could keep the apartment after this is all over? I really love it."

"I'm glad you're enjoying yourself. Just don't get ahead of where we are in this game. That's how mistakes happen."

"I know." Claire yawned. "I'm going to shower and fall into bed. I've got another brutal day ahead of me tomorrow. Remind me again why I'm hopscotching across continents and why we aren't handling all this through the post and FedEx like normal people?"

"Because they lose things, and we cannot afford for that to happen. More important, you and Benedict need the dry run. Especially Benedict." Then his voice softened. "I'm very proud of you. You're doing fantastically well."

Claire laughed. "You're supposed to say that. If you expect any marital privileges ever again, that is."

"Cheeky mare."

Chapter 17
January 18

Benedict had spent the last two days in Baltimore, Maryland, visiting the Johns Hopkins archives for his academic research. He was also there to connect with Claire, per their plan.

It had been almost three months since Peter Gardiner gave Benedict the green light to buy grey market antiquities, and it seemed to Benedict that he had spent most of that time on planes. He'd lost count of the number of times he traveled to Europe and Asia. Even Jennie acknowledged that replacing him as chief of staff was the right thing to do.

It was time to go. Benedict surveyed his hotel room to make sure he didn't forget anything, hefted his bag onto his shoulder, and left for the train station.

The 11:03 a.m. Northeastern Regional train to New York was twenty-two minutes late. Benedict tried to pass the time by perusing the *USA Today* provided by his hotel, but gave up after reading the same sentence four times and still not comprehending what it said. All he heard was ABBA's "The Day Before You Came" running through his head. It was his mother's favorite when he was growing up, played in especially heavy rotation when Her Majesty's Government dispatched his father to unsafe locales.

Benedict savaged himself for turning sentimental at exactly the wrong moment, when he needed to concentrate on the mechanics of the task before him. This wasn't the time to become nostalgic, for Christ's sake. He forced himself to listen to Brahms's *Piano Concerto No. 1*. It was stormy enough to fit his mood, and once the volume was sufficiently loud to damage his eardrums, it even managed to drown his memories.

When the train pulled in, Benedict counted the cars and got on the third from the end. It was crowded, without a single two-seat bench available. He stopped in front of a woman in the aisle seat who had her handbag on the seat next to her.

"Is that seat taken?" he asked.

Claire, as Sylvia Morrison, bitch-on-wheels edition, glared up at him. When he didn't seem to take the hint, however, she started clearing space for him with a great show of irritation. She closed her netbook and lifted it off the foldout table in front of her, pushed the table up, rose, and stepped into the aisle to let Benedict in. "I'm getting off at Newark Airport. If you're going all the way to New York, you might as well sit by the window," she said.

Benedict thanked her and attempted to stow his bag on the shelf above them among a clutter of luggage.

"Careful!" Claire exclaimed. "You're not moving potato

sacks, you know." Benedict apologized and moved her belongings more carefully. He finally managed to arrange space for both his bag and his coat, and took his seat.

He stole a glance at Claire, who was immune to his presence as she continued whatever she was doing on her netbook. He was astounded by the acting chops she displayed.

When the train neared Newark Airport and Claire was getting ready to disembark, Benedict offered to take her belongings down. He was rebuffed with a frosty "No, thank you" and was left to watch Claire struggle with her heavy luggage, coat and umbrella. She left the train without looking back.

⸺⊷⟨◉⟩⊶⸺

Benedict stepped off the train at New York's Penn Station carrying his bag, his coat, and a dark blue rucksack that Claire left him when she disembarked. He took a taxi to his place on the Upper West Side, a brownstone on Eighty-Second Street between Amsterdam and Columbus. Pushing the gate open, he gave the stone lion on the left gate post an affectionate pat on its head, and walked inside.

Of all the incongruities in Benedict's life, perhaps the most glaring was his ownership of the house in which he lived. Although his salary was handsome, it could by no means support this kind of real estate in New York. His real estate taxes alone were close to $40,000 a year. Benedict had often considered selling the townhouse, but couldn't pull the trigger.

The house had belonged to Jon and was left to Benedict in his will. It took Benedict six months to become comfortable with the idea of living in a place where every piece of furniture and every choice of wall color was Jon's, and would remind Benedict on a daily basis of the void left by his passing. Once he did move in, though, Benedict had to admit that the 4700-square foot mansion was a marked improvement over his previous abode, a seventh floor studio walkup in Soho.

As he entered the house, Benedict heard Latin music blaring from a radio. It was Rosa, the probably undocumented cleaning lady whom he'd inherited along with the property. He cursed himself for not remembering that Wednesday was Rosa's day to clean.

He found her in one of the guest bathrooms causing her to jump back in fright and nearly overturn a bucket of diluted bleach because she didn't expect him to be home. Through a conversation conducted half in mime and half in Spanglish, Benedict learned that she wouldn't get to his study for at least another hour—plenty of time to do what he needed to do and leave.

Benedict emptied the rucksack on his desk. He took out jewelry boxes, a folder with Turkish documents, banknote bundles in several currencies, and a parking stub attached to a note explaining where the car to which it belonged was located, as well as the car's registration and title. Keys to the Friendship Heights apartment in which Claire stayed the night before, and which was to serve as a safe house in case Benedict needed it, completed the contents.

Each jewelry box contained gold artifacts, some with

stones and glass. He examined each piece with a magnifying glass, and was pleased with what he saw. For the first time that day, the deep frown lines on his forehead started to ease. He secured several of the artifacts into a velvet roll he retrieved from a drawer, and replaced the others into their boxes.

He added a thick manila envelope from a wall safe to the items already on his desk, then meticulously packed his briefcase in the order in which the items would be required. Minutes later, carrying the briefcase, he opened the front door, calling out to Rosa that he was leaving.

Chapter 18

A wide smile spread across Peter's face when he saw the boxes Benedict was holding. "Presents? For me? You shouldn't have!" he said, laughing.

"I took the liberty of not wrapping them in flowery paper," replied Benedict, matching Peter's tone. With a magician's flair, he put on his white cotton gloves and took the lids off the two boxes in wide, sweeping arches. Peter gasped when he saw the twelve objects in front of him. He eagerly reached out for them, once again ignoring Benedict's proffer of gloves. He picked up a brooch in the form of a horse, with a cabochon stone for an eye.

Benedict grinned. "Your very own Trojan horse. What do you think?"

"You're sure they're the real thing?" asked Peter, as he put down the horse and turned his attention to a cuff in the shape of a snake. "They're so bright and perfect. Not a scratch on them. How can something so delicate survive thousands of years without a dent?"

Benedict tapped on the manila envelope. "I'm as sure as I

can be," he said, taking out the envelope's contents and placing them in front of Peter. "Provenance. Chemical analyses, including inert gases and dirt traces. Anything and everything that historical research and modern science can bring to bear." Peter picked up some of the papers but didn't even bother to skim them. He then gathered the documents and handed them back.

"You know as well as I do that this is all Greek to me. Or Turkish," he said and chortled.

"Under the terms of the deal I've brokered you can seek a second opinion. Do you want to find another independent expert?"

"No. What am I paying you for? Besides, the more experts we contact, the more likely we are to chance on somebody honest who might have a problem with these being in private hands."

Benedict allowed his annoyance to register.

Peter shook his head. "You're annoyed at me because I'm implying you're not honest? Of course you're not honest. Neither am I! But there are degrees, and as you yourself told me, these were stuck in some Turkish backwater where they were viewed by all of 300 visitors in the seven years they were on display. That's less than fifty visitors a year! Not a huge loss to humanity. Anyhow, I don't need a second opinion. I trust yours."

"You authorize the release of the escrowed money?"

"Yes."

"Do you want to hang on to these reports?" asked Benedict.

"No. I think it's best if you keep them somewhere. Better yet, shred them."

"Very good. I'll take care of it," said Benedict, then chuckled. "Just don't try to put these artifacts into an auction without this documentation. Or, come to think of it, with it either." He turned to leave Peter's office, then turned back. "Shall I keep these artifacts in my safe, then transfer them to your apartment?"

Peter laid a possessive paw on the jewelry boxes. "No, I'll keep them in my safe here for the time being."

Benedict nodded.

"I think this calls for a drink." Peter got up. "Have a seat. I don't have champagne here in the office, but I have Louis XIII cognac. That's an acceptable substitute?"

"Perfectly adequate in my book. Thanks." Benedict sat in an armchair near Peter's desk.

Peter crossed to a credenza that opened to a fully stocked wet bar. He took down two snifters hanging from a rack and splashed a generous portion of the cognac into each, then brought the snifters with him to the desk and handed one to Benedict. Raising his own, he said, "Here's to you, Benedict. To the best consigliere a man could ask for." Benedict pretended to be nonplussed by the praise and mumbled something about it all being in a day's work.

The trill of Peter's telephone interrupted, and Peter punched the speaker button. Mary informed him that the potential investor he was meeting at 3 p.m. was in the lobby.

"Hate to break this up, Benedict, but I need to shoo you out of here. You've made my day. Perhaps even my week, but it's only Wednesday, and I prefer to be conservative." He drained his snifter and rummaged in his desk drawer for a breath mint.

Benedict said, "If you don't mind, I'm going to take to-morrow off. It's been a pretty intense couple of months. Arranging shady deals really takes it out of one."

"Now you know what my world feels like and why I look like I'm a hundred years old."

Walking back to his office, Benedict pulled out his BlackBerry and scrolled through the messages that had queued up since that morning. He was still being copied on everything the Gardiners were e-mailing Anastasia, and now that it was no longer his responsibility, Benedict read it purely for its entertainment value.

But the e-mails were boring, without a single crisis. None of the Gardiner children swallowed a toy or got stung by a bee or scraped an elbow. Jennie was delighted with her new florist, had complimented Anastasia on how smoothly the family's weekend trip to Martinique had gone, and even loved the children's new, gluten-free cereal, selected by the medical department after three weeks of researching cereal nutritional and taste profiles. None of the children were al-lergic to gluten, but why take the risk, was Jennie's prevailing philosophy.

In his office, which he'd kept, Benedict found the phone number of the Bahamian private banker who acted as the escrow agent for the acquisition of the artifacts. He dialed the number, and reflected on the evolution of the black mar-ket in antiquities. In the good old days, such transactions were strictly cash-based. Now, he was calling a banker in the Bahamas who shortly would wire money to a bank in Jersey in the Channel Islands, and from there, it would go on a tour around the world, touching down in various friendly jurisdictions where money laundering wasn't a crime.

The banker asked a battery of questions designed to confirm Benedict's identity before he was allowed to provide the instruction that would initiate the money's journey. The call lasted three minutes and sixteen seconds. And just like that, $5 million changed hands.

Chapter 19

With the call behind him, Benedict left the office. He wanted to do something purely mechanical to help clear his mind, and walking always fit the bill.

It was one of those beautiful January days when even New York City loses some of its grittiness and the air shimmers with uncommon freshness. His route wound through Central Park, and he slowed down to admire its serene beauty. A thick white carpet of undisturbed snow lay on the lawns of the park, dampening sound and creating a pool of calm in the middle of the frenetic activity of the city.

The last thing Benedict wanted to think about was his brother's death, but the snow triggered his memories, and he found himself gasping for breath as a wave of loneliness and grief washed over him, the feelings as raw as they were on the day of the accident over eighteen months before. He saw his brother ahead of him, tethered to him with a rope as they were returning from summiting Gasherbrum II, the 26,000-foot peak in the Himalayas many considered a more technically difficult climb than Everest. One moment Jon had been in front of him and the next he was gone. Benedict had felt a sharp tug at his rope, then a slackening. His brain had taken a few seconds to process what he had just experienced but when it did, he knew with sickening certainty that his brother had fallen into a crevice and that somehow he wasn't roped in properly. Instinct and training took over and he immediately radioed what had happened to his climbing mates and to their base camp. Unable to move, he listened to the rapid radio traffic, which indicated that a search and rescue operation got underway within minutes of his distress signal being received.

Even months later, when he was able to bring himself to think about that day, he could remember nothing else. He didn't know how long he stood there and he drew a blank when he tried to think about how he made it down to base camp. He had been in shock.

Jon was a better climber than Benedict and more fanatical about safety. But in the months leading up to the expedition to Gasherbrum II, Jon had started making uncharacteristic mistakes, the kind an inattentive rookie would make. He was also spending fifteen to twenty-hour days at the lab, and his mood was unusually sour. When Benedict had suggested that perhaps they should postpone their planned climb, Jon snapped at him that he was fine and that everyone was entitled to have an off day.

Since the day Jon fell to his death, Benedict had carried the guilt of not having canceled the climb. No matter how he tried to reason it away, he'd known before they left the U.S. that his brother was in no shape for this undertaking and that, had Benedict canceled his participation, Jon wouldn't have gone either. But the truth was that Benedict was competitive, he wanted to test himself against the Himalayas, and he willed himself to believe Jon's excuses and explanations so he could attempt the climb.

His cell phone vibrated against his coat pocket and interrupted his train of thought. "Hello, William," he said but the words caught in his throat.

"You all right? You sound off."

"No, I'm fine," Benedict answered, knowing he wasn't fooling William but hoping that the white lie would signal to his friend that he'd better move on. It didn't.

"Benedict, you've managed to keep your emotions at bay for all this time, and you need to keep a lid on them until we're done. I know it sounds harsh, but you've got no choice. Can you do that?"

Benedict nodded. "I promise to pull myself back together. I'm walking in Central Park now and the snow..." He trailed off.

"I understand. I have moments when I'm out with my nippers and I hear something, or I see a particular color, and I'm suddenly hit with an overwhelming sense of loss because I remember one mate or another who was shipped back home in a body bag. But you learn to compartmentalize. And then you find a good psychiatrist to speak with. Preferably one who'll prescribe lots of different drugs in liberal doses. But all of that will come later. Right now, we have work to do and not enough resources with which to do it, and we all need to stay sharp and unmedicated. How did it go today?"

"It was brilliant." Benedict shifted gears and recounted his interaction with Peter, his mood brightening as his story progressed. "I can't wait for the next step! I'm becoming an adrenaline junkie," he concluded.

"Did you say 'becoming' an adrenaline junkie? Am I speaking to Benedict Vickers, the licensed paraglider and former motorcycle racer?" William ribbed Benedict. "Now let's go over the plan for this evening."

"Again? You're turning into a worried old woman, William."

"Better a free worried old woman than an incarcerated young stud. Humor me." Benedict did. "Much obliged," said William when Benedict finished. "As I tell Claire every time she complains about not doing things like normal people and forcing you two to go through dry runs, one cannot predict what a cornered man will do, and when Peter understands his predicament, we need to be prepared for however he lashes out and causes all our plans to go tits up."

Benedict smiled with disdain. "William, you don't know Peter like I do. He'll be absolutely no trouble. The man has spent his entire life calculating odds and living according to them. He'll roll over."

"Nothing will make me happier than you being right. But allow me to be skeptical. And allow me to propose a wager. If Peter fights back, you'll watch an Arsenal game of my choice wearing an Arsenal jersey."

"Oh, no. That is something I cannot possibly agree to. Even though I'm certain it'll be you wearing a Manchester United jersey to a game of my choice, I simply cannot chance so much shame."

"Good, then the stakes are appropriately high."

Chapter 20

Back from his walk, Benedict called Mary. "Would you do me a favor? Could you please bring me the two leather jewelry boxes from Peter's safe?" Even though both Benedict and Mary had access to the safe, Benedict had often pulled rank and asked Mary to bring him the items that he needed.

A few minutes later, Mary brought the boxes to him. When she left, Benedict closed and locked his office door. He donned gloves then took a cardboard box out of his briefcase. From it he extracted a velvet roll, which he opened to reveal twelve gold objects identical to those he had earlier presented to Peter.

Careful to pick Peter's artifacts by their edges, Benedict swapped them for the artifacts in the roll. When he was finished, and the velvet roll was securely encased in its cardboard box, he asked Mary to put the boxes back in the safe. After she had come and gone, Benedict took a Saks Fifth Avenue shopping bag from his briefcase and placed the roll and the manila envelope with the reports attesting to the authenticity of the artifacts in it. Then he left the office.

Benedict walked to Grand Central Station. He stopped at a corner store to buy a dozen red roses, asking the clerk to wrap the flowers in clear cellophane rather than paper.

An observer of Benedict's movements at Grand Central would have concluded that they were decidedly odd. He spent ten minutes randomly walking around and darting into various gates where trains stood idling. He even got on one, walked through a couple of cars, then got off and reentered the main terminal. He felt silly engaging in these maneuvers but also duty-bound to do exactly as William had instructed him.

After his walkabout, Benedict made his way toward the information booth, making sure he was holding his briefcase and the Saks shopper in his right hand and the bouquet in his left.

A woman in a voluminous overcoat was walking toward him in a great hurry while searching for something in her purse. She collided with Benedict and knocked the briefcase and the shopper out of his hand.

"Oh, shoot! I'm so sorry! I'm such a klutz!" she exclaimed, bending down to pick up Benedict's stuff. As if by magic, she also made the manila envelope and the cardboard box with the velvet roll in it disappear into her internal coat pockets. She straightened up, handed the shopper and the briefcase to him, and apologized again.

"It's quite all right. Really. The roses weren't harmed, so everything's fine," Benedict assured her. The woman smiled at him and hurried away. Benedict went to the subway, threw the shopper into a trash bin along the way, and handed the roses to an elderly woman.

Chapter 21
January 19

The next morning at 6:30 a.m. Benedict left his house carrying an overnight bag and his briefcase. He hailed a taxi and asked to be taken to Fifty-second Street near Broadway. As the cab sped on, Benedict wondered what genius chose to park what was essentially a getaway car at that location. With the tourists, the tour buses, and the closure of Broadway around Times Square, that area of Manhattan was a virtual parking lot more often than not.

This early in the morning, however, there was practically no traffic and he arrived at the garage less than fifteen minutes after leaving his house. Handing over the parking stub to an attendant, Benedict wandered to a nearby coffee cart and newsstand to buy supplies for his trip. He came back about ten minutes later to find a black Mazda 626 waiting for him.

He lit a cigarette, tuned the radio to NPR, and hit the road. He crossed into New Jersey through the Lincoln

Tunnel and continued south on the New Jersey Turnpike to Exit 13A in the town of Elizabeth. He traveled through the industrial landscape of containers, cranes, and transportation-related businesses to a self-storage facility, and parked the car in its empty parking lot.

Getting out of the car, Benedict picked up his briefcase from the front passenger seat and walked into the facility's reception area, where he was buzzed through the security door after showing his ID. An elevator took him to the third floor. He unlocked a door with the key he'd brought with him and entered a twenty by twenty-five foot room filled with document boxes. At last count there were 1021 boxes in that room, holding approximately 2500 double-sided pages each.

Benedict walked to one of the stacks and took two boxes down. He stood the third box on its side so that the papers inside were stacked on top of each other, removed about a quarter of them, and neatly placed them on the box's lid. From his briefcase he took what looked like a hand-written letter and placed it into the box. He then put back the pages he'd taken out, and put the boxes back where he found them. He repeated this exercise five more times, placing various documents in seemingly random boxes. Each time he took careful note of where the document had been left.

The whole stopover took less than twenty minutes and Benedict continued his journey south on the New Jersey Turnpike, using his travel time to make a few calls. He had plenty of time before his next appointment, at 3 p.m. in Washington DC.

The Washington office of Kress, Rubinoff, Twist & Andrews occupied seven floors in a recently-built midrise in Chinatown. Expense was definitely spared on every detail. In the reception area on the tenth floor, visitors were treated to an arrangement of plastic flowers and a cheap and uncomfortable set of furniture. The glass and peeling chrome coffee table was strewn with Kress Rubinoff marketing materials with a single copy of the *Wall Street Journal* in the mix.

Benedict recalled the story Olga had told him about how Kress Rubinoff finally decided to subscribe to the *Wall Street Journal*. Apparently, the issue had taken two weeks of increasingly acrimonious debate to resolve. It was initiated by a New York partner who was then treated to a full cross-examination by the New York managing partner on the need for such extravagance. Once the MP was satisfied that there were legitimate reasons for the request, he kicked it upstairs to Kress himself, because per Kress's decree any matter that involved the expenditure of more than $200 had to be personally approved by the founder of the firm. When Kress got involved, he directed his assistant to canvass the entire partnership, in eight offices spanning six continents, about what reading materials the competition had for their visitors. Only after the polling revealed that yes, indeed, the *Wall Street Journal* was a fixture in practically all law firms, did Kress relent.

Benedict was trying to make up his mind whether he thought Kress was to be admired or scorned for this stunning display of penny pinching when the great man himself came out to the reception area to greet him. Martin Kress strode toward Benedict, his arm outstretched in anticipation of a handshake, wearing a rumpled off-the-rack suit and looking exactly like his picture on the firm's brochure. Benedict, at 6'3", towered over the pudgy older man.

"Benedict Vickers? Martin Kress. It's a pleasure to meet you!" Kress treated the younger man to a double-handed shake and his friendliest smile.

They walked into Kress's office as Kress continued to play the gracious host.

"Please sit down. Would you like anything to drink?"

"Not yet, thank you." Benedict didn't attempt to match Kress's bonhomie, giving Kress permission to drop his own act and become all business.

"You asked for this meeting, Benedict. Why don't you tell me what we're talking about."

"It's about the Gardiner New Horizons Fund and its founder, Peter Gardiner. I want to sue them."

Benedict had the distinct impression that Kress would have licked his lips had it been a socially acceptable thing to do. "If your case has merit, you've certainly come to the right place. As you know, we don't exactly carry a torch for Gardiner. In fact, we've sued him and his various funds on three prior occasions on behalf of disgruntled investors."

Benedict arched a brow. "You lost all three, if I recall. In fact, you didn't even get a hearing on the merits in any of them, yes?"

"Well, investor suits are notoriously difficult. You're coming up against the business decision rule, even though the funds must act as fiduciaries. We did a masterful job on each of these cases. The facts were what they were," Kress protested, getting more heated with each sentence. "Quite frankly, Benedict, I do not feel the need to justify or explain how they all went down," he finished with obvious irritation. Benedict admired the man's stagecraft and surmised that he was now expected to offer a hurried apology for questioning the firm's competence.

But he offered no such apology, and a silence stretched awkwardly. Benedict remained as he was, leaning slightly forward in his armchair, elbows supported by his knees, fingers forming a steeple and resting on his nose. He continued to regard Kress with the same look of mild curiosity he wore since sitting down, until he felt that Kress was about to snap. "Forgive me if we got off on the wrong foot. If I had any doubts about your firm's ability, I wouldn't be here in the first place." He then offered a smile, leaning back and crossing his legs.

"No problem." Kress visibly relaxed. "We're used to savvy and sophisticated business clients, and we fully expect to be poked and prodded and have our tires kicked before you buy what we're selling. Why don't you tell me what your case is about, as you see it?"

"Certainly." Benedict took out Jon's contract and will from his briefcase and handed them to Kress while launching into the story he'd told Olga in Istanbul.

Kress listened without interrupting. He occasionally made some notations on the notepad in front of him, but in general he just listened, nodding empathetically, pursing his lips, and shaking his head at the most egregious wrongs that Gardiner had committed against Jon.

When Benedict finished his story, Kress again offered him refreshments, and Benedict agreed to tea. After buzzing his secretary, Kress picked up his notes, leaned back in his chair, and began asking questions. His manner was friendly but the questions were sharp and probing. They were also unpredictable. To his surprise, Benedict found he was starting to like and respect Kress despite expecting not to. He also noticed he was volunteering more information than he wanted to. It took a couple of additional parries and thrusts to understand it was due to Kress's habit of remaining silent for several seconds after Benedict finished an answer. Benedict began taking this tactic into account.

Nearly two hours later, Kress dropped his notes. He rested his elbows on the table and massaged the bridge of his nose. "This is an interesting case. Very interesting. And I'm happy to see you've come to grips with the realities of the situation and aren't still dwelling on the injustice of it all. It's important to separate one's feelings from what the law can reasonably compensate you for, and many clients aren't able to do it well, so you're ahead of the curve already. There are a lot of complex issues here, and it's not without some factual pitfalls, but there's nothing here that we haven't dealt with before. No one, of course, can guarantee a result in an adversarial proceeding, but I think you have a good chance at a favorable outcome. Especially with us representing you."

"Of course."

Kress suddenly thumped himself on the forehead and laughed. "Can you believe I forgot to ask you the most important question in all of this? What's the original 45% of Sliema pharmaceuticals worth?"

"That depends. I had a friend run some numbers with forward projections under various assumptions. Right now, simply by the amount of money invested in Sliema, the 45% would be worth about $35 million. If you take into account what the IPO is expected to bring, the number jumps a good ten-fold. Once the drug hits the market, we're talking billions. You know what the obesity market is like; a safe and effective drug will practically print money."

Crescents of sweat began forming on the underarms of Kress's shirt, and his rimless glasses fogged up a little. He took out a handkerchief and started polishing them absentmindedly.

Benedict hesitated a moment before speaking again. "There is one other matter. I can't pay your rates. If you decide to take the case, you'll have to take it on contingency. But please rest assured that I will not be one of those contingency clients who bellyaches about the thirty percent fee when the case reaches a successful conclusion."

"It's not going to be thirty percent," Kress said quietly, shaking his head for emphasis.

"Oh? That's awfully decent of you. Twenty percent?"

Kress laughed. "No. More like fifty percent."

"Fifty percent!" Benedict looked positively scandalized. "Is that even legal?"

"This is a high risk litigation, Benedict," Kress said, spreading his hands, palms up, and sounding regretful. "Moreover, it is likely to have a lot of expenses associated with it. Wouldn't surprise me if the costs run in the millions. Please correct me if I'm wrong, but you won't be able to cover our expenses along the way either. If we take this case on, we're going to have to use our own money, thereby adding to our risk."

Benedict hung his head. He sat in that position for a few minutes, studying the carpet and thinking. Mostly, he wondered why someone as rich as Kress had such old and stained carpeting in his office.

"Fifty percent it is, then," he said eventually.

Kress smiled. "Thank you, Benedict. Your agreement on the percentage will go a long way toward getting approval for this matter in the contingency committee. Something else that would help is involving a third party payor to provide money to support ongoing litigation for a percentage of the recovery. We will, of course, reduce the percentage of the overall contingency fee if we get an entity like that on board."

Kress's secretary brought a fresh thermos of tea and Benedict waited until she poured it and left before continuing. "Sorry, a third party payor is absolutely out of the question," he said.

"May I ask why?"

"Because those who pay eventually want a voice in how the case is managed. If Kress Rubinoff is fronting the money, it has the professional ethical rules that force it to act in my best interests and to listen to my instructions. Third party payors have no such requirements, and they have been known to press on litigants."

Kress whistled. "I'm impressed. You know a lot about how this game is played."

Benedict shrugged dismissively. "I read." He took a sip of his tea and then continued. "Please forgive my bluntness, Martin, but I have four other law firms wanting to discuss this case with me. At least two have confirmed that they won't seek to include a third party payor in whatever deal we finalize."

"May I ask which firms you're talking to?" asked Kress. "As I'm sure you appreciate, not all firms are equipped to get you the result you want. They can promise you all sorts of pie in the sky outcomes, but what's their track record?"

Benedict nodded his agreement even before Kress was done speaking. "You're absolutely right. That is why I only went to firms like yours. Blakely Morris is one. Finch Horowitz is another." He noticed that Kress's face palled at the mention of Blakely Morris. Just as Olga had predicted, thought Benedict. "Frankly, I'd rather go with Kress Rubinoff, but the third party payor is a deal breaker."

Kress reflexively passed his finger over his upper lip several times before speaking. "I won't beat around the bush," he said. "I want this litigation. For a variety of reasons it would fit well with the sensibility and capabilities of this firm. I'll take it to the contingency committee today. Can you give me until tomorrow before you continue talking to other firms?"

Chapter 22

Martin Kress wasted no time convening a special meeting of the contingency committee. The committee was made up of the seven most senior partners of the firm. Because the partners' risk was proportionate to their equity stake in the firm, it was only right that the partners with the greatest share would make the contingency calls. Five of the seven were in the Washington DC office, with the sixth in New York and the seventh in San Francisco.

The five in Washington met in a conference room adjacent to Kress's office. It was the only conference room in the Washington location with adequate soundproofing to maintain the confidentiality of the conversations within, even when these conversations became shouting matches. Kress had it soundproofed the year before after the secret deliberations of the partnership regarding which associates to lay off leaked and became public.

It wouldn't have been so bad had the snippet appearing on the legal blog *Above the Law* not included Partner A shouting that "If you had learned to respect deadlines, we wouldn't be settling malpractice claims all over the place, and we could keep some of our people a bit longer." The statement ricocheted in the blogosphere and the legal press with gleeful speculation as to which partner was the one who did not respect deadlines. The firm was forced to go into a massive damage control operation to keep its current clients and to convince future clients to trust it again. True to Kress Rubinoff form, there were also repercussions for the partners involved. The deadline-missing partner, who was a major business generator, received a mild reproof. Partner A, who wasn't as prolific, was fired.

Once the committee members were in the room or connected via phone conferencing, Kress called the meeting to order. He briefly described Benedict's case and made the recommendation that they take it on for a 50% cut. He told them that, having reviewed Jon's documents, he felt that it was a challenging case but one that would settle on favorable terms. He was confident that Gardiner would be happy to pay Benedict to make the suit go away and that they could probably settle the case before any serious spending on discovery got underway.

Kress's reputation as one of the top trial lawyers in the United States was fairly earned. He was a forceful and convincing advocate who had often managed to convince juries and judges of the seemingly preposterous. As he was finishing his presentation to the committee, he saw his partners nodding in agreement with each point he was making and assumed that the vote was in the bag. He would have preferred to go straight to a vote, but tradition dictated he ask if there were any questions.

Paul Anderson, an intellectual property partner, was the first to pipe up. "You mentioned that the potential client expressed an interest in getting the patent rights back. What if he decides that that's what he truly wants even if there's a cash or stock settlement on the table? You know that clients often change their minds and balk at what would have seemed like a dream settlement only a few weeks before."

"True," replied Kress, "but let's face it, usually clients are full of principles and hurt feelings at the outset, and have to get the anger out of their system before they'll agree to settlement. My impression is that Mr. Vickers has gone through the principles and hurt feelings stage already and we're getting that rarest of all clients here, a realist. Besides, even if he suddenly regresses to an earlier stage, I'm sure he'll get back to reality quickly again. For one thing, I can't imagine that Gardiner will keep him employed once we make his demand for him, so he's going to be out of a job. For another, when he begins to understand the hardships of this undertaking, in terms of time and nerves and intrusiveness, he will see the light."

"What if he doesn't?" Anderson persisted.

"Then we go through some more discovery. We make it a bit awkward and uncomfortable for him, expose him to a deposition with slightly less than perfect preparation, and give him a mild taste of what trial is going to be like. It's our job to protect our clients, sometimes from themselves."

"Then let me ask the question differently. What if Gardiner doesn't back down and offers no settlement?"

"Then he'll experience a world of hurt because this is a case I'd be more than happy to see through trial. We're great lawyers and we've won some unwinnable cases before. Just imagine what we can do with this matter, where We. Are. In. The. Right! This is that one-in-a-thousand opportunity to make money while doing good. How often do we have the facts and the moral ambiguities all arrayed on our side?" Kress paused, ostensibly to drink some water but in reality to provide time for his partners to consider his argument. "So it might cost us some of our own money up front. We can afford it. We're not leveraged like a lot of our competitors are. We have no debt. If there ever was a case on which I'd be willing to stake some of my own money, this is it."

Anderson still didn't give up. "I want us to be aware of all the risks. What if Gardiner says 'a pox on you and your lawyers. Here you go, here are some of your dead brother's patents, now go do your worst. I'm not giving you cash and I'm not giving you stock.' What if this is the settlement offer that's finally on the table and the client wants to accept it?"

Myers, the San Francisco partner, spoke up. "I don't think it'll ever happen. That kind of settlement will gut Sliema's worth. Gardiner will never go for something like that. But on the off chance that hell freezes over during this litigation, we'll just need to pound sense into our client. Early and often. He needs to understand that his best bet is a cash and stock settlement. As Martin said, sometimes our job is to protect our clients from themselves."

Anderson fell silent but remained visibly worried. Some of the partners in the Washington conference room shot him unhappy glances, and Kress sensed it was time to move in for the kill. But Jack Rubinoff, the firm's second name partner and Anderson's closest personal friend, raised his hands and cleared his throat. Kress sighed, realizing that Jack was about to derail the pack mentality developing in the room.

"We all understand this is a huge opportunity. If we get a good settlement, our contingency fees could be north of 100 million dollars. And that's a fantastic outcome we all want," Jack said. "But if we're trying to run a business here, we should do a cost-benefit analysis, not just a benefit analysis. What's our exposure? What's the worst case scenario? How much of a haircut are we going to take if, when all is said and done, there's no money on the table or by some calamity we lose the trial?"

Kress obliged him by going through the calculations. He thought that the partnership could be in for as much as two million in out of pocket expenses and five million in lost revenues for billable time. In a classic closing argument maneuver, he got the bad news out up front, acknowledging that these were not insignificant numbers, and then finished with the strengths of his case.

"We need to think of this as an investment opportunity. We invest at most seven million for a better than even chance at a payout that is more than twenty-five times that, a payout that will materialize in just a few short months because no one is going to have the stomach to litigate this case. I may not be certain about a lot of things, but I'm willing to guarantee that Gardiner won't want the publicity of a trial.

"But this committee is a democracy and I am just one member of it. Majority controls. I won't hide my disappointment if we decide we're too risk averse to take on a virtually guaranteed case because our draws in the next couple of quarters might be short a few thousand each, but I will abide by the majority decision. Are we comfortable voting now, or are there any other issues that we need to discuss?"

No new issues came to the fore, and the committee voted. Benedict's case was approved. The vote was unanimous.

———————— ⇒((◐))⇐ ————————

After the meeting broke up, Anderson and Rubinoff took the elevator to the twelfth floor, where their offices bracketed the eastern corridor. Rubinoff noticed that Anderson was looking grim and commented on it.

"I just have a gut feeling that it's too good to be true," Anderson replied. "Sometimes it's like we're on a speeding train and I don't understand where the train is headed and why we're on it. We've had a good thing here for a long time, yet some of us keep pushing to take on riskier and riskier cases to post bigger and bigger numbers. For what?"

Rubinoff sighed and nodded in agreement. He accompanied Anderson to his office. After closing the door behind them, Anderson headed to his minifridge and came back with a couple of beers. He tossed one of the bottles and the opener to his friend and dropped into an armchair. "Something has definitely changed in this firm," Rubinoff said after uncapping his beer and taking a long pull from it. "There are moments when I wonder if it's time to look at other opportunities."

Anderson kept his gaze on the building opposite. "I was approached by Berger Fleming a couple of weeks ago," he said. "They want to build their intellectual property practice.

They're willing to guarantee a very nice minimum for the next five years and they're willing to accommodate five to ten of my people. I think their bankruptcy practice might use some help as well. Can you imagine what a coup it would be for them to get *the* Jack Rubinoff of Kress Rubinoff? I'll bet they'll give you anything you want just to come over. Do you want me to broach the subject with them?"

Rubinoff was not surprised by Anderson's confession but was blindsided by his own rising excitement about the possibility of bolting from the firm he'd helped build from the ground up. He thought about his people, whom he tried to protect as much as possible, but who had recently become part of the general pool of associates and had been subjected to abuse that they never experienced in their formerly sheltered existence. As a consequence, several had openly threatened to leave as soon as the economy picked up and lateral hiring picked up with it. Then he thought about the years he spent nurturing a bankruptcy practice that was admired and envied nationally.

"Sorry, Paul, I can't commit to something like this yet. I need to mull it over," he said, shaking his head sadly. "I might be too old and too tired to start at a new place. I might decide to retire instead."

"Sounds like whatever decision you make, staying here is no longer an appealing option," observed Anderson.

Rubinoff couldn't really argue. "Sure sounds like that, doesn't it?" he said.

Martin Kress reached Benedict immediately after the contingency committee's vote, while Benedict sat at the bar at Match Box, a popular hangout on H Street, waiting for his dinner and flirting with a couple of comely Department of Agriculture employees, trying to decide which of them was the easier lay. Kress's call cleared all thoughts of extracurricular activities from Benedict's mind. The second prong of the scheme was now set. The litigation would go forward according to plan, with Kress Rubinoff at the helm. He thanked Kress for the committee's speedy decision and asked what the next steps would be.

"I'm going to put together a team. It'll be based in New York because that's where all the parties are, even though the action will have to be instituted in Delaware. But I'll continue to personally be in charge of this case. Are you free next Tuesday for dinner? I'll be in New York myself then and will introduce you to the people with whom you'll be interacting on a day-to-day basis. We'll also have you sign a representation agreement."

"Right. I'll mark my calendar."

"Great. One more thing. Don't destroy any documents from now on. Who knows what Gardiner will ask for once this case gets underway, and you need to preserve everything now that you're on notice of a possible litigation."

"Does that include not deleting e-mails?"

"Absolutely. Unfortunately you need to let your inbox overflow for now."

Chapter 23
January 23-24

"**M**artin will be in the office tomorrow and wants to meet with you," the New York managing partner told Eric McIvor. No words could induce greater anxiety in a Kress Rubinoff partner. Rivulets of sweat started running down McIvor's back even before the call was over.

I'm too old for this crap, he thought. How was it possible that after a solid, even excellent, 25-year career as a litigator, he still found himself this afraid of Kress? He knew the answer, of course. If anyone was going to give him the boot from the firm it would be Kress, in person.

He pretended to himself that his living standard was prudent, even frugal, a lie he almost believed. But all it would take to upend his world was a single missed quarterly partner's draw.

On his desk was a photograph of his wife in front of their home, laughing and holding the leash of their champion Great Bernese Mountain Dog. He snapped that picture on the day they moved back into their Long Neck, Long Island colonial after an eight-month renovation that doubled their living space and tripled their mortgage.

On the bookcase directly facing him was a pair of photographs of his five children. In the one on the left, each wore a private school uniform. In the one on the right, taken last summer, they were all on horseback, lined up in a row, dressed in English riding gear, grinning widely because he'd surprised them with the gift of a horse for each of them that morning. On the wall near the window hung an original oil of his pride and joy, a 1926 BMW R32 motorcycle he had bought at an auction three years before. His wife did not look too kindly on the purchase, which grew his collection of vintage motorcycles to an even dozen, especially when she learned that it came with a six figure price tag.

McIvor sighed. Overall, it was an exceptionally good life, and if all it cost him was a quarterly bout of panic when Kress reviewed the firm's numbers, the price was well worth it.

But this visit wasn't for the quarterly chat. McIvor tried to calm himself down so that he could think properly. He looked out the window. Normally, the view from his 32nd floor office, a panorama of New York City's skyline with the East River shimmering in the background, worked better than the antianxiety pills his doctor prescribed for just these kinds of days. But even the elements conspired against him today—fog was obscuring the view, turning his world claustrophobically close.

His premonition that this time he'd be sacked wouldn't let go, but he couldn't think of a reason for this impending catastrophe. Kress Rubinoff was driven purely by the numbers, and last quarter was a strong one for him, certainly much stronger than a few previous quarters he'd survived.

He ran down a mental checklist of possible other grounds for dismissal, but found nothing. He had even made a conscious effort to kiss his new practice group leader's ass and help him in every possible way. Just thinking of Mike Tajerian raised McIvor's blood pressure even higher.

Perhaps Kress's visit was related to Mike. Perhaps Mike had thrown him under the bus to make himself look better. It was something Mike would stoop to. McIvor turned away from the window with growing determination. He'd given years of his life to Kress Rubinoff, and he wasn't going to be pushed out without standing up for himself. He was just as good at placing blame elsewhere as Mike was.

McIvor took no chances on the morning of his meeting with Kress. He'd taken an antianxiety pill before leaving home and was chugging chamomile tea in a further effort to calm himself down. Still, his stomach clenched and he felt his breakfast come up when he saw that the electronic invitation to his meeting with Kress had been amended to include Mike Tajerian.

Yet at the appointed hour he went to the conference room and pretended it was the best day of his life. "Martin!" he boomed, walking into the room. "What brings you to New York?"

"Hi, Eric. Thanks for meeting me on such short notice." Martin was at his most frightening when he was friendly. "Let's wait until Mike gets here, so I don't have to tell the story twice and bore you. How are Gail and the kids?"

"They're doing great. No complaints. I hear Jake got into Yale Law. You must be so proud of him."

"All I want is for my kids to be happy. But, it's obviously better to get into Yale than into, say, Georgetown." McIvor winced. He wondered if the derogatory reference to his alma mater was deliberate.

Mike's entrance prompted another round of fake camaraderie but Martin cut it short and got to the reason of his visit. "We're taking on a contingency case against Peter Gardiner and one of his funds. Maybe against a pharmaceutical company too. We'll need to make that decision after we review the documents more carefully." Mike and Eric exchanged a confused look. Both were patent litigation specialists who had not worked on a financial or corporate matter in years.

"There might be a patent component to this case. I'm hoping to dissuade the client from making this about the patents, but we need to be prepared and understand all the angles, and that's where your expertise comes in. You're looking light with your billables this quarter, Eric, so I'm going to have you run the day-to-day operations on this case. Don't worry, you won't have to think too hard. I'll manage the strategy and the big picture aspects personally."

Chapter 24

Benedict entered the Serenity Tea Shop fifteen minutes before his 2 p.m. meeting with Peter. The shop took up the second floor of an unremarkable building on Fifty-fourth Street and its entrance didn't offer much encouragement to those seeking either serenity or tea. Inside, however, the room was spacious and inviting. There were wooden tables set at intervals that suggested respect for privacy, an area in which teas and tea accessories were displayed in open cabinets, and a small book section. Benedict surveyed the room and chose the most secluded table. He put a folder on the seat next to him, then covered it with his camel-hair overcoat.

He perused the menu of astronomically expensive teas and frowned at the flowery paragraph-long descriptions typed under each of them. *Whatever happened to plain old tea?* he thought. He eventually settled on the Earl Grey, deciding to order without waiting for Peter.

His tea arrived quickly, and attending to the ritualized mechanics of dressing his drink acted to settle him. He wished William was there to back him up, and this thought bothered him. Benedict didn't like feeling dependent on other people.

He ran through his talking points once again, playing out the various scenarios that could unfold.

"This is highly unusual," Gardiner's voice said. Benedict had been so wrapped up in his thoughts that he failed to see him arrive. "Even though I like you, Benedict, I still prefer not to mingle socially with the hired help. No offense."

"None taken, Peter," said Benedict. "Thank you for meeting me here. You'll see that it's a conversation best had outside the office."

"Is this going to take long?" Gardiner asked. He sat down across from Benedict without taking off his coat, and waved off an approaching waiter.

"I'll get right to the point." Benedict said. "I'm the executor of Jon's estate. You know that means I'm responsible for acting in its best interests, right?"

"So?"

"As executor, I have the full power of the law to right certain wrongs."

Gardiner snorted. "Sorry to be so cynical, but the law has long belonged to those who can pay for it."

"Possibly. But I'm willing to test this hypothesis."

"How are you going to do that?"

"By suing you, for starters. You and the Gardiner New Horizons Fund. For fraud. You diluted Jon's stake in the company he sweated blood to create. That wasn't the deal he agreed to when he allowed you to invest. You swindled him out of hundreds of millions, if not billions."

Gardiner began drumming his fingers on the table. "This

is what this meeting is about? You're wasting my time over Jon's shares?"

"I take it you don't think it's anything for you to worry about."

Gardiner didn't disguise his disdain. "For a minute there I thought you had something serious to sue me for. Jon was a sophisticated party with access to lawyers and he signed a proxy before he went off to the Himalayas. Have a lawyer look at whatever documents you have."

"I did. Martin Kress of Kress, Rubinoff, Twist & Andrews, in fact. He was particularly fond of the e-mail Jon sent with the signed proxy. The one saying that the proxy is not carte blanche and that Jon would not agree to his share being diluted to anything under 20% or to having any major drug company invest in Sliema."

Gardiner sighed and affected regret. "You've escalated it from a minor misunderstanding into a mountain of legal bills. Well done."

Benedict held Gardiner's gaze but didn't speak. He was surprised at how reluctant he felt to pull the trigger. It was one thing to fantasize about this moment, but quite another to face the man he was about to ruin.

Gardiner's color rose, and he slammed his open palm on the table. A waiter looked over in alarm. "Don't you forget who I am and who you are. You're my domestic help and you'd do well to always remember that. I've been a fantastic employer to you. I practically bank rolled your Ph.D. and given you unlimited leave to travel for your research. And you get lawyers involved? You don't even bother discussing this with me first?"

Gardiner's outburst stiffened Benedict's spine. This was the Gardiner he knew and loathed. This Gardiner, Benedict had no problem blackmailing. "Peter, I genuinely regret the need to do this," he said. "But I have a duty to my brother's estate that I intend to honor."

"Who are the beneficiaries of his estate?"

"I am."

"You're the sole heir? You're pursuing a suit as a fiduciary to yourself?" asked Peter, his face showing incredulity.

"My duty is to the estate. It's immaterial who the heirs are." Benedict insisted primly.

"Get off it! Who's going to come after you if you don't do your duty? How about we call it what it really is? An attempt to get rich quick off something that your brother and I worked hard to create. Something you've put no effort into and don't even understand. You wouldn't know an obesity drug if one came up and bit you on your ass, and you certainly don't know how to build a company from the ground up."

"You can hurl abuse at me to your heart's content, but it won't change the facts." Benedict said.

Gardiner shifted gears. "This is so out of character for you," he said. "What's going on? Drugs? Money issues? I'm willing to help."

"You cheated my brother out of what was rightfully his."

"'Cheated' is a loaded word. Are you sure you want to put it on the table?"

"I don't care what words we use as long as the situation is righted. If you prefer that I say 'accidentally diluted his shares' or 'made an accounting error that wiped out ninety-nine percent of his equity' I'll be happy to oblige you. As long as the end result is the same."

Gardiner got up and walked around the shop, picking up and putting down various items, as if weighing them in the palm of his hand, and Benedict knew a deal offer was imminent. There were definitely some advantages to negotiating against someone he'd spent years observing in intimate detail, and Peter ran true to form this time, too. After the loud intimidation and the cajoling laced with faux concern, came the pacing, when he was calculating an offer.

Gardiner came back and sat down. "I think we can work something out. The nuisance value of this suit is high enough to make it worth it to me to give you something, even though I view this as the cheapest form of extortion, especially coming from you. Money's cheap, and I can always replenish it. That's the difference between me and you, Benedict. I know how to make money and you don't. That's why the likes of you will always work for the likes of me."

Benedict cocked his head and smiled. "I would never cast aspersions on your ability to make money, Peter. You're truly a titan, and I say that with admiration. But part of your money-making machine is my brother's sweat, for which he wasn't adequately compensated."

"Adequately compensated?" Peter lashed out again. "What do you call the $400,000 in yearly salary he was drawing? Snack money?"

"That's not the issue. We're talking about his share of the company."

Gardiner rose again. "I'm done. Have your lawyers bark at my lawyers. That's what they're happiest doing."

Benedict laid his hand on the sleeve of Peter's coat. "I

wouldn't leave just yet. If this were all I had to tell you, I could have had my lawyers file the complaint and serve you. There's more."

Peter shook Benedict off but didn't walk away. Benedict looked up at him, refusing to speak further until he sat down.

"You have five minutes," Gardiner said, taking his seat again. "And I hope you realize you no longer work for me. You can add your dismissal to your frivolous lawsuit."

Benedict ignored the taunt. "You are no longer in possession of the artifacts I procured for you." Gardiner's face registered the shock Benedict had been hoping to elicit. He quickly continued. "The objects you now have are fakes."

"There better be a good explanation for this. And you can be sure that if it's true and any of my property is missing you will regret it."

Benedict's demeanor changed abruptly. He leaned forward across the table, and Gardiner drew back instinctively. "Don't threaten me, Peter. You are in no position to do so." He took his smartphone out of his overcoat's pocket, picked up the folder he brought with him, and placed both objects on the table. "Would you like to hear what a conspiracy to receive stolen goods sounds like? I've been recording our conversations, and in this state, recordings made with the knowledge of just one participant are legal. And now I have the real artifacts, which you so obligingly pawed without gloves."

"You lying bastard," Gardiner said.

Benedict shook his head. "Not lying. If you check the trinkets in your safe, you'll see that each has a tiny 'Made in Turkey' stamp on the back." He took color photographs out of the folder and pushed them toward Gardiner. Each was an enlargement showing a dusted surface with a prominent fingerprint. "I also have the analysis reports and the provenance documents," he said, watching Gardiner gingerly touch the photographs. "I decided not to shred them after all. As these photographs show, they have your fingerprints on them, too. And of course the money trail tracks nicely with the recordings."

Gardiner sat rigid, transfixed by the images before him.

"If you agree to play," Benedict continued, "I'm willing to give you back the artifacts. After all, you've paid for them and as you said, their loss isn't a crushing blow to humanity."

"And if I don't?"

"The artifacts and the evidence of your knowledge of their origins will be turned over to the authorities." Gardiner turned white. Benedict allowed him to mull this consequence over and waited for him to respond.

After some time, Peter regained his composure and a shadow of his former swagger. "That's a great yarn, but we both know you'll never go to the authorities. You were a participant. You're just as vulnerable."

Benedict sighed. He picked up the smartphone, found the relevant application, and pressed the play icon.

Gardiner slumped in his chair as he heard himself ask Benedict to purchase stolen artifacts. It was clear he was the instigator.

Satisfied that he'd made his point, Benedict stopped the playback. "As hard as it is to believe, Peter, it's not my intention to cheat you, and I would have gladly dispensed with the blackmail had you been amenable to reason. I just want what rightly belongs to my brother's estate."

"You've got a set of cojones made of brass, my friend. Where was all this courage before now? If I'd seen it in you, you could have made real money with me."

Benedict put the photographs into the folder, and returned the smartphone to his coat pocket. Then he turned back to Gardiner. "Let's talk specifics. Here's what I need you to do."

Chapter 25

Peter cancelled his appointments for the rest of the day and told his driver to drive him to Brooklyn Heights. He felt his chest constrict and wondered if he was having a heart attack and should be going to the emergency room instead. He had the driver drop him off at Montague Street with instructions to come back in an hour. For reasons he couldn't articulate, he felt compelled to walk along the promenade and see the Manhattan panorama before him.

He found an empty bench, and sat down, hunching forward and exhaling deeply in an effort to calm his thumping heart. He tried to concentrate on the skyline, a sight that never failed to move him.

Peter loved New York City. In its brashness, drive, and arrogance, it had mirrored him. Until an hour ago.

Perhaps this was a mistake. He needed to be clear-headed and logical. Instead, he was getting emotional at the sight of his city.

The complexity of his predicament was making it difficult to apply his usually reliable problem-solving methodology to it. Normally, he would parse a situation into concrete issues, arranged them in the order in which they needed to be addressed, and chip away at each task without looking at the main goal again until he'd made significant progress. As he reminded his subordinates, putting these blinders on was the surest way to achieve the seemingly impossible.

Yet now he couldn't do it. Peter's mind raced from the fear of being arrested for buying stolen goods, to the shame of being duped by an employee, to the impossibility of doing what Benedict instructed him to do, and back again to the awfulness of being the star of a perp walk. And a perp walk as a common criminal—not for a financial scheme, which would have at least given him a certain cachet on Wall Street, even if he had to surrender his securities license. Every time Peter came back to that scenario his breath caught and his heart rate skyrocketed. He simply couldn't lose face this way and he certainly couldn't subject his family to this humiliation.

This isn't helpful, he thought irritably. He tried to rally himself with memories of his past triumphs. His almost uncanny ability to pick successful startups to invest in. His teaching stints at Harvard, University of Chicago, and University of Pennsylvania business schools. His access to every powerful figure in Washington. His position on the President's Economic Advisory Panel. Yet the more he reminded himself of his current standing and past achievements, the tighter the fear of losing everything gripped him.

After a few more minutes of getting nowhere except deeper into panic, he finally had to admit that he couldn't deal with the situation on his own. He had to talk to Jennie. He thanked God for sparing him from the vanity of some of his peers, who married 24-year-old underwear models and fooled themselves into believing these girls loved them. Had he married one of them, he wouldn't be thinking about sharing his woes with her right now. He'd be taking out the prenup agreement and making sure he wasn't going to lose too much when the shit hit the fan and his child bride filed for divorce.

He called Jennie and asked her to meet him at home in two hours. He told her that something serious had happened and he needed to talk to her, but not over the phone. Peter was gratified that "Are you all right?" was the first thing she asked, and he teared up with relief at not feeling entirely alone anymore.

⸺⸻«◉»⸻⸺

Jennie was waiting for Peter in the sitting area of their master bedroom, pacing and twisting a strand of her long, glistening blonde hair. When he walked in, she ran over and hugged him. He hugged her back, then went to sit in an armchair. Jennie arranged herself on the chaise longue, kicking off her heels and tucking her knees into her chest. She watched Peter intently, her warm brown eyes wide with apprehension.

Peter didn't mince words. He laid out the situation to Jennie, fully expecting her to ream him out. She didn't. Instead, she sat still, digesting what he had told her. He was about to speak again, but she held up her hand to shush him.

"I just thought of something—can we be sure the house

isn't bugged?" she asked. "I feel stupid saying such melodramatic things, but how do we know what Benedict did? He had access to everything."

Peter groaned and covered his face with his hands. "You're right! We'll have to review everything—bank accounts, credit cards, passwords, keys…" He paled, and beads of sweat appeared on his forehead as a new horror occurred to him. "Do you think he has somebody else on the staff working with him?"

"Let's discuss this outside," Jennie suggested, putting on her shoes. She got up and moved toward the French doors leading onto the terrace. "On second thought, if the spy thrillers I read are to be believed he could have wired our outdoor spaces as well. They're all small enough and partially enclosed. We better have our private conversations in Central Park from now on."

———((()))———

Seven listening devices were detected when the Gardiners' co-op was swept later that evening, in Peter's office and in the Gardiners' drawing room, solarium, private dining room, and master bedroom. Walter Dunleavy, the expert conducting the sweep, said they were of the type used by private individuals, not law enforcement.

Chapter 26
January 25

Benedict's phone rang while he was in the shower. He cursed the caller, thinking it was William, and ran, dripping wet, to pick it up in the bedroom.

"What?" he demanded, only to hear crying on the other end. "Who is this?"

"Benedict? It's Mary. Mary Olsson," Peter's secretary said between sobs.

"What's wrong?" Benedict asked. He sat on his bed, gripped by fear.

"Peter fired me. He's been a total jerk this morning. He's been grilling each staff member individually about whether we've done anything for you recently. When I told him that you asked me to get you the jewelry boxes a few days ago, he hit the roof and fired me. What am I going to do? I'm fifty-eight years old, and he said that he won't give me a recommendation and . . ."

Benedict cut her off. "Mary, please calm down. This is all

a terrible misunderstanding. I'm going to call him right now and straighten it all out. Please don't cry."

Mary sniffled. "Thank you. I didn't know who else to call." She erupted in a fresh jag of crying. "I don't want to tell Frank I got fired. He's going to have a fit. As it is, he gets so angry whenever I tell him about how Peter treats me."

"I promise I'll take care of this," Benedict said, attempting to keep his own growing anger out of his voice.

———=»«(0)»«=———

Benedict wasted no time calling Peter's direct office number.

"It's Benedict."

"I know. I have caller ID. What do you want?"

"I want you to reinstate Mary."

"Why? So she can continue to spy on me for you?"

"Let it go, Peter. She's not involved in this. You know she routinely brought me things from your safe. I was in charge of packing your briefcase daily, for Christ's sake. She had no idea what this was about."

"Well look who suddenly developed empathy for the little people," Peter mocked him. "If you're that concerned about Mary, why don't you give her some of the stock you're blackmailing me for." The line went dead.

Benedict was appalled. He also noticed the blinds weren't closed and he was stark naked. He hastily put on a robe then called William.

When he'd explained the situation, William said, "What

was it that Comrade Stalin used to say? Chop a forest and kindling will fly?"

"Fine, William. If you want to say 'I told you so,' go right ahead."

"I'm not going to say that. What I am going to say is that we need to help the woman out. Could you use a personal assistant?"

"To do what?"

"Fucked if I know. Think of something and hire her to do it at her current salary. If we don't fix her situation she'll eventually blame you for her problems, and we can't afford the distraction."

Benedict thought about it for a while. "I know where she can be useful," he said.

"Good. Problem solved. Care to lay odds on whether it's the last one?"

PART IV

Chapter 27
January 26

Jennie was flicking the French manicured nail of her left thumb against her left pointer finger, and Peter knew not to interrupt. It was her tell for when she was deep in thought.

They sat at the kitchen island having breakfast. It was 6:30 a.m., their usual time for starting the day.

"I find the whole thing so odd," Jennie mused. "You said yourself that cases like this always settle and he'll get something. Why stack the deck like this?"

"I don't know. His behavior is wholly irrational. Either blackmail me properly and don't institute a lawsuit, or just sue me."

"Well, he is kind of new at this," Jennie pointed out, hoping to elicit a smile from her husband, but not succeeding.

"The weirdest thing is that if I follow his instructions, it'll make the litigation more protracted and costly. He told me to hire Fields Stanhope, that I should ask for the moon and the stars in terms of discovery, and that both sides will load up on experts, including Nobel Prize-winning biologists and economists. What's the point of that?"

Jennie dangled her shoe from her foot. "Do you think Benedict's threat would be significantly neutralized if we could get hold of the original items?"

"Probably not. I was thinking about it last night. He taped the conversation in which I crow about having the stuff in my office already, not just plans to acquire them. And he has the conversation about shredding the documents. How could I have been so stupid?"

Jennie set her white Wedgwood coffee cup in its saucer and laced her fingers through her husband's. "Do you think Dunleavy can help at all?" Walter Dunleavy, the security specialist who found the bugs in their home two days before, was ex-special ops, rumored to have done all kinds of extracurricular security jobs for those who could afford his services.

"Maybe, but I'll need to come up with a plausible story to feed him. I don't want him to know what's really happening here. I don't want anybody else knowing anything about this." Then a grin spread over Peter's face as a new thought occurred to him. "Benedict warned me that if he dies or is detained everything will be released to the public. But it doesn't mean that I can't make his life unbearable to a greater degree than he's screwing with mine. Two can play this game. That's the flaw of mutually assured destruction; the threat only works as a threat."

Jennie was alarmed. "What do you have in mind?"

"I think someone needs to pay Benedict's place a visit. Take a baseball bat to his belongings. Maybe a couple of guys can shadow him conspicuously. Maybe bug his phones. Up his misery index a hundredfold. The beauty is that he can't go to the authorities without losing his hold on me."

"Baseball bats? That's very Little Italy mafia circa the Seventies, don't you think? What will it achieve?"

"Leverage. It'll make him want to negotiate more rationally. And it'll make me feel great."

"Wow. Benedict is bringing out the badass in you." Jennie fluttered her eyelashes, "and I kinda like it." She smiled and ran her fingertips along his thigh.

"You do, do you?" Peter matched her tone, but a glance at the clock made him turn serious again. "Wish I could stay and see just how much you like it but I've got a conference call in twenty minutes."

"How disappointing." Jennie pouted.

━━━━━━━ ((◉)) ━━━━━━━

William's emergency cell phone, which he took to keeping under his pillow, rang at 4:15 a.m. He picked it up, got out of bed and padded barefoot into the study.

"I'll be wearing that Arsenal jersey to a game of your choice after all," said Benedict. He was somewhere outdoors; William could hear traffic noise and sirens, typical New York background music.

"What's happened?"

"Someone broke into my place. I don't think they took anything, but they destroyed just about everything and they did a very thorough search. Even my marmalade has

— 173 —

finger tunnels in it."

"You sure they took nothing?"

"I can't be absolutely sure. The place is unrecognizable. But there wasn't anything for them to find. I kept it sterile, as far as this matter is concerned."

"I'm going to get Claire and the children away from here."

"I'm sorry." Benedict said miserably.

"I don't want to hear it," said William, not unkindly. "We all knew what we were getting into. Now the issue is how we get out of it. It's time to activate the reinforcements. I'll take care of it. In the meantime, you know what to do, right?"

Chapter 28
January 27

"Good morning, Mr. Gardiner. Today it is my turn to give you instructions. You understand what we are discussing?" said a gruff basso with an unmistakable Russian accent.

It took Gardiner a couple of seconds to realize that the voice was tormenting him on Benedict's behalf. "Benedict is too high and mighty to make his own calls these days?" he asked.

"Do you have pen and paper?"

"I have a computer. I live in the twenty-first century."

"Mr. Gardiner, please, no sarcasm. People from Russia find it rude and not funny. Please take these names down. They are the experts your lawyers will retain. There are seventeen of them." The voice dictated and Peter dutifully typed them into a new document.

"Do you have them all?" asked the voice when he finished reciting the names.

"Yes, I do. Anything else?" asked Gardiner, trying to keep his irritation under control.

"Just one thing. We do not appreciate it when our friends are harassed, burgled or followed. This is just business, and we are all businessmen, so let us act like it." The voice hung up.

Peter immediately called Jennie. "I think Benedict is involved with the Russian mob."

"Why do you say that," Jennie asked.

"I just got a call from one of their gorillas," said Peter, then repeated what the caller told him. "The Russian mob is the scariest thing there is, except for the Russian security forces. Shit. Until today, I didn't realize it was possible to be this frightened and this furious at the same time. My blood pressure is through the roof," he added.

As was always the case in their relationship, the more worked up Peter got, the calmer Jennie was. "Peter, get a grip. Let's think this new development through. Does Russian involvement make it easier to cut a deal? If they're in, then it's not personal anymore. How does it change our exposure if these people, and not just Benedict, own a large chunk of shares in Sliema?"

Peter was back in control of himself. "You're right. So far, all we have is a foreign-sounding voice identifying himself as Russian. I'll see if Dunleavy can trace the call."

"Olichka, I did it!" Olga's father informed her in Russian

when she answered her apartment landline, his pride unmistakable. "This guy who's playing the Gardiner character is doing a great job! He sounds like a Wall Street asshole with a capital A. Your friends are really onto something with this fantasy spy game they're developing."

Olga felt her skin turn cold and clammy. "Papa, what phone are you calling me on?" she asked, knowing the answer but willing it not to be true.

"Oy!" he exclaimed. "I was supposed to throw it away right after the Gardiner call. Sorry, I just got so excited."

"No problem, but throw it away now, and don't call me until you leave the U.K., okay?" Olga tried to keep her voice steady. The last thing she wanted or could afford was to make her father worry.

"I guess I'm not cut out to be a spy." He father's hangdog guilt would have been comical had the consequences not had the potential to be so dire.

"No, you're not. But I'll keep you anyway. You're a decent father, all things considered." Olga forced herself to laugh, and was gratified that he did, too.

Of all the insane aspects of their plan, she always worried about her father's involvement the most. But Benedict thought his deep, Russian-accented basso would frighten Gardiner into towing the line. Now look where Benedict's obstinacy got them.

As Olga rummaged in her handbag for the cellphone on which she was to call William and Benedict, she chastised herself for being an idiot to agree to it. What was she going to do now?

William's panic phone was getting far too much traffic for his liking. When he saw it was Olga, his heart gave an extra-painful lurch.

"Please tell me you're calling for no reason other than that you're missing my sharp wit."

"The phone used to call Gardiner was used to call my home number immediately afterward."

William heard the tremor in Olga's voice and breathed deeply to steady himself. "Remind me to kill Benedict the next time I see him. And remind me to kick myself for listening to him on an operational issue," he said.

"I know the drill. I'm going to lose this phone and make sure there's nothing linking me to all of you except for the couple of days in Istanbul."

"Whatever happens, don't be a heroine. If they use physical violence, cry, faint, don't pretend to be tougher than you are. The more you hold out, the more damage they may inflict." He heard a sob on the other end of the line. "But maybe they won't trace your father's call to you. After all, they'll need access to nonpublic phone records," William added in an attempt to calm her down, sounding false even to himself.

"I wanted an adventure and I'm getting it," she said. "Rest assured that I will remind you to kill Benedict."

Chapter 29
February 3

Walter Dunleavy presented himself at the Gardiners' apartment at 9 p.m. sharp, and was escorted into the library by the butler. Jennie and Peter were enjoying some brandy and listening to a blues recording. When Dunleavy was announced, Jennie got up, shook his hand, and excused herself. Peter turned off the music and asked Dunleavy what he wanted to drink, and Dunleavy chose a club soda. Peter poured it for him and invited him to sit down.

"Found anything?" he asked before Dunleavy's behind had a chance to hit the chair.

"Yes, we did. We can't put a name to the phone number, but we know it was a prepaid phone, bought for cash, in London, and that the caller was in London when he used it." Dunleavy sipped the club soda.

"So it's a dead end."

Dunleavy put his glass on the coaster on a side table and opened his briefcase. He took out several sheets of paper before answering Peter's question.

"As far as the identity of the man who called you is concerned, yes. Although we have some ideas about him. But there's an interesting twist." He handed Peter a formal headshot of a smiling woman. "Dr. Olga Mueller."

"Who is she?"

"The same cell phone made only one other call, to her home number." Dunleavy saw Peter's puzzled expression and smiled. "I'm sorry. I shouldn't be drawing my explanation out this way, but it's a textbook case of tugging on one thread and suddenly everything unravels. Breaks like these are so rare in my world that I can't help savoring it."

"I understand professional pride as much as the next guy, but you're killing me, Walter. What's the bottom line?"

"Until less than a month ago Dr. Mueller was an associate at Kress Rubinoff." Peter leaned forward at the mention of Benedict's lawyers, a reaction that wasn't lost on Walter. "Kress Rubinoff means something to you?" he asked.

"We've tussled." Peter didn't elaborate.

"Anyway. While an associate at Kress Rubinoff, she traveled to Istanbul on October 18 last year, on the same flight that Mr. Vickers took. But that's not the cutest part." Walter smiled as he presented the next photograph to Peter. The photograph showed Benedict and Olga sitting in the lobby of Benedict's hotel, sharing coffee and pastries. "From the hotel lobby's security camera," Dunleavy explained.

The following photograph showed Olga and Benedict standing with two other people at the same lobby. "The Ashford-Crofts. Colonel Sir William and Lady Claire. Colonel Ashford-Croft and Mr. Vickers were classmates in school, and they've stayed friends. The Ashford-Crofts live in Brussels. Colonel Ashford-Croft is stationed at NATO headquarters there. In the last three months, Mr. Vickers made over 200 calls to the Ashford-Croft residence and to Colonel Ashford-Croft's office and cell phone.

"The Colonel's military service record is classified, and even my most highly-placed sources can't get access to it. That suggests either special ops or intelligence work. He's fluent in Russian, and he was in London on the day the cell phone was bought."

Peter raised his glass to Dunleavy. "I'm truly impressed."

Dunleavy acknowledged the praise with a nod, but otherwise retained his neutral expression. "That's what you pay me to do, Mr. Gardiner. I take my work seriously. I understand that people don't come to me unless regular channels aren't sufficient."

Dunleavy handed over his last two photographs. "Dr. Mueller, the evening of October 30, and Dr. Mueller the morning of October 31. She's wearing the same clothes and she's leaving Mr. Vickers's hotel in the morning." Years of experience had taught Dunleavy not to elaborate on the evidence. Let the client draw his own conclusion.

Peter chuckled. "Well, well. So he's straight after all." He looked up at Dunleavy. "So what does all this tell you?"

"Finding Dr. Mueller was complicated enough to make us work for it, but easy enough that any professional would know we could. It either tells me that Colonel Ashford-Croft is getting sloppy in his old age, or that this is an elaborate setup designed to sacrifice an innocent bystander to slow us down and waste our resources."

"How do you plan to find out which it is?"

"I think we should interview Dr. Mueller."

"I don't need to know the details," Peter said. "Do what you think is best."

Walter collected the photographs and returned them to his briefcase.

"What's happening with Benedict?" Peter asked. "Did you find anything interesting at his place?"

Dunleavy shook his head. "No. We went through all his electronic media. There was nothing relating to your issue. Also no physical clues to go on—no keys, tickets, stubs, receipts. He's been careful to keep his home clean."

"Where is he?" Peter asked. Walter reached back into his briefcase and took out a more photographs. The first showed Benedict exiting a building. The next was a zoom-out of the same location, showing the building to be a residential high-rise.

"He's in Washington DC, holed up in an apartment in Friendship Heights rented to a Sylvia Morrison. He can't go anywhere without us knowing about it."

"Very good. Who is Sylvia Morrison?"

"She appears to be a freelance journalist. Writes fashion articles. She flew out to Bangkok on January 17. We haven't looked for her there because, frankly, we think she's just a friend or a past girlfriend. She travels a lot, so Mr. Vickers probably asked to crash at her place and she said yes. But if you'd like us to investigate this angle further, we can."

"No, it doesn't sound like there's a need to do that. I'd rather concentrate on Olga Mueller and the Ashford-Crofts. And don't let up on Vickers. Can you up the pressure on him? Not destroy the DC apartment, but maybe something more personal?"

"Yes, Mr. Gardiner. We certainly can. One more thing you might be interested in. We discovered that he recently mortgaged his townhouse. The bank approved a $700,000 mortgage and he took the whole amount."

Peter sighed. "Please don't take it the wrong way, Walter. I wish I didn't need your services, but you've surpassed my expectations, and they were quite high to begin with."

"Thank you, Mr. Gardiner. That means a lot to me. In my line of work, reputation is everything. May I suggest that you beef up your own security? We can provide bodyguards, property protection, et cetera."

"I don't think it's necessary. We have state-of-the-art alarms here and we changed the codes since we fired Benedict. Our chauffeurs are licensed bodyguards."

"With respect, Mr. Gardiner, I have to differ. Nothing about this feels like a homemade, small-time operation to me, and it would be prudent to take the appropriate precautions."

Chapter 30
February 4

It had been more than a week since Olga's panicked call to William and nothing had happened to her thus far. As hard as she tried to be vigilant, she saw no signs she was being followed or that her apartment had been tampered with, or any other indications that her connection to Benedict had become known. She was beginning to hope that William was right and the call hadn't been traced, and found that hours went by during which she forgot to be afraid.

It was a cold, sunny day in New York and Olga reveled in the ability to be outside during normal business hours. Other people were hurrying along, phones stuck to their ears or fingers frantically scrolling their smartphone messages. She just walked—slowly, looking up at the buildings, irritating the natives no end for impeding their pace. She used to be one of those people, often muttering that all tourists should be herded and quarantined in one section of Manhattan so they not interfere with people who had work to do. She marveled that taking ten minutes out of her day to walk around the block at lunchtime used to be an unimaginable waste of time.

Since she resigned from Kress Rubinoff, her life was unrecognizable. There was no structure to it. She did what she wanted to do, and mostly she wanted to just be. She slept a lot. She cooked. She went out. She started going to the gym to which she'd belonged for three years, but which she had visited only once, the day she had signed up. She met Brian Keller there. He asked her out, she said yes, and they had been dating since. It was a simple and happy relationship. No drama, no angst, no demons. Olga was certain it wouldn't last but was willing to be proven wrong.

When Olga walked into her apartment building, the concierge handed her a package that had arrived for her that morning. It was a dress Brian had ordered for her online after she told him how much she coveted it. Olga suppressed the desire to clap. Presents were always welcome.

She took the elevator to the eighth floor and walked down the long corridor to her apartment. As soon as she unlocked the front door, she sensed that something was wrong. The lights were on in the living room, but she knew she hadn't left any lights on. Before she had a chance to process this information fully, she was yanked into the apartment and the door was slammed behind her. She froze in terror.

Olga dropped her coat, her handbag, and her parcel by the door as a barrel-chested, bald man shoved her roughly forward through the hallway toward the living room. Two other men were sitting there, but Olga's attention was first drawn to her coffee table, on which a kit of what appeared to be surgical instruments was laid out. Her knees buckled, and she leaned against the wall to support herself.

"Move it, sweetheart," said the man who was shoving her along. Olga complied and stepped into the living room. She was ordered to sit, and she sat on the closest chair.

"Benedict Vickers," said one of the men sitting on the couch. "Name mean anything to you?"

Olga found it difficult to look at his bloodshot eyes, but forced herself to do so. "Yes. I met him on a flight to Istanbul a few months back."

"And?"

"And he showed me around."

The man who had shoved her snorted. "Is that what you kids call it these days?"

Olga turned around. "I don't understand," she said.

"You fucked him."

Olga blushed and was about to launch into an explanation, but thought better of it. Surely whether or not she slept with Benedict was tangential to what these men wanted from her. By the look of disgust the man with the reddened eyes shot at his colleague Olga surmised he thought so, too.

"Are you in touch with him?" He asked, apparently in charge of her interrogation.

"No," said Olga. "That seems to be a very popular question. You're the second person to ask me recently," she added.

"Who else asked you that?"

Olga did her best to appear cooperative. "A man called and asked me all kinds of questions about Benedict and a pending litigation involving my old firm. He spoke in Russian. That was downright odd."

The silence stretched after her answer and Olga felt

beads of sweat gliding along her back. She watched the man questioning her warily, while being hyperaware of the man who had shoved her, standing close behind her chair.

The questioner gave a slight nod, and Olga was jerked back by her hair, the movement sufficiently violent to raise the chair's front legs, causing Olga to flail as she tried to keep her balance. She saw the man who had been sitting until then near her questioner get up and take a shiny metallic object from the coffee table, then advance toward her. She fainted.

She came to in an armchair a few seconds later. She didn't feel pain, and concluded that no one had touched her with what she thought was a scalpel.

"You don't exactly have nerves of steel, do you?" observed her interrogator.

"No," admitted Olga, wiping her tears with her sleeve.

"I'm going to ask you, again, about your interaction with Vickers."

"I've told you everything I can. I promise."

"The problem is that I don't believe you."

"I don't know what I can do to convince you I'm telling the truth. You're asking me to prove a negative hypothesis. It can't be done." Olga's tears turned into sobs.

<hr>

The questioning went step by step. An hour into the interrogation, they had only gotten through the flight to Istanbul and the visit to the Hagia Sofia.

Olga hewed close to the truth, omitting only the conversations relating to Sliema and Jon Vickers. In parallel, she debated with herself the pros and cons of attempting to escape. Her captors were willing to show her their faces, and this made her worry that they weren't going to let her live. She came to the conclusion that she must run.

The first step was to steal a few moments to be unobserved. "I need to go to the bathroom," she said.

Her interrogator looked up at the man who had manhandled her. "Go with her."

"No!" Olga cried.

Her designated escort grabbed her upper arm, forcing her to stand, and they walked to the bathroom together. Olga went in and her captor allowed her to partially close the door.

Her brain kicked into overdrive. She sat on the toilet and surveyed her surroundings methodically, inventorying the various objects that lay at hand's reach from her perch. She quickly discarded the nail clippers, tweezers and toothbrush as possible weapons.

Her eyes locked on the cabinet underneath the sink, where she kept the laundry detergent and bleach. She gently opened one door, thankful it didn't squeak. Then she stood, flushed the toilet and turned on the water in the sink.

She quickly bent down, uncapped the detergent and the bleach simultaneously, utilizing the one-handed uncapping methodology she perfected during her years in the lab, then poured a generous measure of bleach into the large cap of the detergent bottle. Taking a deep breath, she closed her eyes and visualized what lay between her and the door to her apartment. The bathroom was at the end of a short corridor branching off from the one that led to the living room right from the front door. With luck, she'd get to the door before the two goons in the living room had a chance to react.

Olga held the cap in her right hand and opened the bathroom door with her left, as she said a short prayer to an amorphous, nondenominational god.

She splashed bleach into the face of her guard, pushed past him and was at her apartment door in five steps. She heard him emit a horrible sound, part sob, part scream, all pain, and knew she had mere seconds before the two men in the living room would come after her. It took what felt like eternity to grab her handbag from the floor, open the door, and run into the hallway.

Olga heard the shouts of the men as they reached their comrade. She ran as fast as she could, stopping briefly to push open the door to the first stairway that she came to. She rounded the corner and kept running down the hall to the second stairway, listening to the heavy metallic thud she hoped would tell her pursuers she must have used that door to escape.

She closed the door of the second stairway behind her quietly, then ran down the stairs, her breath burning her lungs and throat. She heard the door slam above her, then the sound of running feet. She seethed with frustration. Her captors must have split up, and all she accomplished was the waste of precious seconds. She sped up, keeping close to the wall and hoping that she wasn't visible through the stairwell.

She reached the main floor, burst through the emergency exit door to the street outside, then ran along the street looking over her shoulder for an empty cab. There were usually plenty of them driving along her block because it led away from the hospitals on First Avenue. When she swiveled her head the fourth time, she caught a glimpse of the man who had questioned her, and her adrenaline level surged. She forced herself to sprint, nearly knocking down a dog walker, and reached Third Avenue just as a cab pulled up.

Olga jumped in and screamed at the driver to just drive and that she'd tell him where to in a minute. He obliged and hit the gas.

After a few breaths, Olga calmed down enough to take stock of her situation and became conscious of how cold she was. She had no coat, and the sweater she was wearing was no match for the sub-freezing temperature and biting wind. She told the driver to take her to Bloomingdale's on Lexington and Fifty-ninth Street.

Her cell phone rang, causing her to start. Her caller ID displayed a "number blocked" message.

"Hello?" she said tentatively.

"Olga, come back." Olga recognized her questioner's voice and her heart hammered in her chest.

"No."

"You have a bad attitude. I hope you haven't called the police or your boyfriend, Brian. We'll kill him if you do either. In fact, we might have to lean on him a little to make you see reason and answer our questions."

"I have to call Brian. If I don't, he'll call me. We have plans for this evening."

"Just keep in mind that we're listening. If we think you're tipping him off in any way, it's not going to be pretty." Olga disconnected the call and tried to keep her panic at bay.

There wasn't a plan in place for this eventuality because she never mentioned Brian to the others. But she could never forgive herself if anything were to happen to him—he was a civilian and didn't ask for this.

At Bloomingdale's, while hurrying to the coat department, Olga reached a decision. She would have to call Benedict and alert him to the fact that another person was now in danger. Then she realized that the call could serve another purpose—making Peter Gardiner believe that she hadn't been in contact with Benedict since Istanbul and that she was angry at him for putting her in danger. That last one certainly wasn't going to require much acting.

First, however, she called Brian's home number, knowing he wouldn't be there at that time of the day, and left a message. "Brian, it's me. Something's come up, a possible new client, and I need to go out of town. Don't try my cell, it's running low and I forgot my charger. I'll call you when I'm back in town, in a couple of days. I'll miss you. Bye." Olga didn't sound convincing to herself, but it was the best she could think of and it would have to do.

Next, she called Benedict. She was transferred to voice mail, and left another message. "Benedict, this is Olga Mueller. I don't know what you're involved in or what you've done and quite frankly I don't give a shit. But whatever it is, my life is a living hell right now. Call me back at this number, ASAP. This isn't a joke!" She disconnected then found a large, warm coat with a hood and bought it, along with gloves and a scarf.

Her phone rang while she was putting on her new purchases in the ladies' lounge. "Olga? It's Benedict."

"You asshole! You're a complete and utter jerk!" Despite promising herself she wouldn't do this, Olga couldn't resist venting her frustration to its maximum degree.

"I probably deserve that. Not quite certain why, though."

"Because after not hearing from you once since coming back from Istanbul, I come home to find three animals in my apartment. They held me captive and kept interrogating me about you—about us—while threatening me with a scalpel. And a Russian guy called asking about you and Kress Rubinoff out of the blue before that."

"Are you all right?"

"I managed to escape but they're threatening Brian, my boyfriend, if I don't go back."

There was a pause before Benedict replied. "Olga, listen, I promise to get it all straightened out. You absolutely cannot go back to your apartment, though. Do you think they know your cell phone number?"

"Oh, I know they know my cell phone number. One of them called me. They said they were listening and if I go to the police they'll kill Brian."

"Don't call the police, and lose the cell. It's a beacon for your location. Just dump it wherever you are and move. Find another phone and call the number I'm going to give you." Benedict gave her an 800 number.

"Fine. I'll call you soon," Olga said with resignation. She turned off her cell and threw it in the nearest garbage bin.

Walking out of Bloomingdale's, Olga saw the man again. He was standing across the street, speaking on his cell. She quickly turned the corner onto Fifty-Ninth Street, hailed a cab and asked the cabbie to drive her to Fifty-fourth Street and Sixth Avenue.

When the cab dropped her off, Olga put up the hood of her new coat against the whipping wind, and walked south. She reached her destination, Forty-second Street and Park Avenue, twenty miserably cold minutes later.

The guard on duty asked Olga where she was going and she gave him the name of a law firm in the building. He didn't even call upstairs before issuing her a pass.

She rode the elevator to the reception area on the fortieth floor. A trim middle-aged woman sat at the reception desk, and Olga asked her to let Pam Kensington know that Olga Mueller was there to see her. Pam walked out a couple of minutes later.

"This is a nice surprise!" Pam smiled and hugged Olga before escorting her into the firm's offices.

"I thought I'd come see how Big Law partners live. I haven't seen your ilk for nearly a month now." Olga grinned. "Also, I came to ask for all kind of favors, first of which is to stop at the pantry and get me a large cup of coffee. I'm freezing."

"Absolutely," said Pam and veered to the left.

Once the coffee was poured and the two women were seated in Pam's office, Olga asked to make a call from Pam's phone. "Sorry. I lost my cell phone and I absolutely must call this person back. My first potential client!"

Pam hooted. "Woo-hoo! You go girl. I knew it wouldn't

take you long to get your practice off the ground." She pushed the instrument toward Olga as an invitation to use it. "Do you want some privacy?" she asked.

Olga nodded. "Just for a few minutes."

"I'll step out and find some hapless associates to terrorize."

When Pam left and closed the door of her office behind her, Olga pulled out the number Benedict had given her and dialed it. He picked up immediately.

"You all right?" he asked.

"Fine. No thanks to you."

"Can we stipulate to the fact that you're furious with me and move on, please? Your hissing is a bit distracting."

Olga opened her mouth to respond in kind, but thought better of it. She took a deep breath instead and tried to stop wanting to shove a knife into Benedict's stomach and turn it several full rotations. "What do you suggest I do now?" she asked instead.

"Get yourself down to DC. The apartment here is clean. No one knows I'm here. I can protect you better if you're here with me."

"Really? You and what army?"

Benedict ignored Olga's question. "I'd rather you not use credit cards. And come to think of it, I'd rather you not get on a train or a bus either. Any way that you could borrow a car?"

"How serious is their threat to Brian?"

"Brian? Oh, yes, the boyfriend. The threat is serious." The stress she heard in Benedict's voice frightened Olga and took the fight out of her.

"Okay," she said. "I'll drive down." Then a new worry

made her stomach lurch. "Did I give away your location when I called your cell?" she asked.

"No. My cell is back in New York. The calls are routed through a series of internet phone numbers, then eventually end up on a second cell I carry. But William still thinks the number we're using now is more secure."

"Give me the address of the apartment." Olga said.

Benedict did. "Olga, I'm sorry about this," he added. "I know nothing I say right now is going to make a difference, but I could never imagine you'd find yourself in so much danger."

———————

"All done?" asked Pam, peeking in her office.

"Yes. Sorry for commandeering your office like this." Olga pulled a face. "And now I'm also going to try to commandeer your car for a couple of days." Like most Manhattanites, Olga didn't own a car and had to resort to borrowing or renting a set of wheels whenever the need arose.

Pam narrowed her eyes. Olga was certain that this was the look Pam used to give uncooperative suspects during her years as a Federal prosecutor. She hoped her own face wasn't betraying her agitation and discomfort.

"Why do I get the feeling you're in trouble?"

"I'm not. Honestly. I just need to go to Boston for a couple of days to interview a potential client. It's a whistleblower case and I'd rather not have a record of renting a car or of where I went with it." Olga couldn't recall the last time she'd lied so glibly or so abundantly.

Pam sat back in her chair. "I have Ed's car here today." Ed was Pam's husband. "It's a manual. Can you drive it?" Olga nodded, and Pam continued. "Let me drive you out of the building because the parking attendants can be overzealous if they see a stranger driving a car that belongs to one of their regulars." She picked up her purse and found her keys, then turned back to Olga. "For the record, I don't believe a word you told me just now. But I have faith in you, and I know you wouldn't ask if it weren't important or for a good cause. Do you need money? I can run out to the bank and get you some cash."

Olga felt an acute pang of embarrassment and could barely bring herself to meet Pam's eyes. "I'm sorry for lying to you, Pam. Thank you for being such a good friend. I'm okay in the money department." She got up and put her coat on. "I promise to get the car back in a few days. And I promise, promise, promise to tell you everything as soon as I can."

⟶ ⟨⟨◍⟩⟩ ⟵

Pam drove Ed's black Beemer, with Olga in the passenger seat, out of the garage and onto Forty-first Street. Both women got out, and Pam hugged Olga. "Promise me you'll be careful."

"I'll be very careful. After all, I know how much Ed loves this car, and I want to be invited back to his fabulous BBQs," Olga joked lamely.

Olga got into the driver's seat, put the car into gear and

eased into traffic. As she waited to turn left onto Third Avenue she saw the man who had wielded a scalpel at her. He was standing by the main entrance to a building two blocks away from Pam's office, pretending to smoke but really observing every person entering and exiting.

With a feeling of nausea, Olga realized that her BlackBerry was on. Then she began laughing with relief, thankful for the inaccuracies of the BlackBerry GPS that she and her friends often found so annoying, but would now put distance between Pam and any danger.

Steering with one hand while navigating onto westbound Forty-second Street from Third Avenue, Olga pulled the device out of her bag and shut it off. She was certain that it would no longer give away her position, but didn't want to take any chances. She opened the window and threw it out into the oncoming traffic where an SUV drove over it.

Olga willed herself to concentrate on the mechanics of driving to avoid her anxiety over how wrong things were going. Luckily, it didn't take much effort to be consumed by her task. It was dusk, the traffic was bumper-to-bumper, and she hadn't driven in months.

Chapter 31

It was approaching 11 p.m. when Olga pulled into the visitors' parking at the Friendship Heights condominium. The drive had taken nearly seven hours, partly because she took care not to speed and partly because she made several stops along the way. She'd gotten off the highway in Wilmington, Delaware, to hit a mall on Route 202 where she bought some essentials. Her grumbling stomach reminded her that she hadn't had anything to eat since picking at a salad as an early lunch. On her way back to I-95, she stopped at a Bertucci's and scarfed down a pizza. Stops at rest areas for gas and coffee followed in Maryland and by this time, Olga couldn't pretend that she wasn't stalling.

Her anger at Benedict was disproportionate and she knew it, but she couldn't reason it away. Yes, he was wrong to insist they use her father, and he was too optimistic about how meekly Peter Gardiner would accede to their demands. But deep down, she had known all along that there was potential for danger, and it had thrilled her. Now she learned that the thrill of theoretical danger quickly morphed into uncontrollable and uncomfortable terror when the danger turned real, and feeling afraid made her furious. Benedict was just a convenient target—easier than raging at herself.

By the time she arrived, she was exhausted. She dragged herself to the front desk and asked the attendant to call apartment 27H. Benedict answered the intercom and said he'd come right down.

Olga slumped onto a bench and stared into the middle distance for the two minutes it took him to get to the lobby.

"What took you so long?" he demanded as he approached her.

"I left my place without any spare underwear, if you must know, so I stopped to shop in Delaware. No sales tax," Olga shot back, getting on her feet.

"It's going to be a very long evening." Benedict sighed and extended his hand to take the car keys while offering her his apartment keys. "Why don't you go upstairs. I'll park the car and bring up your shopping bags."

Olga swapped keys and walked off toward the elevators without a word.

Benedict came about ten minutes later. He found Olga standing by the window in the living room, looking at the panoramic view and nursing a large tumbler filled with cold, clear liquid.

"I see that you found the most important provision in the place," he said. "Where's mine?"

Olga stared straight ahead. "In the freezer. It's your place. You can pour your own drink."

Benedict attempted to put his arm around her shoulders, but Olga twisted to evade him. "And she's royally pissed," he said as he headed to the kitchen.

When he came back into the living room, Olga had turned away from the view and was leaning against the windowsill. He dropped into an armchair, draping his legs over the side. "To borrow your phrase, I can't unscramble eggs. We didn't expect Gardiner to react so badly, and I can't take back the ordeal you experienced today."

"Yeah, right. It was completely and utterly unexpected that Gardiner would not like being blackmailed." Olga's anger kept gushing. "You're being cavalier, which is your prerogative as far as your own safety is concerned, and perhaps even mine. But you've no right to be this nonchalant about the wellbeing of innocent bystanders like Brian. But I'm tired and I can't form a coherent sentence right now, let alone argue with you. Go away so I can go to sleep on the couch."

"I don't recall you being so bossy in Istanbul. Were you this bossy? I made the bed up for you and put your bags in the bedroom. I'll sleep here."

Olga looked at the couch and back at Benedict. "You're longer than the couch." She smiled properly for the first time that evening. "Good. You should have a truly uncomfortable night. Couldn't wish it on a more deserving individual."

Chapter 32
February 5

Walter Dunleavy called Peter Gardiner at 7 a.m. to ask for a meeting at Gardiner's earliest convenience. Peter told him to come over to the apartment as soon as he could, and Dunleavy arrived fifteen minutes later. He was led to the solarium where Peter was waiting.

Dunleavy made it a practice to remain impassive no matter how spectacular and opulent his clients' homes and offices were, but the solarium left even him unable to conceal his astonishment. It spanned the full length of the apartment's east side and the full height of its three floors. The glass outside wall provided a spectacular view of Central Park, and the cheerful yellow walls and heated terra cotta floor gave it a Mediterranean feel, heightened by original Tuscan furniture and textiles. Olive, fig, and lemon trees were thriving in that room, as were the two dozen rose bushes planted in barrels along the glass wall.

Peter noticed Walter's expression and smiled. "Jennie's

responsible for this corner of paradise," he explained. "She and our girls spend quite a lot of time here, working with our landscaper. We want our kids to understand that hard work produces great results, and there's something elemental about investing sweat equity into a growing plant and seeing it respond to the effort. But you didn't come here to hear me expound on my philosophy of education."

"No, Mr. Gardiner, I didn't, but it's interesting nonetheless."

"So what are we discussing this morning?"

"Dr. Mueller, Mr. Gardiner. We had almost concluded that she wasn't involved, but her recent movements give us pause.

"Our initial assessment was based on the fact that our approach was a complete surprise to her, and when she got a chance to speak with Mr. Vickers, she was clearly upset with him for putting her in a situation where she was being asked questions about their association. She hasn't been in contact with him since Istanbul, and the first words she had for him weren't exactly friendly.

"There were other factors, too. We searched her apartment, and there was nothing linking her to Mr. Vickers or to the Ashford-Crofts or to any of the issues you told me about. Her behavior was also different than the Ashford-Crofts'. When our people paid their apartment a visit, it was clear they had evacuated it. Only the most basic furniture remains there now. Everything of value has been moved. We spoke to the concierge, who told us that Lady Claire and her family left the day after we searched Mr. Vickers' townhouse."

"Sounds like the Mueller thing was a red herring, then."

Peter distractedly plucked some dead leaves from a nearby rose bush.

Dunleavy shifted in his chair. This was the part where he was going to lie to the client. "Perhaps. But it wasn't a waste of time and effort. We let her have some running room while limiting her options so that it would be inevitable that she contact Mr. Vickers, and that's exactly what she did. She drove down to DC and is staying with him." Dunleavy saw no need to complicate the story with the facts of Olga's escape or the bleach burns suffered by his employee, or the nine hours during which he had no idea where Olga was. All's well that ends well, was Dunleavy's philosophy in these situations, and once Olga was seen entering Benedict's building, all was right in his universe.

"The fact that she went to him gives me pause about clearing her entirely," he explained. "Although it's possible he's convinced her she's safer with him. But regardless of the level of her involvement, I think the two of them being in the same place will work to our advantage. We're planning a couple of events today that should increase their fear, and now that they're together, their reaction will be amplified. I can all but guarantee that Mr. Vickers will be willing to see reason soon."

—— ((●)) ——

Over breakfast, Benedict handed Olga a cell phone. "Another of our cache of untraceable phones," he explained. Olga took it without speaking. Benedict exhaled impatiently.

"The cold shoulder is getting old."

"This isn't the cold shoulder. This is me, self-censoring."

"As wonderful a concept as that is, I'd rather get back to the way we were."

"That's just it. We weren't."

Benedict watched Olga spoon far too much sugar into her coffee and stir it with determination. He was tempted to offer to pour more coffee into her cup, but refrained. She was having a contrarian moment and any offer from him would be rebuffed.

"What are your plans for today?" he asked, to change the subject.

"Shopping." Olga scrunched her face when she tasted her coffee and reached for the coffee pot herself. "That's what I love about Friendship Heights, the concentration of high end shops. Although maybe I'll spend the morning at the National Gallery of Art."

Benedict waited a beat to see if Olga would ask what his plans were. She did not. "Would you like to know what I'm planning to do today?"

"Nope."

"I'm going to the climbing gym. Then I'm going to a meeting with my Kress Rubinoff friends. I'm going to give them my opinion on the demand letter to Peter. I should say, I'm going to be parroting your opinion on the demand letter. You're welcome to come climbing with me."

Olga got up and took her dishes to the sink. She poured soap on a wash cloth and began washing her mug. "I don't want to climb with you. I want to know how you're going to make Brian and me safe again."

"William and I will take care of it, I promise. Besides, I'm certain that even if Peter thought you were involved, he can't think that any longer. Anyone listening in on your cell conversation would have realized that you're furious with me."

"What if he's not convinced?"

"You worry too much."

Olga whipped around to face Benedict, her face betraying her surprise and annoyance. "I what?" She exclaimed as she dried her hands energetically.

Benedict raised his hands in supplication. "I do sometimes say things flippantly. Give it a day or two and everything will get back to normal again, I'm willing to guarantee it. Besides, this apartment is rather nice, isn't it? Can't you think of this as a mini vacation?"

Olga glared at him for a couple of seconds, then stalked out of the kitchen into the bedroom and slammed the door behind her.

Benedict watched her go then, sighing deeply, walked to the bedroom and tapped on the door. "Olga, you're being childish."

The door opened and Olga pressed past him, dressed to go out. "I was changing and didn't want to give you a show. Nothing particularly childish about that, I don't think."

"No. I take my comment back."

"If only you could take the past few months back and rethink the probability of this situation happening." She paused before putting on her coat. "Have you gotten in touch with Mike Adams from the Justice Department yet?

"Yes, and they are launching an investigation. I spoke with him again yesterday, and he assured me that they will

be ready to process whatever information we get to them."
He smiled. "It pays to have law school classmates in high
places, doesn't it?"

"Sure does," Olga agreed.

Benedict suppressed a happy smile. He didn't want to
alert Olga to the fact that she forgot to be mad at him.

"Has Kress Rubinoff engaged Delaware counsel yet?"
She asked.

"I don't think they settled on one yet."

"Make sure they hire R.J. Drummond. They have used
him before and think highly of him. And get him in the loop
before sending the demand letter, first, because he would actually know if the arguments make sense in view of Delaware
law, and second, because he's going to have to sign each and
every filing with the Delaware court once this thing goes
into litigation and they take their signing responsibilities seriously up there."

"I'll raise it first thing. Thank you."

"You're welcome. I'm still pissed at you." Olga had put on
her coat and was walking toward the door.

"Why can't you be pissed at someone else? Like William
and Claire?"

"Because they're not here."

"Precisely. You get to be pissed at someone, I get to have
a pleasant house-guest, and the Ashford-Crofts are not affected by your bitterness. Works for everybody."

Olga took the Red Line down to the National Gallery of Art on Constitution Avenue in downtown Washington. She'd spent five years in the DC area before moving to New York and still felt at home there. Her comfort with the city and her certainty that no one knew where she was allowed her to relax somewhat and think about Brian. Brian didn't know about Benedict nor would he need to if Benedict kept his promise to clear everything up in the next couple of days.

But Olga's mind kept drifting to her recent interaction with Benedict. She was remorseful for being such a shrew despite his obvious concern for her welfare. He'd been adamant things would not spiral out of control any further and she believed him, but she didn't know why she had this confidence in his ability to deliver on his promise. She just had the sense that he would do his best, and it was enough to make her feel protected. Olga grimaced. Just because he's tall and striking doesn't make him Prince Charming, she reminded herself sternly.

Olga walked into the gallery and checked her coat, then proceeded upstairs to the room where her favorite painting in the entire institution was displayed, Botticelli's portrait of Giuliano de' Medici. She sat on a bench in front of the picture and promptly got lost in it.

"They say it's a death portrait," said a man standing next to her. She hadn't heard him come in.

"Yes. I've heard it described that way before."

"If you don't want to see Brian Keller's death portrait, it would be a good idea to convince Benedict Vickers to change course," the man said and walked away.

Olga was stunned. Her breathing became quick and

shallow. She gripped the edge of the bench, afraid she might faint and closed her eyes, trying to settle her nerves and stop the rush of tears. Then she heard a cell phone ring and was startled by a hand touching her shoulder.

A guard was frowning at her disapprovingly "Ma'am, you can't use your cell phone in the picture galleries. You can take the call in the main hallway."

Olga mumbled an apology, picked up her purse and walked out of the room. She went to a stairwell, took out her new cell phone, and redialed the number that had just called it.

"Are you at the gallery." Benedict's voice sounded odd and Olga's panic reached fever pitch.

"Why?"

"Stay there. I want you to be where there are lots of people. I should be there in about half an hour. Let's meet by the water cascade by the cafeteria. Know what I mean?"

"Yes, I do." Olga noticed she was twisting a strand of hair compulsively and stopped it. "Benedict?"

"Yes?"

"They found me here, too."

Benedict groaned. "That doesn't surprise me after my own morning," he said. "But I stand by what I said. We'll make it right, and you'll be safe soon."

"I trust that you'll try."

Benedict chuckled. "Ah, there's the lawyer I know. Can you please lie and say that you have every confidence I'll do what I say?"

"I have every confidence that you'll make it right and that I'll be safe soon." Olga found that she was smiling despite herself. More inexplicably, she found that she believed what she'd just said.

——————※《◎》※——————

William's emergency cell phone vibrated in his pocket in the middle of a meeting attended by two officers of general rank. He quickly stood, let them know it was for an operational emergency, and left the room.

"And today's calamity is…" he said into the phone.

"They know where I am. I don't know how. I did everything you told me to do, and I could swear that I wasn't followed down to DC, so how do they know?"

"Truth be told, you were followed, but by friendlies. I put a security watch over you after the incident at your home. Leaving aside your less than impressive countersurveillance skills, your watchers confirmed that no one else followed you. Which brings us back to the question of how they found you."

"It's more than just finding me. I had a pretty close call today."

William reached his office and collapsed into his chair. "Tell me," he said, shutting his eyes and massaging the bridge of his nose to ward off an approaching headache.

"I went to the climbing gym this morning. The regulars were there. One of them offered to belay me. I've seen her do it before and she's good. When I reached the top of the wall and swung out for her to lower me, she dropped me. Not much, but enough to have my life and Jon's death flash before me. I swung myself back onto the wall, cut the rope, and descended on my own. She just stood there, waiting for me to come down! When I confronted her, she said, 'This is a message, Mr. Vickers. Play ball or it's not going to be such a harmless prank next time.'"

"Where's Olga?" William asked.

"She's at the National Gallery. Apparently she was approached as well and she sounded awfully shaky when I spoke to her just now. I'm on my way to meet her. I'm still very much on her shit list at the moment."

"I need to puzzle this through," said William. "A couple of things don't add up and I need to think. Will call you back as soon as I have something."

William put his feet on his desk and leaned back in his reclining office chair. He'd learned a long time ago to trust his gut instincts, and despite the apparent escalation in Gardiner's tactics, he didn't feel that either Benedict or Olga were in imminent mortal danger. On the other hand, the fact that their location was known despite all efforts to keep it secret worried him a lot.

He thought about the ways the apartment could have been compromised, from the mundane to the fantastic. Did Benedict's use of the computer at the apartment lead them there? Did someone in Gardiner's network spot him by chance? Did Olga lead their pursuers to DC? No, that last one didn't match something Benedict had said. He said that the woman who belayed him was a regular. She had been planted at the gym before Olga ran.

William's thoughts came back to the most likely option. Somehow it was Benedict himself who led his pursuers to his hiding place. But how?

"Oh! How clever," William muttered as a new possibility occurred to him. He called Benedict back.

"When you drove down from New York, did you take your own clothes with you?"

"'Course I did."

"Let me guess. Your shoes and clothes had been strewn about but they weren't damaged."

"Right. Actually, a couple of jackets were cut through and some shirts landed in bleach, but otherwise my clothes were fine."

"And you packed your things in one of your suitcases?"

"No. All of them were shredded. I used grocery store paper bags."

"As Sherlock Holmes said, 'Eliminate all other factors, and the one that remains must be the truth.' When you find Olga, go shopping. Buy yourself all new clothes and shoes. Especially shoes. In the meantime, one of my contacts will deliver a transmission detector to you. If the shoes or clothes ping, get rid of them."

"They put tracking devices in my shoes?" Benedict sounded incredulous.

"Yes, I think that's exactly what they did. If the detector doesn't find anything in your clothes or shoes, then we have another data point to analyze. So looking at your things is a good exercise either way."

"I'm glad you're able to see the bright side of life."

William heard the bitterness in Benedict's voice and realized he'd forgotten to elaborate on his second conclusion. "You're not actually worried for your safety are you? Because you shouldn't be. Look at how Gardiner's played it so far. It's all threats and low grade violence. With you it's understandable because you let him know that the information will be released if you're harmed. But they also only minimally roughed up Olga and mostly threatened her friend. This suggests to me that Gardiner hasn't got much taste for gore."

"Except for the drop this morning. I don't see how it can be classified as anything other than significantly dangerous."

"You see, but you…"

"'Don't observe'" Benedict cut William off irritably and finished the sentence for him. "I swear, William, if you don't stop quoting Sherlock Holmes stories I will reach across the ocean and strangle you."

William chuckled. "The harness clearly tugged on your good humor as well as on your privates when you were dropped this morning." Then he explained, "You said yourself the woman was an expert belayer. She knew what she was doing and consequently you were never in any real danger. Just like Olga being threatened with the surgical instruments. They weren't likely to be used. And the more I think about it, the more I'm convinced they don't even watch Olga's boyfriend. They terrified her enough that they don't have to.

"Gardiner is walking a tightrope. He wants to engender sufficient fear to cause you discomfort so you capitulate and leave him alone. But he doesn't want so much fear, or so much damage, to cause you to become an irrational actor."

"I'm thrilled you're so sanguine and that you've been able to reason away whatever danger we feel we're in. But can you and I agree that this situation, no matter how theoretically safe it may be, cannot go on? I cannot be held captive by my own clothes and Olga cannot walk around afraid of her own shadow."

"I agree. This game is escalating and sooner or later somebody might make a mistake. I vote for the nuclear option. It's time to finish Gardiner's rebellion once and for all."

Chapter 33

The Metropolitan Opera's new modernist staging of Tosca wasn't the Gardiners' cup of tea. Nonetheless, they had to stay to its conclusion because they were hosting some of Peter's biggest investors. It was nearly 1 a.m. by the time they got home.

Peter took advantage of being up at such a late hour to go into his study and check on the trading action in the Asian markets, while Jennie went straight to their bedroom. She turned on the light and would have screamed with fright had not a gloved hand clamped over her mouth. She was dragged through the room and dumped on a chaise. Her captor then expertly taped her mouth and bound her hands behind her back, taking care not to overtighten the restraints to minimize Jennie's discomfort.

"Good evening, Mrs. Gardiner," Jennie turned to see a bearded man in full battle gear with camouflage paint streaked on his face. He was half reclining on the Gardiners' bed, his back supported by pillows and his boots leaving dark streaks on the white Frette duvet cover. "Allow me to introduce myself: I'm Alpha. The gentleman who prevented you from screaming is Beta, the gentleman pointing a gun at you is Gamma, and the gentleman who'll join us shortly is Delta. Let's just sit here in silence until your husband arrives."

Jennie slumped back into the chaise, too shocked to cry. She wished Peter would hurry up and get to the bedroom so this nightmare would be over quicker, but at the same time she wanted desperately to warn him not to come up. She wasn't at all sure that his heart could take the sudden shock.

The door opened and the man they called Delta came in. He held something in his gloved paw that Jennie couldn't make out. He handed it to Alpha, along with an envelope he pulled from his pocket, then dragged a chair close enough to the bed to raise his legs and plant them on the duvet cover as well. Jennie found the quartet's casual ease to be the most frightening thing of all. The next most frightening thing about them was that they were Australians. She couldn't conjure up a reason why armed Australians would be holding her captive in her own bedroom.

The door opened again and Peter stepped in. Beta grabbed him and shoved him toward the chaise on which Jennie sat. Pushing Peter down he promptly tied his hands.

"What is this about?" asked Peter, his face pale and covered in a sheen of cold sweat.

"Consider this an instance of cooler heads prevailing, Mr. Gardiner," said Alpha. "You've been trying to play in our league and we don't appreciate it. Call off your hounds, follow instructions, and everything will work out just great for everyone concerned. Do you understand me?"

"Or else, what?" Peter's natural combativeness asserted itself.

Alpha tossed Beta the envelope and the small plastic bag Delta had handed him. Beta took several photographs out of the envelope and laid them on the chaise between Jennie and Peter, then added the plastic bag to the exhibition. Jennie screamed hysterically, her voice muffled by the tape on her mouth, and Peter turned ashen.

Each photograph showed a gloved hand holding a knife near the head of one of their sleeping children. The plastic bag contained locks of their hair.

"Get them some brandy, and slap Mrs. Gardiner. She's in hysterics," Alpha directed his team. Delta left the room, while Beta shook Jennie roughly. It seemed to do the trick. Even though she still cried, she was under control.

They sat without speaking until Delta returned with the brandy. He helped Peter take a drink, then ripped the tape off Jennie's mouth and gave her some as well.

Alpha continued. "Here's what's going to happen. We push the reset button on this whole situation, as if we're back to the day after your chat with Mr. Vickers at the tea shop. You do exactly as he says from now on. And no more interfering with him, his friends, or any other random civilians you planned to terrorize."

Alpha got to his feet, and his men followed suit. "Our job is done here. If we don't hear you call Dunleavy to cancel his contract within the next eight hours, we'll be back. If we see any of Dunleavy's people sniffing around the folks we're protecting now, we'll be back. And if you deviate from Mr. Vickers's instructions, we'll be back. And next time, we won't be in the business of cutting hair."

Beta sliced off the plastic ties holding the Gardiners' wrists and the four intruders filed out of the bedroom. At the door, Alpha turned.

"The security in this apartment is woefully inadequate for someone of your wealth and prominence. You should give serious consideration to upgrading."

Jennie immediately ran to check on the children as Peter sat still, dazed. When Jennie came back, she set on Peter, kicking and scratching him until he got hold of her hands and pinned her legs.

"You put my children at risk." she shouted, fighting to free herself. "If anything happens to any one of them, I'll never forgive you. I don't care how much money or pride or whatever else you're going to lose. I don't even care if you go to jail for buying stolen goods. The safety of my children comes first!"

<hr />

The four intruders listened to the argument transmitted an hour earlier from the Gardiners' bedroom. Sitting in their hotel room, scrubbed clean of camouflage paint, they were glued to the playback. "Ah, motherhood," said Alpha. "God bless it. When was the last time you guys visited your mums?"

Chapter 34
February 6

B enedict got the all-clear signal early the next morning. He heard Olga moving in the bedroom and knocked on the door to tell her the good news. Considering that she was still treating him like her worst enemy, albeit with flashes of occasional friendliness when their interaction returned to the easy banter of their days in Istanbul, he half-expected her to ignore his knocking. But she opened the door.

"You're a free woman," Benedict declared, massaging his lower back. Two nights of sleeping on the couch were beginning to take their toll.

"How did this happen?"

"I'm not a lawyer, but I suspect it would be healthier for your law license if you didn't know."

Olga shrugged and walked back into the bedroom to pack her things into the suitcase she bought the day before. "You'll want breakfast before you go," Benedict called out to her as he moved into the kitchen.

"I'll grab something on the way, thanks."

"Quit being an idiot, Olga." Benedict banged the coffee pot on the counter in frustration. "I said I was sorry. I said that none of this was supposed to happen. I fixed the situation. I even listened to you wax poetic about the mythical perfection that is Brian."

Olga came out of the bedroom and sat at the breakfast nook, her arms crossed. "The fact that I'm dating Brian really rubs you the wrong way, doesn't it?"

"Of course not, though it would have been nice of you to mention him before, rather than spring him on me at the most stressful moment possible. You know the available assortment: frozen waffles, yogurt, toast, cheddar, eggs. What do you want?" he asked.

"A waffle and yogurt, please." Olga paused for a moment, then continued, "You act like you're the aggrieved party in this."

Benedict turned to face Olga. He was furious and let it show. "I took responsibility for my actions. I solved the situation. I apologized. What else do you want? Money damages? How much do you reckon your pain and suffering are worth? Tell me. I'll write you a check."

Olga looked down at the counter and didn't respond. The ping of the toaster brought Benedict's attention back to breakfast. He dropped the waffle onto a plate, which he then set on the table before Olga with a crash.

"You're right," Olga said quietly. "You did do everything possible to fix things and I do sometimes have a tendency to grouse."

Benedict put his hand on Olga's. "Given what each of

us needs to do next, and how imperative it is that Kress Rubinoff not get wind of our connection, William insists that you and I cut off all communications until we're done." he pressed Olga's hand lightly. "I'll miss you."

"I will, too," Olga admitted. She raised her coffee mug. "Here's to the adventures ahead, and to coming out alive and in good health."

Benedict clinked his mug with hers. "I'll drink to that."

PART V
Chapter 35
February 10

B enedict had arranged to stay at a friend's place in New York while the damage to his townhouse and its contents was being repaired. As he was driving back to the city, he called Peter to set up a meeting; he suggested lunch at *Les Sans Culottes*, a French bistro near Gardiner's office. It was neither chic enough nor fast enough to attract the venture capital or Big Law lunching crowds.

When Peter arrived at the bistro, Benedict was sitting at a corner table perusing the menu. When he saw Peter, he got up and offered his hand. Peter hesitated for a moment before shaking it.

The two men sat down, and the waiter brought the charcuterie tower and the basket of fresh vegetables the place was known for, and took their orders. He also brought a carafe of the house red wine, which Benedict had ordered.

After the waiter left them, Benedict tasted the wine and frowned. "Not exactly Chateau Margaux 2000, but it'll do.

Thank you for meeting me."

"You know I didn't have a choice."

"Right. I'm glad you understand that now." Benedict cut off a piece of salami from the charcuterie tower and bit into it. Peter followed suit.

"At the end of the day, Peter, we both want the same thing. We want the Sliema IPO to be wildly successful. I want my piece to be bigger than it is right now and protracting our litigation will intensify the investing public's interest in the IPO."

"Clearly you haven't done your homework. Lawsuits are not an aphrodisiac to investors."

"True, most aren't. But this one, especially if it's sufficiently bitter, will be. Think about it. Would you and Correx put up fierce resistance to giving up some of your shares if those shares weren't valuable?"

Peter had to admit there was some logic in Benedict's reasoning, but he was still not convinced. "The problem with lawsuits, though, is that they're unpredictable. Things happen, information is uncovered. It's a can of worms."

"We'll shut it down before it gets out of hand. We'll settle before the deposition stage. This way no one is on record saying something that can come back to bite us."

"Are Kress Rubinoff coaching you on this?"

"No, they don't know about our discussions, and I want it to stay that way. I also don't want you telling Fields Stanhope about our chats either."

Peter agreed to this.

"Here's the general outline of how it's going to go," Benedict continued. "Martin Kress will send you a demand letter later this week. He'll ask for Jon's full 45% share back. He'll rely on the fact that Jon gave you only a limited proxy and you deliberately flouted the limitations he set when you voted his proxy along with your shares to issue a massive number of new shares to dilute him out. The letter will also state that we believe Correx knew your actions with respect to Jon's proxy were illegal and that they participated in the fraud by agreeing to buy the newly issued shares. Upon the receipt of the demand letter, you, through your lawyers, will tell us to go jump in a lake.

"We'll file suit in Delaware. The complaint will be filed under seal, ostensibly to allow settlement negotiations to continue, but really to pique interest in the story. We'll seek a declaration that the vote to issue new shares is void and an injunction directing Sliema to return to how things were before that vote.

"There'll be extensive document discovery but all the documents will be protected by a confidentiality order so the public will have no access to them. You'll ask for everything Jon had and I now have that relates to Sliema. I'll ask for all your communications with Jon, with other people at Sliema, and with Correx. I'll also ask for financials, including past, present, and future projections, and for all scientific data since Jon died."

"Why do you need the scientific data?"

"Because the success of the Phase II trial going on now will determine the success of the IPO. There are rumors that it's going spectacularly well, but I need substantiation."

Peter sipped his wine. "What's the end game? How much do you want?"

"I'll settle for twenty percent, and I expect it to come proportionately out of your and Correx's shares. I want SEC-registered shares, the kind I can sell immediately. Restricted shares, which is the only type Sliema's shares are at the moment, do me no good. And the twenty percent have to be iron-clad."

"What do you mean by that?"

"I don't want to be diluted out again or have to play a game of chicken with you delaying the IPO, waiting for me to be desperate for money so that I sell the shares back to you or Correx at a discount. There will be a poison pill provision."

Peter arched an eyebrow with some amusement. "For a historian, you're remarkably up on the lingo."

Benedict shrugged dismissively. "I've mastered several dead languages. Wall Street vernacular is nothing compared to Assyrian. I am, however, beginning to have a greater appreciation for the excitement and profitability of your world. Maybe once I cash out my Sliema stake after the IPO, I'll use the proceeds to start a venture fund of my own."

"Here's lesson number one for you. Don't count your chickens before they hatch. You still have only 0.5% of Sliema, and we're still waiting for the Phase II trial results. It's a long way between you, here and now, and you, venture fund titan."

"Duly noted."

"Back to the poison pill. What do you have in mind?"

"I want a provision saying that in the event my shares are diluted before the IPO, or if the IPO doesn't happen in say, six months, all Sliema's patents and patent applications will be automatically reassigned to me."

Peter nearly choked on a piece of roll. "You're insane! Correx will never go for that."

Benedict smiled. "First, I trust your power of persuasion. I've seen you twist arms and bang heads and get exactly what you want. Second, once you produce your communications, we'll be able to add to the pressure, because they knew you didn't have Jon's authorization to sell Sliema stock to them, and went ahead with the purchase anyway, didn't they? They participated in the scheme with you. Isn't that right, Peter?"

Peter didn't meet Benedict's gaze. "Isn't that right?" Benedict insisted. "Don't worry, I'm not recording this conversation, you can tell me the truth and it won't affect anything."

"Yes," Peter nodded, straightening an imaginary crease in the white tablecloth.

"What else will those e-mails show? Give me a preview."

Peter sighed. "Here's lesson number two in venture funding. Companies have a life cycle. The people who get it going, who have the initial spark to start it, are often not the right people to grow it, and certainly not the right people to run it when it's a mature company. The back and forth with Correx was about easing Jon out. He had served his purpose. He had already been handsomely compensated for it. Townhouses in New York City aren't exactly for paupers, and he would have made a killing even if he owned just 0.5% of the stock.

"He needed to go. He was stuck in an unending research loop. Paralysis by analysis is the term for it, if you want to add it to your venture cap dictionary. With him at the helm, you wouldn't be looking at a successful IPO in the near future. Correx had the right personnel for where Sliema was at that time and is now."

"That's awfully cold." Benedict could not control the upset flush that spread over his face. He thought back to the years that Jon had willingly, even joyously, sacrificed to his work because he felt that he was doing something worthwhile, helpful to humanity. Benedict was certain that even in his worst nightmares Jon had never imagined that he would not continue to direct the research at Sliema, no matter how much his shares were diluted. The gulf between his brother's scientific brilliance and his business naïveté astonished him.

"I could say something clichéd like 'that's business' or 'that's just life,' but it wouldn't be the truth. The difference between the Correx people taking over at Sliema and Jon still heading it is the difference between a successful, blossoming enterprise with many employees and a failed entity that's no good to anyone. It's not all about brilliant ideas and science. It's about execution, and logistics, and navigating regulatory minefields, and knowing how to price the product. And that brings me to lesson number three. Don't get emotionally involved. Don't do business with family members. And don't get in if you don't have an exit strategy."

The two men sat in silence for a while, each lost in his own thoughts. Finally, Benedict stood and put enough cash on the table to cover the bill and the tip. "Thank you for the lessons in venture capitalism, Peter. On second thought, you were right all along. I'm not cut out to swim in your shark pool after all." He left before their entrees arrived.

Chapter 36
March 1-20

At 3:46 p.m., a hand-carried complaint naming Gardiner, the Gardiner New Horizons Fund, Sliema Pharmaceuticals, Correx Pharmaceuticals, and several Correx executives as defendants, and requesting expedited review and injunctive relief, was filed by R.J. Drummond in the Chancery Court of Delaware, the venerable leader in U.S. corporate jurisprudence. The complaint thus starting the *Vickers v. Gardiner* litigation was filed one week after Gardiners' lawyers rejected any and all allegations contained in the demand letter sent by Martin Kress on behalf of Benedict Vickers as the representative of Jonathan Vickers's estate.

At Benedict's insistence, the complaint was filed under seal. He explained that he didn't want news organizations to publish sensationalized versions of what the dispute was about. He wanted to keep the bad blood between him and Gardiner to a minimum, even as they were embarking on a potentially bitter and acrimonious litigation.

Kress vehemently disagreed with Benedict's request to file under seal, arguing that embarrassment could be a potent weapon in their push to get Gardiner to a settlement, but it soon became apparent that Benedict wasn't asking for his opinion; he was the client and he was giving instructions. This was hard to swallow, especially from a contingency client. Regardless, the client's word controlled and Kress Rubinoff were obligated to honor his instructions.

The defendants were served with the complaint shortly after it was filed, and Kress and company settled in to wait for the inevitable motion to dismiss for failure to state a claim from the defendants. They were certain that the defendants would argue that the allegations in the complaint were not sufficient to allege a legal wrong. To their surprise, the motion didn't materialize.

Gardiner's attorneys were surprised by this turn of events, too. They were flabbergasted that Gardiner didn't want to file a motion to dismiss. But he insisted. In his opinion, it would have been a waste of time. The judge was virtually guaranteed not to rule in their favor, and Gardiner wasn't going to pay for low-percentage plays costing tens of thousands in attorneys' fees. Instead, he directed his attorneys to file an answer.

Per the agreement under which Correx bought into Sliema, Sliema and the Gardiner New Horizons Fund were responsible for any and all legal bills that Correx incurred in any suit stemming from that transaction. Because Gardiner was footing the legal bills, and because Correx's and Gardiner's interests were intimately aligned, Correx agreed to let him take the lead in defending the suit and not to field its own set of lawyers.

Once the answer was filed, Kress and McIvor, along with R.J. Drummond dialing in from Wilmington, got on the phone with Gardiner's attorneys to discuss settlement talks.

"What can I tell you folks?" said Brandon Ogden, Gardiner's lead attorney. "My client isn't budging. He insists this suit is so much crap and that there will be no settlement. He doesn't even want to hear offers. As I see it, the only thing we have to discuss is the joint schedule we must present to the Court. Shall we leave it to our respective associates to draft?"

Kress agreed. The call ended amicably enough, considering the simmering blood feud between Kress and Ogden, the origins of which were rooted in competing accusations of willful misconduct and fraud on the court lobbed by the two men in a case they had tried against each other eighteen years before. Ogden even managed to sound sincere while congratulating Kress on the birth of his new grandson.

McIvor convened an all hands on deck meeting for 6 that evening. All invited knew something serious was up for McIvor to call a Friday evening meeting. He usually couldn't be found at the office past noon on Fridays.

The team of seven associates and four junior partners in addition to Kress and McIvor assembled in the large conference room. Martin Kress's presence was terrifying to all, even those who knew that the meeting was only to discuss the Vickers-Gardiner litigation.

Kress opened the meeting by explaining what the litigation was about. He emphasized the fact that the litigation was taken on a pure contingency basis, including costs, and that they needed to keep expenditures to a minimum. To that effect, whatever could be done by associates, rather than third party vendors, would be. One of the associates asked for specific examples and Kress obliged.

"Let's say we get a hundred thousand documents from the client, and it would cost twenty-five thousand to process all of them, load them into the document review program, and use search terms on them to cull down the number to fifteen thousand before you guys start reviewing them. Let's say that instead you review the full batch of the documents before they are processed, and it will take you much more time, but the firm will spend a lot less money because it'll only be for the processing and loading of the small fraction you mark relevant, say, eight thousand documents. We're going with the second option."

When he saw that his words produced general unhappiness among the associates, he added, "We're a bit slow right now, and you guys are a fixed cost, so you either sit around doing nothing and draw a salary or you do this document review and draw the same salary. As long as you're moving this litigation forward, it's much easier for the partnership to justify carrying your salaries even if some of you are not bringing revenue in client billables." Kress's statement went a long way toward creating fake enthusiasm in the room.

Chapter 37
March 23-25

Benedict was inclined to let the incoming call go to voice mail. He'd sworn that he'd finish the first draft of the third chapter of his dissertation that day. But he could not help throwing a glance at the caller ID and immediately picked up. It was Kress Rubinoff.

The caller identified himself as Jeff Thompson, an associate working on Benedict's litigation. With him in the office was another associate whose name Benedict promptly forgot. Jeff was calling to talk about document collection. Benedict saved the four sentences he'd managed to add to his dissertation chapter in the three hours he'd spent working on it and settled in for a long conversation.

Thompson was an impressively organized young man. He explained to Benedict that he had a list of places where documents could usually be located and had created a master chart that he wanted to now go through with Benedict.

The chart was thorough. It listed electronic media,

including personal computers, laptops, BlackBerries and other smartphones, thumb drives, photo storage media, printers and copiers with memory storage, external hard drives, external servers, backup tapes, backup Internet-based storage, and a host of other options that Benedict had never heard of before. Then they turned to hard copies. Anything in your filing cabinets? Garage? Basement?

Finally, Jeff asked, "Any other place you can think of that I may have missed?"

"Actually, yes. I feel privileged to add to your chart. I've rented two storage units out in New Jersey and they're full of document boxes. Printouts of data in spreadsheet form, reports, graphic representations of the data, multiple copies of protocols, and other things I don't understand. As you may know, I'm not a scientist."

Benedict heard a sharp intake of breath and thought he heard the nameless second associate mutter, "Oh, crap."

"How many boxes are we talking about?" asked an obviously rattled Jeff.

"About fourteen hundred, I think."

"Full boxes?" Jeff asked.

"Yes."

"About 2500 pages per box. That's about 3.5 million pages."

Benedict was impressed with Jeff's computational skills, but he needed to correct him. "More. Many are double-sided."

"WHY?" The nameless second associate almost wailed in his anguish.

Benedict fought an impulse to smile. "Concern for the environment, I suspect. Single-sided printing is such a waste, don't you think?"

"Listen, let me jump off the call with you for a sec and talk to Eric McIvor. I'll get back with you right after I speak with him. Is that cool?"

"Totally cool," said Benedict, finding it amusing that under stress Jeff's professional demeanor crumbled and he reverted to what he was, a scared twenty-something kid without any real authority.

It was useless to get back to his dissertation because Jeff's second call could come at any minute, so Benedict brewed a pot of coffee and settled in with the *New York Times*, which he insisted on reading in the old fashioned, newsprint form.

The news that there were more than three million pages of possibly relevant documents in Benedict's control didn't make anyone at Kress Rubinoff New York happy. The associates did a quick mental calculation of how much of their collective lives they would waste reviewing spreadsheets that none of them understood. McIvor did a quick mental calculation of how high the cost of producing these documents would run and wondered if it would be possible to shift the cost of handling them to the defendants. He spent an hour writing meticulous notes to himself about all the possible issues this new revelation raised and another half hour debating whether he should call Martin Kress directly or talk the situation over with another partner first. He eventually settled on calling Kress directly for fear that someone else might beat him to it first.

Kress hit the roof, showering McIvor with abuse for his incompetence and hanging up on him. Then he shifted his rage to Benedict, who was quickly proving to be the worst contingency client in the firm's history.

Kress allowed himself to indulge in this mental tirade for five minutes, then stopped. He was an old enough hand to know that railing against Benedict and McIvor wouldn't solve his problem. He needed to act rationally, and he needed first-hand information.

He called Jeff Thompson and made him repeat what Benedict had said, then instructed him to arrange to go out to New Jersey with Benedict as soon as possible to bring back a few boxes so they could make an informed decision.

In the meantime, he called McIvor and asked whether they'd identified or signed up any experts for the litigation. The document situation made the retention of experts a higher priority because the firm had to know whether its experts would require any of them. McIvor told him that several prominent candidates had been identified, but that they were running into conflicts with all but the most expensive ones.

"How much are we talking about?" Kress asked.

"Salk wants two thousand an hour. Corbett wants two thousand five hundred and a non-refundable retainer of $50,000. Brackman is a bargain at seventeen fifty an hour, but he wants a non-refundable retainer of $75,000. We've expanded our search to Canada and the United Kingdom without much luck. All but a handful are conflicted out."

"How is this possible?" Kress demanded.

"Four of them told us they've been signed up to help

Gardiner right after he received the demand letter."

"I guess it really does mean he has no intention of set-tling this case. This could get far more expensive than we expected."

"It's not too late to back out," McIvor pointed out. "We're nowhere near the trial, and I'm sure the Court would let us get out of the representation."

"There are many reasons why we're not going to do that. For starters, I don't want to give the impression that Kress Rubinoff cuts and runs. Especially not against Gardiner. We've lost too many cases to that asshole, and if we bail now it'll look like we brought yet another loser against him. I'm not going to risk our reputation. We need to see this case through."

"Understood."

"In fact," Kress mused, "their signing up of about every available expert is overkill, and it tells me they're not as con-fident as their posturing suggests. This may be the first sign of fear we've seen from them. It's what we'd do if our case was shit. No, we're going forward. Sign up whatever experts you think we need."

———◦《◦》◦———

Benedict dutifully agreed to tromp out to New Jersey with Jeff. He was amused by the thought that he was living out the stories Olga had told him. He hoped that Jeff would be as vocal, disloyal, and entertaining in his bellyaching as Olga had been.

But he turned out to be disappointingly loyal and proper, one of those perfectly wholesome Midwestern specimens, down to the cowlick in his hair. Benedict was certain that Jeff had never missed a dental checkup appointment in his life and that he had married his college sweetheart mostly because being married was the right image to project if one wanted to make partner at a law firm.

They drove out in Benedict's car and quickly realized they had nothing in common except the case. To make matters worse, Jeff explained that he had asthma when Benedict took out his cigarettes, sentencing Benedict to a smokeless drive. When they reached the warehouse and opened Benedict's storage area, Jeff couldn't suppress his dismay. "That's a lot," he said dejectedly.

"Sorry," said Benedict, aiming for an apologetic tone. "Do you want to look at random boxes or shall I tell you what's generally where?" he asked.

"If you can direct me to the corporate stuff and any correspondence your brother had with other people about Sliema, that would be great."

"That's actually a tiny minority of the boxes here. Only number one through six." Benedict pointed to a stack close to the door. "I made sure to keep them at easy reach. The rest relates to the science. We can take them back now."

"Great," said Jeff.

"Do you want to take a couple of the science boxes just so you have a sample?"

"Yeah, good thinking. One more thing. Do you mind putting me on the list of approved people to get into your units? I don't want you to have to come out here when we start moving all these boxes to our offices."

"Brilliant idea. Let's take care of it right now."

⸻ «(()» ⸻

Jeff's haul was quickly reviewed by the associates on the Vickers-Gardiner litigation team. The 4,000 documents, comprised of 30,000 pages, were reviewed by the seven of them in less than five hours. Jeff was invited to participate in a call between McIvor and Kress to summarize what the associates had found. He spent an hour carefully crafting his talking points before the call. This was his moment to shine before the big guy, and he wasn't going to blow it.

"So, Jeff, what's your general take?" Kress asked.

"The docs are pretty good for us. We were all pumped when we found the correspondence between Dr. Vickers and his attorneys during the original negotiations with Gardiner. It's clear that he was afraid of being diluted out and wanted to retain some control over the decisions of the corporation. He insisted on a requirement for a supermajority of 75% of the shares to be voted on any matter relating to the issuance of additional shares or for the sale of a block bigger than 15% to a third party. Which means that Gardiner was in no position to take a unilateral decision even though he had the majority of the shares and controlled the board."

"Very good. Prepare me a binder of the most useful documents you've found, please, and the most damaging, if there are any."

"Sure thing. Eric, do you want one as well?"

"Yes, that would be great, Jeff." McIvor sensed that Kress liked Jeff and decided it was important to show that he, too, could spot talent. "You've done a super job."

"Thanks!" Jeff was glowing.

"How many documents are in this category?" asked Kress.

"About 4,000. Approximately 30,000 pages."

"What about the rest of the 1400 boxes?"

"All relating to science. I took the initiative and brought back a couple of representative boxes from that category. We've quickly gone through them, and they are as Benedict described—charts, graphs, and experimental protocols."

"Nothing that looks like it might have been sent to attorneys or be otherwise privileged?" Kress asked.

"No."

"Okay. Then I'm going to make the call that we don't review these boxes. The science is immaterial to the question at hand and there's no point in burning hours reviewing it. If the other side wants it, we'll oblige them with a document dump. Just do me a favor, Jeff. If these boxes are ever sent out, take a peek at each box before it goes out for processing so we sort of know what's in it."

"Definitely. In fact, I was going to send one of the paralegals out to New Jersey to catalog the boxes. I think it would be useful to have an index."

"Hold off on that for now. Let's see what the other side asks for. No sense in burning paralegal hours unnecessarily."

Chapter 38
March 25-29

Margaret Drewry walked out of the Wood Basic Science building on the John Hopkins Medical Center campus and turned left to the market where she bought her lunch daily. A tall woman in skinny jeans, slouchy brown leather boots, and a dark parka, her hair held back in a ponytail, detached herself from the wall near the door and hurried after her.

"Mrs. Drewry?" The woman called out

Margaret became immediately suspicious and groped for her keys in her pocket, gripping them like she was taught to do in the self-defense class she took a couple of months back. In this neighborhood, a woman simply couldn't be too careful.

"I'm Daisy Fenton," said the woman when she caught up with Margaret. She extended an ID card. "I'm with the Foundation for Justice in Medical Research, and I'm looking into the M-1752 drug trials. The Sliema weight loss injectable."

Margaret blanched and quickened her pace. "I'm not going to talk to you," she hissed.

"Mrs. Drewry, please." Daisy had no trouble keeping up with Margaret's speed walk. "I'm conscious of the difficulties here. That's why I didn't call you or send you an e-mail or a text. But we need your help."

"I don't know you, and I don't know why you decided to come talk to me, but I'm not interested."

"I know that speaking with me may earn you a lawsuit for breaching your nondisclosure agreement with Sliema and may also cost you your pension. But not speaking with me may cost people their lives." Margaret slowed down and took her first good look at Daisy, noticing her unusually light blue eyes and her open and friendly expression. Daisy held Margaret's gaze unflinchingly. "I'm going to be having breakfast at the Bonjour Bakery Café on Falls Road every day between 8 and 8:30 a.m. until next Monday. It's that small purple house right next to the antique shop. You should try their breakfast pastries, save yourself a trip to Paris."

<hr />

The people at the Bonjour stopped paying attention to Olga by her third consecutive breakfast there. Every morning she ordered a pain au chocolat and a large coffee, then sat at one of the tiny bistro tables writing in a notebook. She was perfectly friendly and polite, but it was clear that she had no interest in any conversation.

On Thursday morning, Olga was buying her usual

breakfast when she heard a tentative "Daisy?" behind her and turned to see Margaret standing by the door, her hand on the doorknob and her entire body speaking of hesitation.

Olga tamped down her excitement. The third prong of the plan, for which she and Claire needed the cooperation of ex-Sliema employees, might be doable after all. "How great to see you!" she smiled warmly, trying to put Margaret at ease. "What are you going to have?"

"I'll have the same you're having." Margaret was still ill at ease, but she had moved into the miniscule café and let go of the doorknob.

Olga pointed to the table with her notebook on it. "Just grab a chair. How do you like your coffee?"

Olga doubled the order, then sat down and smiled at her guest. Margaret was twisting her wedding ring nervously, working it off and on her finger.

"I had my husband check your foundation out on his work computer. He couldn't find much, and your Web site is pretty bare bones."

"Alas, that's so true. We're new and funds are tight right now. We're applying for grants, but with the pharma lobby being what it is..." Olga shrugged to indicate how futile the grant writing effort was.

Margaret stopped toying with her ring and began twisting a paper napkin instead. She still hadn't touched her pastry or her coffee. "I can't afford a lawsuit, and I can't afford to lose the pension Sliema's paying us, which will stop if I violate the nondisclosure agreement I signed when they fired us. I took a huge pay cut when I came to work at Hopkins. You know how it is with academic institutions, a good title and a shitty salary. So now I'm Senior Technician and Animal Protocol Advisor at about half of my pay at Sliema."

"I understand."

"I can't give you data. I didn't take any with me when they asked us all to leave. And I wouldn't give it to you even if I had it because it's easy to trace where it came from."

"I'm not asking you to."

"Why are you going after Sliema?"

Olga smiled mirthlessly. "I know, right? There is, after all, a plethora of choices to go after. Sliema stood out because what they're working on is designed to be taken by a huge swath of the population. And many of the people who'll be taking it are perfectly healthy. Fat, maybe. But otherwise healthy. Except that they won't be for long if they take M-1752, will they?" Margaret inhaled sharply, but kept quiet. "You know about the aggressive liver cancer in a cohort of spider monkeys, right?" Olga pressed.

Margaret stared at Olga. "How do you know?"

"I can't tell you that."

Margaret finally took a sip of her coffee. "Not just spider monkeys." Her voice barely rose above a whisper.

"Oh?" Olga asked. "What else?"

"There were other experiments, after the spider monkey one, in different strains of mice and rabbits, and they also got cancer. But a new directive came down after Correx took over, to keep experimental animals alive just long enough to satisfy regulatory. So they sac the animals before the cancer shows up." Olga nodded to show that she understood the shorthand Margaret was using. She knew that "regulatory" meant a drug company's department charged with putting together the information packages required by the FDA to gain approval for the next step in a drug's journey from lab to market, and that lab people used the euphemism "sacrifice" or "sac" to denote killing experimental animals.

Margaret continued. "They said it was costing too much to keep animals alive past what the FDA was looking for."

"How long between the end of the injection course and the appearance of tumors?"

"In spider monkeys? Twenty to twenty-four months."

"All hepatic?"

"Mostly. Also kidneys, but that's rare."

"The incidence was pretty high, right? A third of the monkeys got cancer?"

"Yes, about that."

"How did Sliema explain these results to the FDA?"

Margaret snorted. "I don't think they reported them."

"I thought they had to."

"I thought so, too. But it was so long after the injection that they could convince themselves it didn't have any relationship to the drug. Except that they also altered the internal Sliema records."

Olga gasped.

Margaret went on. "The records now indicate there was a mix-up and that the monkeys were injected with a different chemical than M-1752, and if it's a different chemical, then the tumors didn't result from an M-1752 injection, right?"

"So there's willful fraud going on, not just the turning of a blind eye. And now they sac the animals before the tumors appear."

Margaret nodded. "You got it."

Olga got up to refill her coffee cup. Coming back, she asked, "Can you tell me a bit about Dr. Jonathan Vickers? Just curious, that's all."

"He was great." Margaret's voice cracked, and she dabbed her eyes with a paper napkin. "Sorry, I still get emotional."

"I apologize."

"You need to know that it's not his fault," Margaret said earnestly. "He was the one who kept the animals a long time because he wanted to be absolutely certain there weren't any adverse events before going further into human trials. And he was just such a fantastic person, totally down to earth. Some scientists are so odd, but he was just normal, if you can say that about somebody who's so brilliant. He wasn't stuck up, either. He respected people. When he asked you a question, he wanted to hear your answer.

"We were a small group, only eight of us, because most of the functions of a drug research company were outsourced. You know, the chemical synthesis, the big animal experiments, all that stuff was contracted out." Margaret sighed. "It was an amazing place to work when he was there."

Olga let some time pass before she asked her next question. She didn't want Margaret to teeter from trusting her to regretting saying too much. "Who should I talk to next?"

Margaret didn't hesitate. "Greg Banting. He's an analytical chemist and a really good scientist. He's also an old, grouchy fart whom people tend to discount because of his age. He's very bright, but he's over 70 now. He lives in Toronto. Both of his kids married Canadians and moved up there many years ago, and once Sliema let him go, he and his wife packed up and went there, too. We exchange e-mails

sometimes, and Christmas cards. He's in my address book."
She took out a well-thumbed address book held together by
three rubber bands and searched for the relevant entry. "Here
he is."

———≫《◉》≪———

The Foundation for Justice in Medical Research occupied
a 1000-square-foot loft-like space in a startup farm near Union
Square. For $6000 per month, with no yearly contract, the
foundation had a large space by New York standards, janitorial
services, a secure T1 high-speed Internet link, and the great
energy that comes from many entrepreneurial people rubbing
together. The office was bright and inviting, with exposed brick
walls, large windows, and lighting that made its three live pot-
ted palms thrive. It was a great bargain for New York.

Olga walked in around noon and dumped her parka and
knapsack on the floor by her desk. She stood for a moment
enjoying the room she and Claire chose for their fake foundation, then sat down and powered up her computer. Twenty
minutes later, she'd reserved a seat on a flight to Toronto the
next day, rented a car, and printed directions for getting from
the airport to Greg Banting's apartment.

"Daisy! You're back."

Olga swiveled to smile at Mary Olsson. "Did you miss
me?"

"You, I missed you. Your mess, not so much." Mary put
her hands on her hips and shook her head at the parka and
the knapsack.

"It's only temporary. We will be gone again before you know it. What's been happening here?"

"We've gotten some more boxes of documents from the printer, which I stacked in our storage space on the third floor. The people from the Justice Department said they'll pick them up tomorrow. And Anne says that she's coming back into town tomorrow." Anne Blakely, the name by which Mary knew Claire, acted as the other principal investigator at the foundation.

"Shit. I'm flying to Toronto first thing tomorrow. Can you ask her to meet me there instead of coming here?"

"Sure, I'll track her down."

Before reaching for the phone, Mary stopped. "Daisy? Can I ask your advice about something?"

"Sure. What's up?"

"Benedict Vickers recommended that you hire me, right?"

"Yeah…"

"Well, while you were out, he called and invited me to lunch. And, of course, I went because he's a nice guy and we were friendly when we both worked for Gardiner, and I owe him for helping me find this job."

"Personally, I'd go simply because he's so good looking. Then again, maybe I wouldn't because men that hot usually need to come with a warning label saying *seriously damaged inside*," observed Olga.

Mary giggled. "That's true. But I'm married, so I can just look at him and not worry about the seriously damaged part."

"Lucky you."

"Well, I'm not so sure. It wasn't obvious at first, but by the main course I got a strong sense that he was pumping me for information about your work."

He's checking up on me, thought Olga, *Maybe he does miss me.* But she made sure not to show how much the idea pleased her. Instead, she said, "I wouldn't be surprised. I kinda figured he was planting you here, so to speak. He has a major economic interest in Sliema, and as quiet as we've tried to be, somebody may well have alerted him to us."

"So why did you hire me?"

"Because you're a great admin and you're honest. And I go with my gut feeling about people. Oh, and Anne likes you, too. So what ended up happening with Benedict?"

"I confronted him about it and he tried to make a joke out of it, but I wouldn't let him. I told him I am very grateful for his help but there are some boundaries I can't cross. He seemed to take that quite well. Although I probably won't be getting any more Cadbury chocolates or lunch invitations from him."

"My heart bleeds for you." Olga smiled. "I promise to bring you some of those chocolates from my trip to Canada. They're available there, too."

Chapter 39
March 30-31

Olga landed at 9:15 a.m., and quickly passed through Canadian immigration and customs. She checked on Claire's flight and saw that it was scheduled to arrive at noon. There was no point in driving away from the airport just to come back for Claire, so Olga waited. To pass the time, she picked up the rental car and parked it at the terminal where Claire's flight would be arriving. Then she settled near the passenger exit doors and read a copy of *Cosmopolitan*, her guilty pleasure.

When Claire emerged, the two women embraced and walked out to the parking lot.

"You're looking well, all considered," said Claire.

"Now there's a backhanded compliment if ever I heard one. But thanks. You're looking quite well yourself. Everything okay at home?"

"Couldn't be better."

"How's Benedict?" Olga asked, trying not to show how

much she cared about the answer.

"He is exactly as you have left him. Smokes too much, drinks immoderately, sleeps around. Not that he tells me about it, but I catch snippets of conversation between him and William, who lives vicariously through him, now that he's domesticated and can't indulge in at least one of these vices."

Olga quickly changed topics. "Any luck?"

"Nothing. Nada. Zilch. Niente. Nulla. Frustrating doesn't begin to describe it. I'm glad your talk with Margaret Drewry got us somewhere."

"Greg Banting was on our list anyway. I hope bumping him up in priority is worth it."

"Is that...?" Claire saw a new ring on Olga's hand and stopped.

"No, no." Olga laughed. "It's just a birthday present. But Brian's done quite well, no?"

"It's gorgeous! Congratulations, you found a man who has good taste in jewelry and remembers your birthday. That makes him a keeper in my view."

Greg Banting lived at the corner of Finch Avenue and Don Mills Road, about ten miles northeast of downtown Toronto. Relying on the maps she'd brought, Olga found his building without trouble. She parked in the visitors parking outside the gates controlled by a guard. The two women got out and were immediately buffeted by strong, cold winds that nearly took their breath away. Olga found her balance again, put her hood on, and stuffed her hands into her pockets. Then she took a moment to orient herself and figure out where she was going.

For some reason, perhaps on the basis of Margaret Drewry's money woes, Olga expected Banting to live in a modest, if not outright run-down retirement community. Instead, they stood at the edge of expansive, well-maintained grounds surrounding two high-rise towers. She surmised that the large curved glass dome between the two buildings covered an indoor pool. She could also see a large outdoor pool covered with a blue tarp for the winter.

Olga and Claire worried briefly about gaining entrance into the compound until Claire pointed out that the gates weren't connected to an outside fence. They could simply walk around them along a well-tramped foot path that lazy residents had carved out to shortcut the way from the buildings to the street.

"Welcome to Canada," Olga said, shaking her head in disbelief. She hunched over against the wind blowing straight into her face as she and Claire walked to the front door of Banting's building.

In the vestibule, Olga found the intercom code for Banting and dialed it.

"Yes?" asked a male voice.

"Dr. Banting?"

"Yes."

"My name is Daisy Fenton, and I'm with the Foundation for Justice in Medical Research."

"I'm not giving you any money. Go away." The line went dead.

Olga dialed again.

"Go away!" The voice was raised.

"I'm not asking for money. It's about Sliema," Olga said

as fast as she could, before Banting could hang up on her again.

"Why didn't you say so in the first place? I'm in apartment 3309. Come on up." There was a buzz, and the door to the building unlocked with a click.

They hurried into the foyer and rode the elevator to the thirty-third floor. They found number 3309 at the end of the corridor and Olga knocked. The door was opened almost immediately by an older man in a plaid workshirt and gym pants.

"Thank you for letting us in, Dr. Banting. I'm Daisy Fenton and this is my colleague, Anne Blakely." Both women extended their IDs for him to read and, when he nodded, put them away.

"Call me Greg." He shook their hands with a surprisingly crushing grip, then led them through a large, beautifully furnished apartment into the solarium. "What can I get you? Coffee? Tea?"

Both Olga and Claire declined, not wanting to be too much trouble.

"Suit yourselves. Then you're going to watch me drink tea because I'm having some."

"Then we'll have some, too. Thank you."

"Sit here," Banting said, indicating a rattan table with a round glass top and four matching upholstered chairs. Claire and Olga complied, but when Banting left them, Olga walked over to the large windows to admire the panoramic view of Toronto spread before her. She could even see Lake Ontario shimmering more than eight miles to the south.

Banting returned with a tray on which he had arranged

tea mugs, sugar, lemon, and cookies.

"You want to talk about Sliema. Why?"

Olga took the lead. "Because it's well on its way to getting FDA approval for a drug that's incredibly dangerous."

"Did you know that I contacted the FDA about it and they ignored me?"

"No, we didn't know that."

"Oh, yes. Once your hair turns white and you need three different pairs of glasses to get through the day, everybody treats you like you're mentally retarded. Or senile." Banting took off his glasses and fixed Olga with his green eyes. He had an intimidating stare made more so by his unruly eyebrows. "What are you hoping to achieve?"

Olga wasn't cowed by the interrogation. She welcomed having a frank discussion with someone who wasn't afraid of Sliema. "We're hoping to get enough concrete information, maybe even data, that we can take to the FDA scientific advisory panel so that it has no choice but to recommend shutting down the M-1752 human trials. Our foundation's mandate is simple. The FDA doesn't have enough resources to do its job, so we're here to do it for them. Albeit one drug at a time."

Banting nodded approvingly. "Good. I like that. Maybe somebody like you is more political and knows better than I do how to get them to listen."

"Or maybe they still won't, but at least we'll give it our best shot."

Banting put his glasses back on, transforming himself once again into a harmless owl, and sipped his tea. "I'm probably responsible for all the original Sliema people being summarily let go. After Jon, Dr. Vickers, died, I continued the line of experiments we'd discussed and got the results that we didn't want to get but expected. And I went to the Correx people who were now running the place to tell them. They listened to me with that glazed look and that fixed smile designed to tell you 'I see your lips are moving but I'm going to make no mental effort to understand what you're saying.' The next day, we were all dismissed."

"We want to know what you told them," Olga prompted.

"How much chemistry do you know?" Banting asked.

"Unfortunately, probably not as much as I should know," Olga said. "I coasted through my undergrad courses. Still don't know the difference between an ester and an ether. And between Anne and me, I'm the expert."

"This is going to be a long conversation." Banting got up with a grunt and walked off to his study. He came back with a sticks and balls model of a molecule.

"Don't worry about what this molecule is. It's not M-1752. I just want to demonstrate some basic principles." He twisted the model into a different shape without breaking or separating it. "Did you see that?" he asked, demonstrating again by twisting it back to its original shape.

"Yes! Cool!"

"Some molecules have the ability to exist in different orientations. The fancy name is stereochirality, and the different forms are called stereoisomers, and they are designated as either R or S. Even though they have the exact same atomic composition, same molecular weight, and same melting point, they can have strikingly different functionalities."

"Do you mind if I take notes?" asked Olga.

"Be my guest. Generally speaking, unless you enrich for one or another isomer, you'll get a fifty-fifty mix at the end of synthesis—half R isomer and half S isomer. In industrial and pharmaceutical situations, you're praying that the functionalities of these two isomers will be the same, or at least sufficiently similar to let it go. Otherwise, you'll have to separate the isomers away from each other with various purification techniques and that's a whole added complication, and complications are synonymous with expense."

"Is M-1752 a chiral molecule?"

"Bingo! Yes, it is. Only in this case, one isomer is highly potent but deadly. The other is much less potent but appears to be completely safe. Just before his death, after the spider monkey fiasco, Jon and I suspected that this was the case."

Olga's brow creased in concentration. "Why did you focus on the stereochirality as the potential cause of the problem?"

"Call it intuition bred by experience. This particular cohort of monkeys was showing a much faster weight loss than previous animals, to the point where we seriously debated whether we should give them the third injection, but we had to, because that was the protocol that all the other animals were subjected to. When we saw the difference in the results and in the side effects, we went back to the batch documentation and saw that in this particular batch, the R isomer was 72% and the S isomer was 28%, not the 50:50 of the other batches. We looked at the synthesis notes, and found that this batch had one step where the temperature was elevated during synthesis, compared to the other batches.

"I don't know if you have lab experience, but so often these stories play out like a cross between a bad joke and a badly-conceived science fiction novel. It's often unbelievable how you discovered things or why a fantastic result turns out to be just an artifact in the end. The chemical company shouldn't have sent us this batch. Once they did, I should have caught the anomalous isomer ratio when it first came to us and rejected it, but I didn't. If only my intentional science was as brilliant as my errors."

"This batch had an elevated ratio, but if one of the isomers is toxic, shouldn't the 50:50 mix have produced some cancers too?" Olga asked.

"Absolutely. You'd expect lower incidence or slower onset, because of the lower amount of the R isomer, but they should be there. Which is why, once we suspected that we had an isomer problem, we decided to go back to the original animal experiments to see if we missed anything. But the mice and the rabbits in those experiments lived out their natural lives without any ill effects. But if you're injecting them with something that's 50% poison, how can that be? We tried to think of an explanation for weeks, until Jon came up with the hypothesis that those strains of mice and rabbits were genetically immune to the effects of the R isomer.?"

Olga was writing quickly as Claire listened with rapt interest. Banting basked in the attention.

"Lab mouse and rabbit strains have been bred for countless generations until they're genetically uniform. That's useful because you don't have to worry about inconsistent results; you can simply concentrate on the question your experiment is hopefully properly designed to answer. Once we came up with the hypothesis that the R isomer was toxic on certain genetic backgrounds, we designed a rough experiment to test it. We ordered seven mouse strains and four rabbit strains, and divided each of them into two groups, one injected with pure R and one with pure S. And wouldn't you know it, our hypothesis was bang on." Banting thumped the glass tabletop for emphasis. "The S isomer was safe for every strain, but the R strain was deadly in several of them. The R isomer was also the main driver of weight loss. The S isomer showed much lower activity than the R. How I wish Jon would have lived to see it."

Claire looked confused. "Let me try to summarize this to see if I got it right," she said. "You have two different versions of the same active ingredient. One causes aggressive cancer and one is harmless. Except that the cancer one is not harmful to all animals. Rather, it depends on their genetics. About right?"

"Yes, you got it."

"How do we know then, if it causes cancer only in some animals, that it'll cause cancer in people?"

"Because monkey DNA is much closer to human DNA than that of mice and rabbits. And animals like monkeys are much harder to standardize, so the cohorts we used were of mixed genetic background, and a third got highly aggressive tumors. This batch had about time-and-a-half the amount of R isomer than the other batches, so with a 50:50 batch you might have fewer tumors or you might have the tumors showing up later, or both. But nevertheless you will have a large number of people with aggressive liver and kidney cancers. They'll be looking good because they'll be thin, but they won't enjoy their new good looks for long."

Olga put her pen down and helped herself to a cookie. "I

don't know where to begin. I have so many questions."

"Why don't you go away and put your questions into an organized list. I'm big on lists. In the meantime, I'll review everything that I have. You like Greek food?"

"Love it!" Claire exclaimed, and Olga nodded enthusiastically.

"There's a great place on Danforth Avenue called Astoria. Meet me there for late lunch tomorrow, say at 2 p.m., and we'll continue."

"I hate to be pushy, especially when you've been so helpful, but would it be possible perhaps to continue now?"

"No. My wife is coming home from the hairdresser's soon, then we have to do some shopping and our kids are coming for dinner."

Claire got up and tugged at Olga to do the same. "I'm sorry," she said to Banting. "Daisy turns into a bulldog when she finds a nugget of information. Useful in our line of business, but totally unacceptable, socially speaking." Olga blushed and mumbled an apology.

"This is killing me." Olga and Claire were in their hotel room. "I can't believe we have to wait another day to hear the rest of the story."

"Patience is obviously not a strong suit of yours." Claire smiled indulgently.

Olga threw her pen across the room in frustration.

Claire decided to take Olga's mind off the unavoidable

delay. "Let's go exploring. There's some excellent shopping here, and good restaurants, and I read that a lot of the Broadway shows get tested here first."

"You forgot to extol the virtues of the Toronto Maple Leafs and the Raptors in your spiel," Olga grumbled.

———

Banting was waiting for the two women when they walked into the Astoria. He was carrying a briefcase and leaning on a cane. "My back gave out this morning. Stepped out of the shower, bent down to dry my right foot, and my back just seized up. My advice to you two is not to get old."

The restaurant was mostly empty, but they were kept waiting. Banting said, "We're waiting for my table. It's that one on the elevation." He pointed at a table set by itself in a railed-off section to the left of the three steps that separated the back section of the restaurant from its front. "It's more private."

The waiter finished clearing Banting's table, and the group was escorted to it. Once seated and their order taken, Olga could no longer contain herself.

"Your letter to the FDA. Who did you send it to?"

"The contact person for the Endocrinologic and Metabolic Drugs Advisory Committee." Banting opened his briefcase, then changed his mind. "I'll give you everything I have when we're finished here, including a copy of my letter."

"Aren't you afraid of Sliema? Didn't you have to sign a nondisclosure agreement to get your severance package?"

"I didn't take it."

"Oh." Olga was surprised. This option hadn't occurred to her.

"You want to know how I could afford not to?"

"No...really... it's none of my business."

"I'll tell you anyway. Jon gave me a huge bonus when he got the first round of funding from Gardiner. He set up a trust so I wouldn't have to pay taxes on the whole thing at once, seeded it with $750,000, and I can draw on it whenever I need to. I was past retirement age when I joined Sliema, and he didn't want me to rely solely on the stock options to hit the jackpot.

"But so far I haven't needed to touch it because my wife and I understand that living within our means includes saving for retirement. I hope you two are putting something aside, too. Retirement can be a cruel place for people who don't think ahead."

The waiter brought three large plates of pork souvlaki, roasted potatoes and rice, and the three concentrated on their food for a while.

"The more I hear about him, the more Jon sounds like a saint," Olga said.

"Oh, I wouldn't say that. For one thing, that boy had a serious skirt problem. He once juggled three girlfriends at once, each of them thinking he was this close to marrying her. I don't think he was ever in a relationship with a woman when he didn't cheat. He was an adrenaline junkie, and maybe cheating was part of his thrill-seeking behavior. He could also be incredibly brash. He didn't suffer fools at all. He hated bureaucracy. Actually the last two points go into the saint column in my book."

Olga laughed. "Mine, too." She paused to take a drink of water. "Do you know what happened to the data from your M-1752 isomer experiments when you left Sliema?"

"I wouldn't be surprised if they were all destroyed."

Claire frowned. "How could that be? I can see a conspiracy of a couple of people, but aren't there a lot of people at Sliema and at Correx who know about your experiments?"

Banting chased a piece of souvlaki down with some red wine before answering. "I think people have a distorted idea of what a drug company looks like. It's compartmentalized. Just like any other science lab, one person or two people work on a line of experiments and report to one person above them. It's amazingly easy to make up results, delete results, or fake whole experiments. And the pressure to get good results is enormous. That's why I'm always amused when it's patient lawsuits that finally force drugs off the market and then, lo and behold, it turns out that somebody at the drug company knew all along that the drug was causing whatever side effect patients eventually complain about."

"But in practical terms, how would they destroy your data?"

"The animals were all sac'd, and all that was kept from them were tissue specimens in wax blocks in case we needed them for future experiments. You'd be amazed at how common it is to mix up such specimens, then lose the log of which specimen was what, then toss the whole rack of specimens because they're useless without the log.

"In terms of the data, my lab books and my computer files went to my supervisor. He was, and still is, a Correx vice-president of something or other, a corporate type through and through who hasn't gotten his sleeves wet in a lab in years. If he deletes my files and shreds my lab books, the data is gone. That's it. Who's going to call him on it?"

"What about backups?" Claire asked.

Banting shrugged. "I don't know what their policy is. But who's going to ask for the backups if they don't have a reason to do so?"

Claire lowered her eyes and shook her head. "I guess no one will," she said quietly. Then a new question occurred to her. "You said yesterday that the R isomer is more potent than the S. But the S does work, right?"

"It works, but not as dramatically. Three injections will result in the loss of only fifteen to eighteen percent of excess weight. So if you're 200 pounds and should be 150 pounds, three injections will achieve a loss of 7.5 to 9 pounds. You could continue doing the injections and continue to lose weight, but you'd plateau at about 40% of excess weight."

"What I don't get is why not purify the S isomer and start over? After all, you and Jon caught this issue so early."

Banting shook his head vehemently. "Not early enough. You'd have to throw away everything that we'd shown the FDA to that point and start from scratch. *In vitro*, mouse studies, big animal studies, stability, toxicity. Everything. It's at least three years of work, and the competition in the obesity field is incredible. You lose three years, you may not get a second bite at this market."

"At the risk of sounding naïve, how can the Correx people live with themselves?" Claire was appalled.

"It's easy for now. People have an amazing capacity for

fooling themselves. Think about it. Everything is going fantastically well. Phase I human trials are hitting the ball out of the park in terms of weight loss, and with no side effects. This is it! This is the drug that will make obesity a manageable problem, if not completely eradicate it. You're doing something glorious for humanity! And then this old clown shows up and babbles about some Rs and Ss and some random strains of mice. Who are you gonna believe? Your fabulous data on which billions of dollars are riding, or me?"

"So they've done nothing to fix this? They haven't surreptitiously told their chemists to purify future batches to pure S form, for example?"

"Of course not. With a pure S solution you're not going to see the jaw-dropping weight loss results that you see with a solution in which the R isomer is present, and the discrepancy will be so obvious that it'll raise major flags, even at the FDA, despite all its shortcomings.

"And there's one other thing. You yank M-1752 now and start tinkering, and it'll be obvious to everybody that there was a massive toxicity problem with it. You wouldn't do it for any other reason. Even if you came back with the safest drug in the world, you have a guilt-by-association problem. You bring out a purified S isomer and many people wouldn't want to touch it. It's like the Phen-Fen fiasco. One part was toxic, the other not so much, but the FDA is now extremely leery of allowing even the benign part in other combinations."

"And presumably even if you were able to get it through the FDA, the public wouldn't be quite so excited about it, and that would hurt the bottom line," Olga mused.

The waiter cleared their plates and they ordered coffee.

Claire said what has been on her mind since the day before. "So hundreds of volunteers have been injected for the Phase I and Phase II trials and they don't know that many of them have aggressive cancer in their near future."

"The Phase II volunteers are the one thing I wouldn't necessarily worry about."

"Why?"

"Correx is all about cost cutting, and when their people took over running Sliema, it became all about cost cutting, too. So they off-shored the human drug trials. You know that's a growing trend, right? Almost 100% of new drug applications contain data from non-U.S. human trials these days.

"It's so much cheaper to test drugs in the developing world, and the results are usually better because the population is drug-naïve, whereas in the U.S., good luck finding volunteers who aren't medicated to the gills. Also, if things go wrong, it's harder to sue U.S. corporations for problems they caused overseas. And even if you can sue them, the cost of a life in other countries is so much cheaper than a U.S. life. It's an economic fact."

"Are you saying we shouldn't try to find those volunteers because they are not Americans?" Claire's voice rose.

"Oh, quit your politically correct liberal bellyaching, I'm not saying anything of the sort. The reason I think there's nothing to worry about is that they outsourced Phase II to Nigeria. Have you ever heard of a fat Nigerian?"

"So how are they getting data?"

"They've signed up a whole bunch of doctors to whom they pay per recruited volunteer. They explain to the doctors quite carefully what results are good. The doctors have every incentive to produce good results or else they won't be on the roster for the next drug trial. And the doctors are responsible for collecting the data. You see where this is going, right?" Both Claire and Olga nodded.

"A couple of other little nuggets," Banting continued. "First, the FDA inspects less than 5% of drug trial sites and this percentage is even lower if you take U.S. sites out of the equation. Second, companies are not required to report trials that took place abroad. So, in essence, drug companies may pick and choose which trials they're going to disclose. How about them apples?"

"So you don't think the Phase II volunteers are actually being injected with M-1752?"

"I'm hoping the doctors they recruited aren't sufficiently diligent for that. Or maybe that's just me being a master of self-deception because I don't want to know I'm partly responsible for a large number of future tumors."

"But the Phase I volunteers?"

"Oh, yes. Those are real future cancer patients. I tried to find out who they were, but the Correx people instituted new security measures and I didn't have permission to get into that database."

"Do you know, or have any way to find out, which doctors are participating in the Phase II trials? We'll try to document the human trials fraud to give the FDA more ammunition to shut this down."

"No, but I know they're concentrated in three Nigerian cities—Lagos, Kano, and Benin."

"Shoot me now. These are big cities." Olga threw her

head back in despair.

"Yes, but there can't be more than a few thousand doctors, if that." Claire tried to be encouraging. "At least we have a geographic start."

"There might be a simpler way than just walking around Lagos asking random physicians if they're M-1752 pushers. You could try to get the information from the contractor who's overseeing these trials," Banting said to Olga.

"Even the oversight is outsourced?"

"Sure. First, it's cheaper, and second, it's another layer of 'hear no evil, see no evil' deniability. If there's fraud in the results, Sliema will simply say that it's the contractor's fault and they didn't know anything about it."

"Please tell me you know who the contractor is."

"I do indeed. It's an Indian company headquartered in Mumbai. My Internet research on them is in the folder I'm giving you." He opened his briefcase and took out two bulging manila envelopes.

"Thank you. I can't believe no one would listen to you about this," said Olga as she stuffed the envelopes into her rucksack.

"Too much hype and too much money. People go deaf."

———————≈《()》≈———————

"Talk about burying the lede. It offends my journalistic sensibilities," said Claire, reading Banting's letter to the FDA while Olga drove the car back to Toronto's Pearson International Airport, where they were scheduled to take a flight back to New York. "He starts with almost a page and a half about how the new Sliema management laid off all the original people and how no one listens to what he has to say, etc., etc."

"You can't blame him. He's angry for a good reason."

"Yes, but being angry usually doesn't get you where you need to go, does it?"

"No," Olga said. "Let's shift gears and talk about what we're doing next. My next task is to get inside the animal lab contractor that housed Sliema's monkeys to see if it has an unaltered version of the work order and experimental protocol that Sliema later altered to show the monkeys weren't injected with M-1752. Right?"

"Agreed." Claire nodded.

"After that, I'm flying to India. No point in going to Nigeria first."

"Right. India's a much better starting point."

"And you're going find an attorney specializing in whistleblower cases to retain for Banting?" Olga asked distractedly, concentrating on the traffic around her.

"Yes. I wonder how I'm going to find someone who can control Banting. The more I think about it, the more I suspect I've gotten the harder task here."

Chapter 40
April 20

The Google Alerts filter that William had set up on his computer flagged a story about a militant animal rights group that the *New York Times* ran that morning on the second page of the main section. Bermuda Labs, a contract lab specializing in animal testing located in rural Maryland was the victim of an attack the night before. The activists overpowered the guards and the four technicians who were at the facility, roughing them up and leaving them tied to each other until the police found them.

The intruders splashed every room they managed to break into with fake blood. They smashed computers, furniture, copying machines, and sensitive and expensive scientific equipment, including microscopes, micro-injectors, and cryostats. Most worryingly, they released many animals into the wild. They were going to release the primates in addition to the mice, rats, rabbits, and pigs, but the locks on the primate enclosure proved too tough for them and they left without infiltrating that section of the facility.

The article quoted the general manager as saying that the attack had created an atmosphere of fear among the staff and that seven employees had quit. "This is domestic terrorism, nothing more, nothing less," he stated. "It's difficult to find well-qualified animal technicians. It took us three months to fill one position, and the woman we hired for it just two weeks ago has now quit. But we're determined not to give in to this type of intimidation and we will redouble our efforts to provide a safe environment for our staff."

Bermuda Labs was the Sliema contractor responsible for its large animal studies.

William smiled and placed a copy of the article into a burgeoning folder. He then picked up one of his cell phones and called Olga. "How does it feel to be hailed as a hard to find, 'well-qualified animal technician,' albeit something of a quitter?" he inquired.

"I love the smell of mouse in the morning," She laughed. "Seriously. Thank you for giving me an opportunity to get over whatever shred of nostalgia I had for my grad student days. The biggest problem was keeping my identities straight. I finally got used to people calling me Daisy Fenton and then I had to become Meg Ridley."

"Then you should be ecstatic that it's back to Daisy Fenton for you."

"Personally, I can't wait for the day when I'm able to return to being Olga Mueller."

Chapter 41
April 23-May 17

The parties to the *Vickers v. Gardiner* litigation exchanged their discovery requests a week after the defendants filed their answer. A few rounds of terse letters followed in which each side protested the overreaching and unduly burdensome nature of the other side's requests and in which they reserved all rights to remedy the situation. Then they got down to the business of exchanging documents, which were produced on a rolling basis over the next six weeks. When all documents had been exchanged, the defendants had produced 4.5 million pages to Kress Rubinoff. Kress Rubinoff had produced the almost four million pages that Benedict had kept in the warehouse, having first reviewed only 100,000 of them—a mere three percent.

Neither side had any interest in reviewing each and every document produced to it, let alone each and every page. After running key word searches and culling the most promising 126,000 e-mails and financial documents, Kress Rubinoff simply ignored the rest. Fields Stanhope also identified the few thousands of documents they wanted to review, but instead of ignoring the rest, they added them to an electronic data room accessible to their experts. They weren't thrilled that all seventeen experts had access to all the documents exchanged in the litigation thus far, and grumbled about contaminating their testifying experts with too much information. But Peter Gardiner proved to be a surprisingly micromanagerial and miserly client, and he insisted that consolidating all information and giving their experts access to it was going to be cheaper in the long run.

——))((◉)) ——

Professor Bernhardt Hoffmeyer was determined to spend the entire day working on fixing the draft paper written by one of his post-doctoral fellows, Jhi Ming Yang. When he first saw the draft, he shook his head in despair. As fantastic a scientist as Yang was, his English was atrocious and the draft was nearly incomprehensible.

Professor Hoffmeyer was tenured faculty at Stanford's School of Medicine, cross-appointed with the Biochemistry Department. His list of accomplishments belied his relative youth. At 42, he was a star in the obesity research world. He ran a lab of almost fifty people, including eighteen post-docs and twenty-one graduate students, which published innovative research at a dizzying pace. He was a recipient of several international prizes, sat on the editorial boards of four highly-respected scientific journals, and fielded more invitations to speak at symposia and conferences than he could accommodate.

His easy manner and photogenic looks also helped propel Professor Hoffmeyer out of the obscurity of academic stardom into the spotlight of the general media, and he was rapidly becoming the go-to expert for stories having to do with obesity or metabolism. In his more reflective moments, he admitted to himself that, as much as he loved his scientific work, he loved the public acclaim even more.

Just as he was getting the hang of Jhi Ming Yang's garbled syntax, his concentration was interrupted by a knock on his door. He looked up to see a woman leaning against the door frame. She wore the typical graduate student uniform, jeans and a baggy sweatshirt, and carried an obviously heavy backpack.

""Yes?" he asked somewhat impatiently, cursing his habit of leaving his office door open.

"Professor Hoffmeyer? I'm Daisy Fenton. I made an appointment with you through your secretary." The woman advanced into his office, hand extended. She seemed oblivious to his distinct lack of enthusiasm.

Hoffmeyer got up and shook her hand out of politeness. He then chuckled and spread his arms to indicate the messiness of his overflowing desk and the piles of documents covering every other surface within his reach. "I'm afraid that I'm going to give absent-minded academics a bad reputation, Ms. Fenton. I'm very bad checking my calendar. I didn't know you were coming today and I don't have the..." Hoffmeyer trailed off, watching with astonishment the interloper's undeterred progress toward a visitor's chair, from which she began clearing books and papers.

After removing the last book from the chair, Olga sat down and flashed Hoffmeyer a smile. "I totally know how it is. I double and triple-book myself all the time. So it's great that you're actually here and we're connecting now."

"No. That's what I mean. I don't have time to speak with you."

"Professor Hoffmeyer, trust me, you do have the time to speak with me. In fact, I'll bet you're going to forget whatever you're doing right now and that you think is so earth-shatteringly important. I need to talk to you about Sliema's M-1752 drug. You're on the FDA's scientific advisory panel for its approval, aren't you?" Olga, realizing that the office door was open, got up and closed it.

Hoffmeyer regarded her with growing dismay, but made the calculation that it might cost him less time to hear her out than to argue with her. "Yes, I'm on the panel. That's public knowledge."

"And you've been retained as an expert in a litigation pertaining to Sliema. Vickers v. Gardiner. On the Gardiner side, no?"

Hoffmeyer bristled. "I followed the ethics guidelines and disclosed it. It was deemed not to be a conflict of interest. Who are you anyway?"

"I'm with the Foundation for Justice in Medical Trials. We figured you'd be the right person to approach with our findings. After all, you're German, so you should be hypersensitive to inappropriate medical experimentation."

Hoffmeyer could feel himself flush as he abruptly stood and glared at her. "You really are very rude."

"That's probably true." Olga shrugged and smiled conciliatorily.

"Just tell me what you want and get out." Hoffmeyer sat back down.

"What if I told you that I know — not think, not wonder, not surmise — I know that M-1752 causes aggressive cancer in a high percentage of lab animals? What if I told you that I know there are serious irregularities with the Phase II human trials now ongoing? What if I also told you that I have some documents and that I can lead you to other documents in the database set up for the litigation? And finally, what if I told you that Sliema knows about its cancer problem and is either willfully ignoring it, or, even worse, actively covering it up?"

"How do you know all of this?"

"Through research. Something that the FDA should be doing, but isn't."

"I can't believe it. I knew Jon Vickers personally and he would never allow something like this to happen."

"He didn't. He was just starting to understand the problems with M-1752 when he died. He was worried about it, but the new powers-that-be decided to forge on." Daisy sat forward in her chair and rested her arm on Hoffmeyer's desk. "Your friendship with Jon Vickers was the other reason we decided to speak with you. It wouldn't be fair to sully his reputation along with those really responsible."

"I need to see data. I need to see experimental designs and outcomes."

Olga nodded enthusiastically. "We're not knee-jerk anti-drug or anti-corporate fanatics, and we're certainly not anti-science. We just want something incredibly dangerous not to get approved for use. Especially an obesity-related product that's going to be popular with the general public." She opened her bag and removed its contents. "I'll give you everything we have. Time is of the essence because the litigation may settle any day, and your access privileges to the data room will probably end right afterward."

———◄《◉》►———

Jeff Thompson, the senior associate on the *Vickers v. Gardiner* litigation, allowed himself some whooping and a couple of fist pumps behind the closed door of his office when he found the e-mails in which Gardiner and Correx executives discussed plans to oust Jon Vickers from Sliema.

You sure Vickers is still going on that trip to the Himalayas? Asked an e-mail from Correx's CEO.

Absolutely. I have his proxy. We're good to go.

Gardiner e-mailed in reply.

I just want to nail down the timing. You're holding the vote on the 20th and issuing the new shares on the 21st, and we're buying on the 21st. And Vickers is coming back about 3 weeks later, after we've changed the locks and cleaned house.

You got it.

And you're still ok with voting his proxy this way?

A proxy is a proxy and I now have control of his voting bloc.

It never failed to amaze Jeff how careless people were

with e-mails, especially C-level executives. It's as if they didn't think the rules of discovery would apply to them. He still remembered an e-mail exchange in another shareholder litigation in which the CEO, corresponding with the CFO, penned the priceless e-mail that ended any chance of their side winning:

I can't believe those financial press geniuses are so dumb that they can't figure out we're underreporting our earnings to get gov't subsidies. How do they ever cross the street w/o being hit by a bus???? How long do you think we have before we need to restate?

After coming down from his euphoric high, Jeff began strategizing about the best way to present his find to the partners. He couldn't sit on these documents too long, but he wanted to make sure the fact that he, Jeff Thompson, found them wouldn't be lost in the ensuing frenzy. He immediately wrote a short memorandum summarizing his findings, drawing the obvious conclusions as to their value, and describing the even more obvious ways in which these documents could be used in the future phases of the litigation.

———⟫•⟪———

Martin Kress wasted no time calling Benedict to apprise him of the documents Jeff found. "Benedict? Martin Kress. How are you?"

"I'm well, thank you. You caught me in mid-run in Central Park. How are you?"

"I couldn't be better. Frankly, I'm floating on air right now. We found the most amazing chain of e-mails between Gardiner and some Correx executives describing their conspiracy to minimize Jon's share in Sliema. Jon's e-mail was helpful, but it's always better to have confirmation that the receiving party actually received the e-mail and read it. Now we have proof that both Gardiner and Correx knew of the conditions attached to Jon's proxy and willfully ignored them. Even worse, it sounds like they wanted to get him out of management altogether."

"No! Those bastards! Sliema was his life. And he, in turn, was an integral part of Sliema, and its public face. I can't imagine how they planned to run it without him up front."

"Nevertheless, we have it all in writing. We'll score some outstanding points during the depositions. Which is the other reason I'm calling. They want to depose you, and we need to give them some dates. You and I should coordinate our schedules because I'll be defending your deposition personally."

There was a short silence on the line before Benedict went on. "Back to the documents for a moment. Aren't you going to let opposing counsel know you found them? Seems to me they might be willing to discuss a settlement once they know we have these e-mails."

"We're not going to do anything of the sort. We're not going to give away the surprise element of introducing them at the right moment during Gardiner's deposition. To do it differently would be tactical suicide. If one of my people ever did something like that, I'd question his or her fitness to be a trial lawyer."

"I understand your reasoning, but I still think we might be able to get to a negotiated settlement quicker and without the pain of depositions if the other side were made aware."

Kress's voice cooled. "Benedict. I understand that you're the client and that you give us instructions. But you're wading far into the tactical realm of this litigation, where you really ought to take the advice of your lawyers. This is what we do, day in and day out. Please allow us to conduct this litigation properly. We've followed your instructions about filing the complaint under seal against my better judgment. But this is a nuts-and-bolts issue that we deal with a lot and that you, quite frankly, don't know anything about."

Benedict matched Kress's tone. "I'm sorry if it appears that I'm stepping on your toes, Martin. But this is more than a mere tactical matter. I know Peter Gardiner personally and you don't. I know how he thinks. If we get into the deposition phase of this case, there will be no settling with him. He'll give no quarter in attempting to save face from that point on."

"Are you afraid of being deposed?" Kress had seen many clients get cold feet at the thought of being questioned under oath and had done a lot of handholding to get them over their fears. His voice grew friendlier as he tried to assuage Benedict's concerns. "You shouldn't have any worries about this. We'll take as much time as we need to prepare you. Even if it takes a week, we'll get you to the point where there'll be no rattling you. And on top of that, I'll be at the deposition with you, and I'm not afraid to get in there and defend my witnesses up to and including halting the deposition if I see the other side engaging in dirty tactics. You'll be fine. That's my guarantee."

"I'm not afraid of being deposed. I'm afraid of missing a golden opportunity when one presents itself. Let me make it simple. Either you discuss these documents with Peter's attorneys or I discuss them with Peter myself. I know I'm well within my rights to talk to the other parties to the litigation. You can't because they're represented by lawyers, but I can because I'm a party. Which will it be?"

"This is the kind of stunt that gets clients fired."

"By all means, go ahead. And you won't see a penny from your 50% contingency fee."

It took all Kress's self-control not to hang up on Benedict. The man had gone beyond the pale. But he was also right. If Kress Rubinoff didn't see the litigation to its conclusion, then according to the retainer agreement, they had no claim on the contingency fee. And although Benedict would have to pay them for their out-of-pocket expenses, Kress was beginning to wonder if he was the type to honor even that part of the agreement without a fight. "I think we're both a little overheated right now. Let's take a day to think this through and resume this call tomorrow afternoon. Can we do that?"

"Of course we can, Martin." Benedict's tone softened somewhat. "Surely you know that I have no interest in switching attorneys at this stage. You've been utterly brilliant. Superb."

Chapter 42
May 18

The next morning, as was his habit, Martin Kress fixed himself a coffee and began reviewing the telephone messages that had come in before he'd arrived at the office. He stopped at the slip telling him to call Brendan Ogden, Gardiner's lawyer, as soon as possible.

Kress couldn't think why Ogden was calling him, and his curiosity was aroused. The two sides didn't have any outstanding motions before the court, and any other possible issues were of the kind that would have been handled at the associate or junior partner level. He dialed Ogden's number and settled more comfortably in his chair.

"Martin. Thank you for calling me back."

"What's on your mind, Brendan?"

"Let's talk settlement."

Martin was rendered speechless for a moment. That was a rare occurrence for him. "I'm sorry, did I just hear you say 'let's talk settlement?'" he repeated to buy some time for his brain to kick back in.

"You heard it. Apparently, your client and my client had a chat yesterday, and my client changed his mind about settling."

Kress hit the mute button on his speakerphone, his face purple with rage. "MOTHERFUCKER!" he screamed. Because Kress was not a yeller, his outburst brought his secretary to his office door to see what was wrong. He waved her off and hit the mute button again to continue the conversation.

"What terms do you propose?" Kress managed to say in a conversational tone of voice.

"Five percent of the current shares."

"That's laughably low and you know it. But I'll present it to my client and get back to you as soon as I have an answer."

"Looking forward to it."

————))⟨⟨(⟩)⟩⟩((————

Benedict drummed his fingers on his desk, staring intently at his cell phone and willing it to ring. He'd been chain smoking since 9, waiting for Kress to call and tell him that the other side had made its move. Just as he ran out of cigarettes and began dressing to go out to buy another pack, the phone finally rang. He would now have to endure the conversation without the comfort of nicotine.

"Hello, Martin."

"That was a schmuck move to pull, Benedict. I sounded like a fool when Ogden called me. I had no idea what was coming. That's not a good position to put me in."

"Sorry about that."

"Yeah? I don't think you understand the full ramifications of what you've done. What did you tell Gardiner? I need to gauge what kind of damage you've done."

"I told him exactly what you told me, including your plans to use those e-mails during his deposition. I also told him about the other documents you've found, so he understands the whole picture and has more incentive to cooperate."

Benedict heard a sharp intake of breath on the other side of the line. "You completely collapsed any possibility of us surprising them with any of the smoking gun documents we found. This is unbelievable."

"But Ogden did call you with a settlement offer, no?"

"How does an offer of five percent grab you?"

"It's obviously too low. Please go back to them with an offer of twenty-five percent and a provision that they forfeit their patent portfolio if they dilute me out again or if the IPO doesn't happen in two months."

"They'll never go for that."

"The results of the Phase II human trials are due in three weeks. I'm sure they're planning to IPO right after that."

"What if something happens and the results are delayed and come out six weeks from now?"

"Fine. Give them three months then."

"Do you want me to come back to you with every counter-proposal or do you want to give me your bottom line and some room to negotiate on your behalf? Or maybe you just want to chat with Ogden yourself and save me the trouble."

"Now you mention it, that's not a bad idea. In fact, I think

Kress Rubinoff's usefulness as my lawyers has reached nil."

"What are you talking about?"

"I'm talking about your style, Martin. Your scorched-earth and take-no-prisoners approach works well for some things but not for others. You also have highly antagonistic relationships with Peter and his counsel. In fact, the more I think about it, the more I'm certain the right thing to do is to fire you now."

"You can't do that!"

"Why not?"

"This is your way of getting out of paying your contingency fee, isn't it?" Martin shouted.

"Actually, that was the farthest thing from my mind, but firing you kills two birds with one stone. How brilliant of me. So, yes, please stop working on this matter immediately and file papers with the court asking to withdraw your appearance as my counsel. You'll get an e-mail from me to the same effect as soon as we get off the phone, and I'll courier a more formal hard-copy letter to you later today." Benedict hung up without waiting for Martin's response.

"R.J. Drummond," a baritone drawled.

"Hello, R.J., Benedict Vickers here."

"Benedict! How are you?"

"I'm very well and about to be better, thank you. And you?"

"Great. Are any Kress Rubinoff folks joining this call?"

"I should sincerely hope not, considering I just fired them."

"I...see." The hesitation in R.J.'s response was obvious and Benedict smiled thinking about the relationship equations that R.J.'s mind was racing to solve. He was Benedict's attorney of record, but he also had a longstanding and profitable local counsel relationship with Kress Rubinoff that Benedict was certain he'd be loath to lose.

"I want you to take over as lead."

"Can you tell me about your decision to fire Kress Rubinoff?"

"Sure. They've served their purpose and are now a hindrance. Purely business."

"It's just that we're entering the deposition phase, and I gotta be honest with you, we don't have the institutional knowledge that Kress Rubinoff has of this case. We've been kept strictly to local counsel tasks and, aside from opining on certain aspects of the demand letter and the complaint, we haven't been substantively involved. That's not to say we can't get up to speed quickly, but as your lawyer I have to tell you that this isn't the ideal moment to switch counsel."

"Thank you, R.J., for being so honest and forthcoming. But the case is about to settle, so depositions shan't be going forward. There's an offer on the table from opposing counsel. I need you to negotiate the settlement for me and to do whatever needs to be done to bring this case to a close."

"Parties often engage separate settlement counsel without firing their litigation counsel. That might be the right thing to do now. Settlements have a way of blowing up sometimes, then the case has to go on. If it happens in your case, you'll find yourself behind the eight ball without your primary litigation counsel."

"Rehiring Kress Rubinoff is off the table, R.J. I appreciate that it might put you in an awkward position, but you've been on the opposite side from Kress Rubinoff on many occasions and they still want to work with you. And I intend to compensate you for this added inconvenience."

"That's not it at all. I'm not concerned about my relationship with Kress Rubinoff—it'll work itself out. I'm concerned about your case being handled well," R.J. bristled, and Benedict, believing him, felt remorse as he realized that it hadn't even crossed his mind that R.J. could put a client's interests ahead of his own.

"I'm sorry, R.J. I've been less than perfectly adroit in this conversation. Will you, nevertheless, handle the settlement negotiations?"

"If you still think this is your best course, then sure, I'll handle it. Tell me what they're offering and what our bottom line is."

"They're offering five percent of their standard shares. That does me no good. I need at least twenty percent, and I need Sliema to register them so I can sell them whenever I want." Benedict decided to give R.J. his true bottom line, instead of the number he threw at Kress. "I also insist on a poison pill provision, through which Sliema's patents will be automatically reassigned to me if my shares are diluted again before the IPO or if they don't IPO in three months."

There was silence on the line, but Benedict thought he could hear the faint sound of pen scratching on paper. "I'm not gonna lie to you, Benedict. That's a tall order."

Benedict laughed. "It's nowhere near as tall as you think." Then he detailed the information in the documents that Kress Rubinoff had reviewed and explained that the other side was well aware of Kress Rubinoff's findings. He concluded, "Do let me know if things ever get sticky between you and Ogden, and I'll speak to Peter directly. It seems we've developed a certain grudging respect for each other and a surprisingly functional, if adversarial, working relationship."

Chapter 43
May 19

The term sheet for the confidential settlement of the *Vickers v. Gardiner* litigation was circulated at noon, and all parties signed off on it that afternoon. Benedict got the twenty percent of registered shares and the poison pill provision he demanded. He wasted no time calling Martin Kress, betting with himself whether Kress would take his call.

Kress did take his call. "You saved me the effort of dialing," Kress said.

"Always happy to help," Benedict answered flippantly, picturing the sour expression his comment must have elicited. "The case settled."

"Good for you. On what terms?"

"Unfortunately, I can't tell you, even though I'm bursting to do so. It's confidential. But if Kress Rubinoff executes a nondisclosure agreement, I'll share the results of R.J.'s stellar efforts with you."

"Send me the agreement and I'll sign it as soon as I get it."

"There was something you wanted to speak with me about?" Benedict prompted Kress.

"There's no point in that conversation until you can share the terms of the settlement with me."

"I see. I'm e-mailing the NDA to you now."

Kress chuckled without much warmth. "Aren't you eager to crow?"

Benedict laughed. "Why keep good news bottled up, I say. Did you get my e-mail?"

"Yes. Give me ten minutes. I'll send an executed copy to you, then call you back."

<hr />

"Hope you're sitting down," said Benedict when Kress called him back. "Here are the terms: twenty percent of unrestricted stock and the poison pill provision I wanted."

"You understand it's Kress Rubinoff's position that half of those shares are ours," Kress said, his voice betraying no agitation.

"That's one point of view."

"If that's the attitude you're taking, you'd better lawyer up again. We intend to come after you for those shares, or whatever they're worth after the IPO. In fact, the team is in the process of drafting the arbitral demand as we speak. Thanks for asking for unrestricted shares, by the way. Makes getting them from you that much easier."

Benedict took his time responding. He lit a cigarette and reclined in his chair so that it balanced on its two hind legs.

"Before you file the demand, let's meet in person and try to solve this situation amicably."

He could hear the smile in Kress's voice. "Excellent idea. How does May 23 at 11 a.m. work for you? I need to be in New York that day anyway, so I'll save you the trip down here."

"Looking forward to it."

<hr />

After ending the call, Kress picked up his coffee mug, poured a refill in the kitchen, and headed to the roof of the building. He wanted to enjoy a few minutes of peace in the warm air of a DC spring day before returning to work. He sat in the sunshine, expecting to savor the satisfaction of knowing that he'd made Benedict quake in his shoes. He had no doubt that having experienced litigation Kress Rubinoff style as a client, Benedict was now sweating bullets at the prospect of being on the receiving end of their efforts. Instead, though, he frowned and wondered why the other side in *Vickers v. Gardiner* folded so quickly. It didn't add up, despite the good evidence that his team had uncovered and that R.J. had undoubtedly used. If he was advising the defendants, he would have told them that those documents were damaging, but that they weren't the end of the world. And whatever else he thought of Brendan Ogden, he'd never thought him to be less than a brilliant lawyer.

Kress shrugged. What difference did it make how it all came to be? The more time he spent in this business, the more he was amazed at the twists and turns that cases took. There was no point in looking a gift horse in the mouth. Benedict got the deal that he wanted, and in a few days the Kress Rubinoff partnership would have an unheard-of profit for a law firm fiscal year.

———— ⟫⟪ ————

That same day, Olga called Professor Hoffmeyer. "I don't know if you heard, but the litigation has settled."

"No, I didn't know."

"Did you get the documents I pointed you to?"

"Yes. I opened and printed a lot of other documents, too, as you suggested, so they wouldn't know what I was looking for. I'm analyzing what I found now, but at first glance it looks horrifying!"

"You have provided the Justice Department access to these documents, as we discussed, right?"

"Of course."

"And you'll honor our deal? You'll sit on this information for the next couple of weeks until my colleague has a chance to write the article and line up the press for it?"

"Yes, yes. I'll not say a word about this until you give me the signal. But remember that our deal is mutual. You will give me credit for finding this information, too."

Olga rolled her eyes; the man was such a publicity hog. But she was careful to keep her voice neutral when she answered, "Absolutely. You'll be given star billing in Anne's article."

"Any chance I can read it before it publishes?"

"Probably not the whole article because it's such a tight schedule and Anne will be working on it right up to deadline, but she'll send you any excerpts in which you're mentioned. Would that be okay?"

"Yes, of course. Thank you for involving me in this project."

"Oh no, Professor Hoffmeyer. We should be thanking you."

Chapter 44
May 23

The day after the Sliema shares were transferred to Benedict and R.J. Drummond filed a stipulated motion to dismiss the action in Delaware's Chancery Court, Benedict arrived at Kress Rubinoff's New York office.

The Kress Rubinoff partnership was in a cautiously celebratory mood. Kress was keeping his partners apprised of every twist and turn in the Benedict Vickers fee saga, and the e-mail he sent that morning explained that Benedict was coming in to discuss settlement and attached a memo prepared by Jeff Thompson summarizing the most recent Wall Street estimates of Sliema's worth. They ranged from the rosy to the glitteringly golden. If Kress were able to negotiate even half the fee owing them under the retainer agreement, it was going to be a handsome payday for a case that had turned out not to have taken that much work after all.

Benedict had chosen to dress well for the occasion, his attire standing in stark contrast to the wrinkled, off the rack suit worn by his host. His tropical wool suit in charcoal grey pinstripe was custom tailored and fit him perfectly, showing just the right amount of broadcloth white cuff fastened by platinum and agate cufflinks. He wore what looked to be his school tie, and his dark brown loafers were burnished to a dull gleam.

After some preliminary pleasantries, the two men settled at the table in a small conference room. Benedict opened the slim leather briefcase he'd brought with him, took out some papers, and smiled at Kress. "First allow me to pay you for all the expenses that Kress Rubinoff incurred on my behalf." Benedict took one of the papers in front of him and handed it to Kress. It was a check for $672,126.90.

Kress put his reading glasses on, reviewed the number, and looked up in confusion. "I don't understand. Our costs were far higher than this, as the monthly bills we've been sending you indicate. And our agreement states that in the event we recover more than two percent of Sliema stock, we won't count the expenses at all and our compensation will be a straight fifty percent of the total. This check makes no sense under either scenario."

"Let me explain then." Benedict said. "As your bills came in, I took the initiative of calling every vendor you listed on them to get duplicate copies of the bills they'd been submitting to you. Would you believe your accounting department routinely overcharges your clients by 500% for every bill? I'm sure you're too shocked for words at such blatant usury."

A muscle spasmed in Kress's left cheek. "We have internal expenses processing these bills and supervising the vendors. If you have a problem with our billing practices, you can take it up with the ethics boards of the bars in the states in which we practice."

Benedict raised his hands in a conciliatory gesture. "I'd rather solve our differences amicably. I totaled the vendor bills and given you a twenty-five percent premium for your internal expenses." He pushed a stack of papers toward Kress. "Here are the copies of the bills along with my calculations. Do let me know if I made an arithmetical error somewhere along the line and I'll rectify it."

Kress was making heroic efforts to stay calm. He took off his reading glasses and fixed his gaze on Benedict. "We'll sort this out later. Obviously, our attorney-client relationship has gotten off the rails and we don't like each other all that much. That's okay. These things happen, and I'm philosophical about it. As long as you pay me what you owe for my work, I'll still consider it to have been a pleasure to work on your case."

"All commendable sentiments, but here's the rub. I don't really want to pay you for your work. I fired you before the conclusion of the case, and according to the retainer agreement, I owe you nothing." Benedict sat back and laced his fingers over his midsection. "As a matter of principle, I find it difficult to stomach that I should be handing over ten percent of Sliema for less than six months of work and a settlement that was eventually negotiated by a different attorney, despite your best efforts to stop it from being negotiated at all."

"This is bullshit!" Kress quickly regretted losing control. He took a couple of breaths before continuing. "We had an agreement. You weren't coerced into signing it, and you had every opportunity to consult another lawyer before agreeing to its terms. We did our best on your behalf, but your behavior clearly shows that you acted and continue to act in bad faith."

"Let's just think the situation through for a moment, shall we?" Benedict's evident refusal to get ruffled tested Kress's ability to stay collected, let alone civil. "Here's my proposal. I'll let you buy the 10% for ten million a percentage point. As you probably can imagine, there's now a bidding war for my shares. Not an hour goes by without an e-mail or a phone call from some money manager somewhere trying to get in before the IPO, so you won't have a problem selling yours at a profit. I will tell you, though, that your best bet is Correx, because they want to be majority owners. They're willing to pay thirteen million a percentage point. So if you buy me out at ten and sell to Correx at thirteen, you'll make tens of millions in a day. Or you'll have an opportunity to make an even bigger fortune once Sliema IPOs.

"I'm giving you the option of buying these shares at a discount as the cost of avoiding the arbitration. I'm not going to pretend that arbitrating against you would be pleasant. No, I'm fully aware that it would be a disruptive shit storm and a massive inconvenience to my life. I'd prefer to avoid it if possible.

"Alternatively, I could sell my shares to Correx myself and give you five million in cash to reimburse you for all your hard work. Those are your options. The option that's not on the table is you getting any percentage of Sliema for free. My position isn't even a clear breach of contract at this point, but even if it were, there's something in your ethics rules that states your remuneration should be proportional to the amount of work you've done. As much as I'd hate to go to arbitration, I will do it if you continue to insist on getting your hands on Sliema stock without paying for it. And if we do go to arbitration, I'll make sure it's as protracted and painful as possible for you. By all means, let's argue about what less than six months of time on your part is worth in terms of Sliema stock, especially when your exorbitant billing practices are brought into the equation."

Kress got up and walked over to the credenza, where the refreshments for their meeting were arranged. He selected a can of seltzer from the ice bucket and popped it open. He'd never felt more inclined to be physically violent with a client than at that moment.

He turned to Benedict and snapped, "Get out of my office. You're nothing but a common grifter, a small-time, cheap con man."

Benedict got up to leave, still maddeningly calm. "Aren't you even a touch curious why I'm doing this?"

"You mean there's a reason beyond your plain greed and lack of morals?"

"I'm glad you asked. Yes, there is. Call it a social experiment. A friend and I have a bet about which way you'll go. Here's my honest, unvarnished, your-best-interests-at-heart advice, which is also going to win me the bet, incidentally: let me give you the five million in cash." Benedict picked up his briefcase and buttoned his suit jacket. "But you probably can't make a decision about this without discussing it with your partners. Let me know how you wish to proceed by the weekend or I'll be forced to make the choice for you, and that would ruin the fun for everybody."

———«◎»———

After Benedict left, Kress sat down, thinking through the choices before him. Soon, however, he decided to seek Jack Rubinoff's advice and dialed his direct line in Washington DC.

"Why am I not hearing fanfares blaring and drums beating for the conquering hero?" Jack asked. "Haven't you just met with Vickers?"

"Conquering was part of my plan. He, apparently, has other plans. He's refusing to honor the retainer agreement."

"What was the point of meeting with you then?"

"He gave me a check for less than 700 grand for our out-of-pocket expenses and told me that we have a choice of either buying the shares he owes us, or him selling them to Correx and giving us five million. We're to let him know by the weekend."

"We can go after him through a binding arbitration."

"True. But it'll take a couple of years, and by then Sliema will have IPO'd, the shares will have changed hands many times, and who knows how much of the money Benedict will have made would be frittered away. He strikes me as a spendthrift and I wouldn't be surprised if he were judgment-proof in very short order."

"If that's a real concern, then we should simply take the five million and be done with it. It's not a bad payout for, what, five months of work?"

"We should leave hundreds of millions on the table?"

"They aren't real right now, Martin, you know that.

Anything can happen between now and the IPO."

"Gardiner and Correx would have never agreed to the poison pill provision if they had the slightest hesitation about the IPO. If they don't become public in less than three months, Benedict automatically assumes ownership of their patents. He will have effectively killed Sliema and their entire investment with it. Yet they're holding on to their Sliema stock even though they could unload some of it now, and Correx, at least, is trying to buy even more."

Kress heard Rubinoff sigh and visualized the sad headshake that accompanied the sound. "We've known each other a long time, Martin, and I know that when I hear you speak this way, you've made up your mind. I'll be the first to admit that your competitiveness and drive have built this firm into something much bigger than I could ever have dreamed of, but those traits have also led us into some seriously risky ventures lately."

Kress squared his shoulders at the challenge in his old friend's words. "You know the drill, Jack. If you think you can do a better job leading this firm, challenge me for the position of managing partner."

"Will you relax? No one's challenging you for the leadership," said an irritated Rubinoff. "I'm just trying to be the voice of reason. Let me ask you this. If there are hundreds and hundreds of millions to be had within three months, why is Vickers selling his shares now?"

"Because he needs the money now. And he definitely strikes me as someone who doesn't see the value of delaying gratification. I told you how he went behind my back and forced this settlement. Who knows what kind of deal we would have gotten if we had kept going through the depositions? We had nothing to lose. Benedict couldn't hurt our case even if he tried, but they could have made all kinds of admissions and driven the value of the settlement even higher. But he couldn't wait."

"I still think that five million is a lot of money. If Vickers writes us that check and it clears we could consider ourselves well rid of a bad situation."

"I'll be damned if I take five million when the most conservative estimate puts the value of the shares he owes us at more than fifty times that amount after the IPO."

"So you're inclined to buy the shares from him?"

"Yes. I'm sure I can bargain with Benedict for a lower price than the 10 million per percentage point he's asking for. He seemed to throw it out as just an idea. Obviously, we'll have to get the partnership's approval, because I'm going to use our cash reserves and our line of credit for the buy."

"I'm sorry, Martin, but this is where I draw the line. I can't support the use of the firm's resources for speculation. You want to raid your own private investments and see if others want to join you? Great. But the line of credit is for financing real litigation, not a Vegas-style gambling spree."

"I'm calling a general partnership meeting for tomorrow evening here in New York. I'll make sure you have an opportunity to present your point of view."

"I'm telling you right now that if I don't prevail and if the majority backs you, I will resign."

Kress paused. He knew his next words could end a thirty-five year friendship that began in law school and had endured through the peaks and troughs of building their firm. "I'll be sad to see you go, Jack. But my first responsibility—no, my only responsibility as managing partner—is to maximize the profitability of the partnership. It's not in my job description to coddle hurt egos or to make this a nice, friendly place to work. The only thing that keeps us together as a firm is money. We need to post bigger numbers every year or else the likes of Tajerian, and Gorsky, and Wilson will walk, and you know it. And I'll be damned if I give other firms an opening to poach our most profitable partners by playing timid and leaving huge sums of money on the table." Kress was shocked to realize that he was pleading. He hadn't understood just how important Jack's approval was to him until that moment.

"Maybe they should walk," Jack said quietly. "A great firm should be more than a collection of money-hungry, self-centered egomaniacs. But that's what we've become. That's the reputation we've earned among our associates. Do you know they're actively encouraging their friends not to apply here as laterals even though we have a recruitment bonus program? Our associates are leaving money on the table to save their friends from coming here."

"Associates are fungible, but rainmakers are not. You can be the best lawyer in the world, but if you can't sell, you won't eat."

"Oh, come on, Martin! We're so far away from not eating that it's not even funny."

Kress paused again. The conversation exposed a rift that had been threatening his relationship with Rubinoff for at least a decade now, but that thus far they had been able to paper over. He now understood that they couldn't avoid the subject any longer. "You and I are on two different sides of a chasm."

"Yes, we are. And if you decide to put your proposal to the partnership, you might find that I'm not the only person who's willing to walk away. Then where will your theory about this move being necessary to keep us together be?"

"Perhaps it'll be for the better. I bet that if anyone else chooses to leave, it'll be the dead weight."

"Then we have nothing further to discuss. In fact, I don't even think I need to be at the meeting in New York tomorrow. You'll have my resignation letter on your desk within the hour."

"Jack, wait." Martin stopped himself. He was speaking to dead air.

⸻ ❖ ⸻

After leaving the meeting with Kress, Benedict walked in the general direction of his townhouse. His path took him along Madison Avenue, where he stopped before the window display at Asprey's, then went into the store. He emerged fifteen minutes later carrying a small bag and a receipt for $60,000 in his wallet.

When he entered Central Park, where traffic noise was less audible, he called William.

"I think he would have decked me had I stayed a couple of minutes longer," he said after recounting his meeting with Kress.

William chuckled. "I've had that same desire myself on

a few occasions. Especially since agreeing to help you with this half-witted exercise of yours. Which way do you think he'll go?"

"I've no doubt he'll buy the shares. He'll probably try to bargain with me first, but he will buy them." Benedict lit a cigarette and watched the exhaled smoke curl up and away from him. "It's almost over."

"Almost being the key operative word, so keep your guard up."

"I intend to. No worries at this end."

Chapter 45
May 24

Martin Kress surveyed the assembled partnership of Kress Rubinoff, who had gathered in a ballroom at the Waldorf Astoria rented for the occasion. He felt a twinge of panic. Attendance seemed unusually light for an all-partner meeting. He did a rough head count and came up with only about 120 partners out of the full roster of 177. One hundred and seventy six, he corrected himself, as he remembered that Jack Rubinoff made good on his threat and resigned the day before.

But his superstar rainmakers were all there. Even if Jack tried to split the firm and get some of the partners to come with him, he hadn't yet been able to convince them to follow him.

He brought the meeting to order. "I've called a general partnership meeting because the firm is facing an extraordinary situation. Whatever we decide here tonight will affect the compensation of every one of you. I feel it's a decision that must be taken by the whole partnership rather than by the one or two relevant committees ordinarily responsible for such matters.

"As you know, we achieved a great result for our client, Benedict Vickers, in the Vickers v. Gardiner matter. But as you also know, sometimes the more successful the outcome, the less the client sees the hard work that went into achieving the outcome and the less he is willing to pay. What are you going to do?" Kress shrugged to indicate that *that was life*. A murmur of laughter rose in the audience as each partner recalled his or her own battles to get clients to pay their bills.

"Benedict Vickers is in a class by himself in that regard. I've no doubt he acted in bad faith when he fired us right before settling in order to get out of honoring the bargain he struck with us. But even now, facing a bitter arbitration battle against us, he refuses to part with any of the shares he owes us. On the other hand, he has magnanimously offered to let us buy what's ours at a discount to the current market price." The audience murmured again, but this time without the laughter.

Kress recounted the options available to the partnership, which were greeted with rapt silence as the partnership waited for Kress's opinion.

"I think we should bite the bullet and buy the shares. It's a short-term commitment of our resources that will have us investing alongside Peter Gardiner. Whatever we all may think of him, the man has an unbroken chain of picking blockbuster investments." Private conversations broke out in the partnership. Kress raised his arms to ask for silence. "We're sitting on some pretty sizeable cash reserves, and we have an untapped line of credit. If we agree to use it, we'll all share in the profits from this venture equally. And each of you is welcome to buy in for a greater share with your own money."

Paul Anderson stood even before Kress finished speaking. He was shaking his head emphatically. "With all due respect, Martin, the cash reserves and the line of credit are there to finance our day-to-day operations and contingency litigation. We have seven of those going on right now and most are expense-intensive. Our burn rate on the patent cases alone will be between four and five million per month for the next six months."

Kress didn't hide his annoyance at the interruption. "Do the math, Paul. We use this money for less than three months and we get a ten-fold return."

"Funny, that sounds similar to the argument you advanced during your presentation to the contingency committee that got us to approve taking on the Vickers case in the first place. It sounded too good to be true then, and it sounds too good to be true now. I won't be signing on to the responsibility of repaying a $50 million line of credit for this exercise in venture capitalism. That's not who we are and that's not what we know."

"It's a majority vote, Paul. You'll be bound with the rest of us if the majority decides to do this."

"No, Martin. I'll leave the firm if this folly is approved. But maybe you can spin that as a good thing, one less snout at the trough for when the bounty from Sliema's IPO materializes."

"This is not a pie-in-the-sky scenario, Paul. Not only is

Peter Gardiner heavily invested in Sliema, but Correx is willing to pay a high premium for the Vickers shares right now."

Anderson smirked. "Who's your source? Benedict Vickers? The guy who swindled us out of our fee and is now about to make a killing on our collective greed?"

"Give me some credit. I've had sources within Correx confirm that they are willing to buy shares at thirteen million per one percent."

"But…"

"Paul, I'm going to cut you off now." Martin raised his voice slightly. "We can go in circles all night on this but I think we all have a clear understanding of the options available to us." He raised his gaze to signal that his next comment was directed at the entire audience. "I've had a ballot prepared with the four choices that I've outlined—buy the shares and hold them until the IPO, buy the shares and sell them to Correx immediately, take a cash payment, or arbitrate the original agreement. If you go with the buy-in option, there's a second section asking whether you authorize the use of the cash reserves and the line of credit for this purpose. Let's break for dinner so you can discuss this before you vote."

⸺ ◆ ⸺

When the ballots were counted, 102 of the partners were in favor of buying Sliema shares and keeping them through the IPO. Twenty-one were in favor of taking the five million payment. No one was in favor of buying the shares and selling them to Correx, and only one was in favor of arbitration as called for in Benedict's retainer agreement.

As the partners filed out of the hotel ballroom, Barbara Wilson, a financial litigation expert who had never lost a trial and had been a top five rainmaker for Kress Rubinoff for the previous seven years, asked to speak with Kress privately.

"I'm afraid I'll be tending my resignation, Martin," Barbara said when the two found a quiet corner. "For what's it worth, I think you're absolutely right about the financials and that Kress Rubinoff will make a killing on its gamble. But I'm worried that it sets a very bad precedent for the future. I was the partner who thought we should arbitrate the original retainer contract because I think clients should be held to the bargains they've struck. I knew it was a throwaway vote because there was no way that would have been the position of the majority, but I thought they'd take the five million."

"You're worried that other clients will learn of this debacle and start playing the same game?"

"No. I'm worried that we'll get a taste for fast money and will be more interested in the next great investment opportunity than in practicing law."

"That's not going to happen. We're dedicated lawyers."

"Perhaps. But there's nothing law-related in us buying into Sliema. It's no different than buying into a prospecting pool on a tip that there's gold in them thar hills."

"Please reconsider your decision, Barbara. This windfall will allow us to take on more of the types of cases you've been wanting to do: civil rights, pro bono, that sort of thing."

Barbara looked away and blinked rapidly. "This is not the firm I joined thirteen years ago, Martin. I can't justify staying."

Chapter 46
June 1

William and Claire descended upon Benedict a week after the Kress Rubinoff vote took place. After dumping their suitcases in the spare bedroom and freshening up from their flight, the Ashford-Crofts joined Benedict in the living room, where he was waiting for them with champagne chilling in an ice bucket and all the ingredients necessary for vodka martinis lined up on the bar.

"Jet lag and alcohol," said Claire, rubbing her hands together and smiling. "My favorite combination."

"Shall we start drinking immediately or wait for the fourth horse of the apocalypse to join us?" asked Benedict.

"I vote for holding off on the champagne until Olga arrives," Claire answered, "but martinis don't have the same imprimatur of official celebration so we can start on them immediately."

"I can lend her to you any time you need a reason or a justification to drink." William put his arm around Claire and pulled her closer to him but she wriggled free and went to help Benedict at the bar.

When they each had a glass in hand, Benedict raised his. "Here's to getting through these past eight months and coming out richer, wiser, and still speaking to each other."

William grimaced. "There were some monumental fuckups along the way."

"And yet, here we are, sitting on nearly 200 million dollars and a quarter of a percent of Sliema stock. As uncomfortable as it is to feel compelled to scan myself every time I leave the house, I'd rather be paranoid and rich than carefree and poor."

The doorbell rang and Claire went to open the door. She soon returned with Olga.

"Uncork the champagne! We're all here now," William said and got up to welcome Olga. Benedict and Olga acknowledged each other with formal hellos and Benedict busied himself with the champagne bottle. The two hadn't seen or communicated directly with each other since leaving Friendship Heights four months before.

"I've always wanted to learn to uncork champagne with a sword." Claire said.

"I'm not sure that swords, or any other weapons for that matter, are a good subject to bring up. Olga might remember that she wanted to kill Benedict not too long ago." William laughed.

Benedict handed a champagne flute to Olga. "Surely I'm forgiven by now, yes?"

Olga smiled. "Yes. I'm over the whole thing, now that I moved into a new apartment and the nightmares have stopped."

William raised his glass. "May I bring this meeting to order by proposing a toast? Here's to the memory of Jon Vickers, the man responsible for everything's that's transpired so far and that will transpire in the next few weeks. I hope we've done him proud. To Jon."

"To Jon," the other three agreed.

A silence descended on the group as each honored Jon's memory. "Has anyone got plans for the money?" asked Benedict eventually.

William and Claire looked at each other and laughed. "We have plans, and we have arguments about the plans. I want to start a girls' school in Zimbabwe," Claire said. "I know it's terribly cliché of me, but that's where I was born and I want to see that country get back to a semblance of normalcy in my lifetime. William objects."

"You're making me sound like an ogre!" protested William. "I have absolutely no argument with the girls' school or even a dozen of them. Very admirable. I do, however, have an objection to buying acreage in South Africa and creating a game preserve. And the yacht. Both things you've conveniently forgotten to mention."

Claire kept going as if William hadn't spoken. "William has decided that the best use of the money is restoring the ancestral pile back to its Elizabethan splendor, drafts and all."

"Darling, watch the inaccuracies. I expressly and enthusiastically endorsed the idea of central heating. There shall be no drafts at Crofton Hall."

"William, Crofton Hall is in East Swampia, just north of damn-all-to-do-town." Claire said, then waved her hand. "I'm sure we'll sort it out. How about either of you? Plans?"

Olga shook her head. "I'm afraid of jinxing myself at this stage so I've deliberately avoided making plans. Beyond fantasizing about a trip around the world, that is." She took a sip of champagne before continuing. "I'm still worried about the trouble Kress Rubinoff could cause us down the line, once they realize their Sliema stock is worthless."

"Yes, but that trouble will only be of the civil litigation variety. And we're certainly prepared for all the ins and outs of that beast, thanks to you," said Benedict, raising his flute in her direction.

Olga acknowledged the accolade but continued explaining her concerns. "Still. Kress Rubinoff should never be underestimated. Despite their flaws, colossal greed, and general uncuteness, they're excellent at what they do, and they'll be extra motivated in this situation."

"What's the worst that can happen?" asked Claire.

"They could get a judgment against Benedict for fraud, then try enforcing it. That could be pretty nerve-wracking."

"But our money is no longer in the United States. In fact, it's not in any institution that has a corporate affiliation with an American financial entity. They won't be able to get to it, again thanks to you," Benedict said.

Olga laughed. "Thank Kress Rubinoff's greed once more. They were so eager to get their hands on the Sliema shares that they even agreed to a non-arbitrability clause in the sales contract. Amazing."

"What does such a clause do?" asked William.

"It forces them to litigate any disputes relating to the sale of the shares in New York courts without recourse to arbitration."

"What's the difference?"

"Thanks to the New York Convention on Arbitration that most nation states are signatories to, if you obtain an arbitration award, you can go to a court in any other signatory country where your opponent's assets are found and the court will enforce the award and help you recover those assets. Totally different story with a litigation win. If you have a judgment, it's not automatically recognized and you'll need to go through yet another litigation to try to get at the assets, and that's only if the other country will allow you into its courts. This is one of the reasons why Kress Rubinoff is so big on arbitration clauses in their retainer agreements and why it's such a glaring error on their part in this contract."

"How wonderful for us," murmured Claire.

Olga walked over to the bar to refill her champagne flute. "I can't believe that, by and large, everybody played the game exactly as we predicted they would, especially Martin Kress and the majority of his partners. Correx bidding up the shares was kind of obvious, but managing to separate Kress Rubinoff from its money still feels like a lucky roll of the dice. It frightens me to think I may have as blind a spot as Kress does and that someone else can read me as easily as he can be read," Olga said.

"Of course you don't. You're a highly complex and intelligent creature with no flaws whatsoever." Benedict smiled at her. "Which reminds me, I have something for you." He handed the Asprey's bag to her. "You won our bet, but we haven't agreed on a prize, so I took the liberty of coming up with one myself. See? I remember how partial you are to sparkling things."

Olga extracted two boxes from the bag and opened

the larger one first. A diamond and aquamarine bracelet of an Art Deco-inspired design glinted in the light from the chandelier. She looked up at Benedict in surprise. "You really shouldn't have! It is gorgeous, though. Thank you." She opened the smaller box, which held matching earrings. "And what are these for?"

"An apology for putting you in danger. I should have listened to you and dropped my insistence that we use your father. He was just so perfect, though!"

"So you said, in Istanbul, when I told you that it would be a mistake. Although my objections had nothing to do with what did finally happen. I just thought he'd either never agree to do it or would go off-script."

"You played your part magnificently, though, Olga," said William. "To know these thugs were coming after you and force yourself to keep to your routine and to give no hint that you're afraid is a hard thing to do."

"Please, go on, William. Tell me how wonderful and brave I was." Olga's encouragement was only half in jest.

"Well, you were. As wonderful and brave as my own wife tends to be through our various adventures. That's as high a compliment as I can come up with."

"Oh, good God, just stop!" exclaimed Claire, rolling her eyes but otherwise looking pleased.

Olga closed the boxes and put them back into their bag. She looked up at Benedict and sighed with regret. "I'm sorry, but I can't accept them. It will be hard enough explaining to Brian how I suddenly became a multimillionaire, but it would be wholly inappropriate to accept such an extravagant gift from another man now that we're engaged." She extended her left hand to show off a gold ring with a small diamond.

Claire jumped up, clapping her hands. "How wonderful! Congratulations! How? When?"

Her enthusiasm, echoed by William, threw Benedict's frosty reaction into sharp relief. He put down his glass rather deliberately. "Ah. Brian. He's still in the picture. I keep forgetting he exists."

Olga took umbrage. "What's that supposed to mean?"

"How can you become engaged to someone you've only known for a few months?"

"It's a matter of cultural norms," Claire interjected, "It's quite common for East Europeans to marry after only months of courtship. And there's a study, Swedish I believe, showing that couples who marry quickly are more likely to stay together."

"Whose side are you on?" Benedict snapped at Claire before turning back to Olga. "He's a horrific mismatch for you."

"How would you know?" Olga was taken aback by the vehemence of Benedict's reaction.

"He obviously has a complete lack of imagination and a slavish adherence to conventional wisdom. He can barely afford a chip of a diamond, but instead of getting a cheaper stone that would look infinitely better, he still chooses a diamond because that's what an engagement ring must have."

"Benedict, stop," William said warningly.

Benedict ignored William's advice. "I've heard enough to form a clear picture of the man. He manages a restaurant, for Christ's sake! Why would you ever consider marrying him?"

Olga got up. "Why wouldn't I want to marry him? He's a

nice, decent human being. He loves me unconditionally, he's loyal, and I feel safe with him."

"Congratulations. You just described a Rhodesian Ridgeback."

"Why can't you be happy for me?"

"What a trite sentiment! He's rubbing off on you already." Benedict stalked out onto the balcony.

"When did you become so cruel?" Olga called after him.

"When did you become so ordinary?" he shot back, not turning to look at her.

Olga's face flushed. She apologized to the Ashford-Crofts and turned to leave.

"Come back," Claire called after her. Benedict reentered the room, and Claire stepped over to him and administered a quick, vicious kick to his shin. "This is a preemptive measure so you don't even think of being the shit you can be in these situations," she said.

Olga hovered uncertainly by the door, and Claire walked quickly to her and pulled her back in. "William and I are going to leave the two of you alone. Benedict will apologize, then you'll attempt to have a civilized conversation and clear the air. We'll be back in a couple of hours. Do try very hard not to kill each other until then."

＊＊＊

Olga and Benedict stood at opposite sides of the living room, avoiding direct eye contact, but stealing surreptitious glances at each other. Benedict finally broke the impasse.

"I'm sorry. I was out of line."

Olga sat down on the sofa and started playing with the hem of her blouse. "Congratulations. Claire will be proud of your apology. Do you mean it?"

"Not really," Benedict smiled. "I'm trying to avert the possibility of you crying. I can't concentrate when there are tears." Olga lifted her head and looked at him angrily.

"And when did you see me cry?" she demanded.

"When the tram nearly ran you over back in Istanbul, actually."

"I have no intention of giving you the satisfaction." Olga said.

Benedict turned to the bar. "I cannot continue this conversation dry." He filled two large tumblers with chilled vodka, then walked over to Olga to hand her one. He took a seat at the opposite end of the sofa. "I thought we had an understanding," he blurted out.

Olga was surprised. "Based on what? One drunken pass you made at me eight months ago? Besides, it seems like you have quite a harem of women with whom you have an understanding. One in every port, if Claire is to be believed."

Benedict shrugged. "I have sex with them. Not an understanding. I never promised to be a monk, and I didn't expect celibacy from you either. But I haven't gone off and gotten engaged to some random individual, did I. You can't accuse me of something that colossally stupid."

"Will you donate yourself to science?"

"Why?"

"Because you're one of the oddest people I've ever met.

Were you born this way or has life morphed you into your current insufferable self?"

Benedict didn't respond. He stared out the window, watching a sparrow build a nest on a branch of a tree in his back yard. "You cannot marry Brian," he said finally, turning to look at Olga. "He does seem to be an awfully decent sort, but he's not too bright. He's not smart enough to understand you. He'll suffer horribly if you do marry. You'll be bored with him in a matter of months. And then what?"

"Intelligence isn't all it's cracked up to be. I'm tired of being a nomad and I'm tired of being alone. Brian anchors me. If I lose him, I don't know where I'd find someone else. I want what Claire has." Olga took a shaky breath but her eyes remained dry. "I no longer have a job, and our adventure is coming to an end. I'm going to be untethered from anything or anyone or anyplace, and I won't know what to do next. That's frightening."

Benedict watched her uncomprehendingly. "Woe is you."

"You may find my worries laughable, but they're real and they cause me sleepless nights."

"So your solution is to marry someone you don't trust enough to discuss what you've been doing the whole time of your relationship?"

"That's different."

"'Course it is." Benedict crossed the room to pick up his cigarettes and lighter from the mantelpiece above the fireplace. "Let's work through your problems one by one, shall we? In order not to be alone, you need to find someone as intelligent as I am and as wonderful in all other respects as Brian seems to be. Granted, William would fit the bill, but he's taken. But surely there are others out there, and now that we've defined the parameters of what we're looking for, it'll be much easier to find one of them."

Olga stood abruptly and headed for the door again. "Find someone else to practice your sarcasm on," she said. Benedict heard the door slam a few moments later.

"Well, that didn't go entirely as planned," he said to the industrious sparrow outside his window.

Chapter 47
June 4

Olga met Claire at Madison Square Park for their long-anticipated First Annual Girls' Day of Shopping and Eating. As Claire had never walked across the Brooklyn Bridge, Olga suggested a leisurely stroll to Brooklyn and back, a distance of approximately eight miles. Claire enthusiastically agreed, and the two women embarked on their trek.

Olga hadn't heard from Benedict in the three days since their argument. There had been no calls, no texts, and no e-mail messages, and she was disappointed by his silence. She promised herself, however, that she wouldn't bring up his name with Claire.

"Can we set some ground rules first?" Claire asked as they ambled along Broadway toward Union Square.

"Depends."

"Shopping trumps serious conversation and eating trumps shopping. We break for every food truck, especially those hawking cupcakes or gelato."

"Those are rules I definitely can live with."

"Good. Let's discuss Benedict before we hit a serious stretch of shops we'd want to visit."

"Oh, look! I must try on that cute yellow dress," Olga pointed at a mannequin in a window display.

"Nice try. It's a children's store."

"You have three of them. Don't they need new clothes for the summer?"

"Olga!" Claire stopped and put her hands on her hips.

"Oh, all right," said Olga with less than perfect grace.

"He told us what happened. I'm sorry he was so difficult. In his defense, however, you caught him off-guard with your engagement announcement."

"Well, he caught me off-guard with his temper. He acted as if I cheated on him, but we were never involved in the first place. He couldn't even be bothered to make a pass at me when sober. I mean, we spent a whole night together in his hotel room, working through our plans for Kress Rubinoff and the Gardiner litigation, and he did nothing. He never gave me any reason to think I was anything more than a business partner and, at most, a friend."

"Yet for some reason you chose not to mention Brian to Benedict for nearly two months, and you probably would have continued not mentioning him had he not been threatened by Gardiner's people. That's a curious omission, wouldn't you say?"

Olga colored slightly and looked at the ground. "Benedict still acted like a jerk."

Claire sighed. "Benedict's problem is that he's used to having to make no effort. He's a fantastic friend, but less than stellar in the way he treats his women. But you're different. Believe me, the bracelet and the earrings were the grandest and most thoughtful gesture I've ever seen him make. It didn't occur to him that you wouldn't be overcome and fall into his arms the minute he snapped his fingers."

"Truth be told, I probably would have were it not for Brian."

"If it makes you feel any better, Benedict is really smarting."

"It's just his pride."

"I don't think so. I've never seen him this cut up over a woman."

Olga couldn't suppress a smile. "Seriously?"

"Seriously."

"I managed to make him miserable?"

"Very much so."

Olga's smile widened into a beam. Claire punched her arm. "Olga Mueller, quit gloating. It's unbecoming."

Olga turned serious again. "It's all part of the same pattern. If he cared as much as you say he does, he'd have apologized. And if he were that interested, he would have found a way to keep in touch through all the months since Friendship Heights. He was in constant contact with you and William."

"You know that's different. You know there could have been no hint of your involvement, especially then. If Kress Rubinoff had an inkling that you were advising Benedict, their antennae would have twitched, and they might have realized something was off and not bought the shares."

Claire and Olga stopped at a gelato truck parked near Union Square. They bought raspberry gelato, found a bench in the shade and sat down to enjoy their treat. Claire licked her spoon with relish. "I never told you how William and I met, did I?"

"No. And I'm dying to know."

"Bosnia. He was stationed with UNPROFOR. I went out to write a couple of stories and was attached to his infantry unit. We spent no more than three days together, and he was so preoccupied that most of his contributions to our conversations were 'yes,' 'no,' and 'perhaps.'"

"The strong, silent type."

"Something like that." Claire laughed. "Anyway, I went back to London and got on with my life. About a year later, I went to a party with a boy I'd started seeing then. The place was a madhouse, lots of Sloane Ranger types. Suddenly the crowds parted Red Sea-like and in walked Benedict and William. You can imagine the effect they had on the female contingent. The collective sound of eyelashes fluttering was as loud as bats flying in a cave.

"I knew Benedict by then. We ran in the same social circles, and I recognized William. So I said hello and introduced Oliver, my young man. A couple of hours later I walked out onto the balcony to cool down."

"Let me guess. William followed you."

"Of course he did. What would a love story be without a cliché? Then he said the most extraordinary thing! 'I guess I timed things wrong. I'm sorry,' and walked back into the party. Well! You can imagine just how gobsmacked I was. And he and Benedict were gone by the time I went back in."

"Why do I think you're making a point with this story?" Olga's face clouded.

Claire shrugged. "Points are highly overrated. Life

lessons, on the other hand, are priceless." She got up to throw away her cup and spoon. "A couple of days later, Benedict called and said he was in my neighborhood and asked if I'd meet him for coffee. We met and had a lovely chat about all sorts of things. And then as we were saying our goodbyes, Benedict said 'William loves you, you know.'"

"Oh, shoot me now," Olga interrupted, rolling her eyes.

"I know! That was my reaction, too. I said 'He doesn't know a thing about me.' And Benedict said, 'You're wrong. And I think you should give him a chance. And I most especially think you shouldn't allow convention and politeness to stop you from doing what's right for all involved.' He gave me William's number, kissed me on the cheek and walked away."

"What did you do?" Olga asked, then laughed at her breathless anticipation of a conclusion clearly obvious, considering Claire and William had been married for a decade.

"I went back to my office, stared blankly at my word processor for a couple of hours, called Oliver and dumped him, then called William and told him he had three months to prove to me that I hadn't just made the mistake of my life by breaking up with a cardiothoracic surgeon. And the rest is history."

"As you said, Benedict can be a good friend," Olga observed drily as the two women continued their walking tour.

"Can I tell Benedict you'll speak with him, then?" Claire asked after a few minutes.

Olga shook her head. "No. He needs to apologize of his own accord first."

"If you two ever do get together and the event is recorded and analyzed, it might solve the age-old mystery of how hedgehogs mate."

Chapter 48
June 6

B enedict called Peter Gardiner and asked him over to his house a few days later. Claire and William had gone back to Brussels the day before, and Benedict was once more alone in his home, prowling around the house for the hour it would take Gardiner to get there.

When Gardiner showed up, Benedict noticed a marked change in him since he had seen him in *Les Sans Culottes*. His innate swagger was gone. Benedict surmised that he was still able to fool most people, but now it was only a show—the inner fire that had carried him to the pinnacle had dimmed.

Benedict offered him a drink, which Gardiner declined. "This isn't a social call. I've done everything you've dictated to me. Don't tell me you're moving the goalpost."

"No. I've asked you here to hand over your gold artifacts," said Benedict, pointing in the general direction of the dining table, on which the twelve objects glittered. "I told you I'd give them back to you, and I'm keeping my word."

Gardiner made no move to collect them. "Not sure I want them," he said. "The bloom is off that rose."

"Entirely up to you. You did pay for them."

"You can say that again."

"Perhaps I should explain," Benedict said. "There's nothing illegal about owning them. They're only replicas of certain artifacts that really were stolen and are yet to be recovered. You'll find the goldsmith receipts and the export control documents in the folder."

Gardiner gaped at him in incomprehension. "These are fakes, too?" he finally managed to ask, looking suddenly unwell.

"I insist you have a drink, Peter." Benedict was genuinely alarmed. "The last thing I want is for you to drop of a heart attack or a stroke." He walked over to the bar and poured a Louis XIII.

"Frankly, I'm insulted that you so readily believed I could be an accessory to the theft of Turkish patrimony," he said as he handed a glass to Gardiner.

"But blackmailing and stealing from me is sitting just fine with your conscience."

"I was in something of a bind because I needed both leverage and cash. Making certain you'd cooperate required leverage, and ridiculously expensive plans that my resources couldn't cover required financing."

Benedict took a sip of cognac and continued. "What was it you said to me when I brought you these artifacts? 'Honesty is relative.' So is stealing, I find. I gave you every opportunity to have the artifacts examined by an independent expert." Benedict furrowed his brow, thinking. "But if you feel strongly that I've taken advantage of you, I'd be willing to return your five million. That money has served its purpose, and I don't need it anymore."

Gardiner sneered. "Shove it up your ass."

Benedict ignored the insult and walked over to the table. He picked up a binder and brought it to Gardiner. "The first item is an article that will run on the front page of the *New York Times*, above the fold, the day after tomorrow. The rest are supporting documents you need to see."

Gardiner blanched when he saw the headline. "FRAUD AND COVER-UP IN SLIEMA'S DIET DRUG TRIALS."

"You son of a bitch!" he shouted, getting up and moving menacingly toward Benedict.

Benedict held his ground. "M-1752 causes aggressive cancer and you know it. You know it because my brother told you before he left for the climb, and you know it because Greg Banting told you of his findings in a memo he e-mailed you one day before he was fired. The e-mail and memo are in the binder as well. Look under Tab 6. It was imperative to stop you and Sliema and to do so before you had a chance to sully Jon's reputation"

Gardiner sat back down, deflated. "This is what the last six months have been about? You think I'm some kind of monster that wants to unleash a deadly drug on the unsuspecting public? For your information, I spoke to the Correx people at length about this, and they said there wasn't necessarily a direct correlation between the drug and the tumors."

"You willfully chose not to worry yourself about that possibility. Despite all the evidence in front of you, you pushed to continue testing M-1752 on humans. Your only concern was to get to an IPO and unload your shares before the side effects manifested themselves. Damn the human consequences, and damn the inevitable product liability lawsuits that would bankrupt Sliema down the line and destroy everything my brother stood for. The cancers and the lawsuits won't happen for another five to ten years, so they're no concern of yours. That is monstrous to me."

His words failed to elicit a reaction from Gardiner, but Benedict willed himself to keep going without raising his voice or physically shaking Gardiner into understanding. "The binder also contains the evidence of what you knew and when: That Jon came to you with the results of the monkey experiment and told you that the Phase II human trials had to be scrapped. That you told him that one experiment shouldn't derail Sliema's future, and Phase II wasn't scheduled to start for another few months, so he had plenty of time to go away and think the situation through. That you told him there needed to be an additional infusion of cash and Sliema had to issue new shares. I have the spreadsheet that made it look like Sliema was going to run out of cash in less than a month."

Peter interrupted him. "If you were that concerned about stopping the Phase II trials, you could have gone public. The truth is that you wanted to get rich, and now you're spinning this wild story to square your behavior with your conscience. Which is surprising, considering I don't think you have one of those."

Benedict kept a tight leash on his anger. "That's not it at all. I thought Sliema was months away from the Phase II trials and I needed time to gather proof. All I had was Jon's story, and some of his notes and e-mails. No one, least of all the FDA, would act under these circumstances.

"Then you sped up the schedule. You lobbied the FDA for an accelerated review of the Phase I results and an accelerated approval of the Phase II design. By the time I got corroboration, the damage was already done. Phase II trials volunteers were supposedly already injected with M-1752."

"You're blaming me for things I had no understanding of and no control over. I'm just the money guy."

"Look under Tab 7. There you'll find e-mail traffic between Correx executives, on which you were copied, discussing the need to get the Phase II trial going as soon as possible. Your contribution to this e-mail chain said that it would be good to minimize the chances of adverse effects in Phase I human volunteers appearing before Phase II was complete and the IPO launched."

Gardiner kept silent, and Benedict sensed that he had still not comprehended the entirety of his problem. "You understand that the IPO will not happen now, and once it doesn't happen, because I've kept a small number of shares instead of selling them all, Jon's patents will revert to me automatically." he said.

Gardiner raised his head and smiled. "I'm not so sure about that. I wouldn't bet against Correx's regulatory guys. They're experts at explaining seemingly bad data to the FDA."

"Peter, Bernhardt Hoffmeyer is on the FDA panel charged with recommending the approval of drugs like M-1752. He's had access to all the litigation documents all along. The day after tomorrow, concurrently with the publication of the *New York Times* article, he's scheduled to have a press conference to take credit for uncovering the fraud and cover-up at Sliema. He will also announce that the FDA panel will be holding an emergency hearing on Friday to pull its approval of Sliema's Phase II trials and that the star of that hearing will be a whistleblower he identified through his diligent research, Greg Banting.

"The Justice Department will announce criminal indictments against you and some of the Correx executives this week, too. They'd like to make this into a high-profile example. You'll be charged with fraud and a laundry list of other charges, including racketeering for conspiring with Correx to mislead and defraud investors."

Sweat broke out on Gardiner's brow and his breathing became labored as he reflexively put his hand on the left side of his chest. "Why are you telling me now?" he asked.

"Because I feel some guilt about how all this will impact Jennie and your kids. I wanted to give you a chance to speak with them and perhaps square away any other dealings that you need to. Maybe make a deal with the Feds. Or even run away, if you think that's the best course."

"Okay, Benedict," Gardiner said. "Let's say it's all true. Why did you sell shares to Kress Rubinoff when you knew all this was coming? When their money goes up in smoke, those barracudas will come after you for securities fraud. Why poke a mad dog with a sharp stick? Why didn't you sell everything to Correx?"

Benedict smiled. "I had an obligation to a friend."

Comprehension dawned on Gardiner. "The Russian?"

"Why, yes, Peter."

Gardiner set the snifter on the coffee table. He got up, leaning on the armrest of the chair to steady himself. "I thank you for your courtesy," he said. "I need to go now."

Benedict watched him leave, then dropped onto his sofa in a funk. This did not feel like the triumph he'd been looking forward to for all these months.

Chapter 49
June 6

Benedict caught the last few seconds of the bulletin as he walked into the living room from the kitchen, wiping his hands after washing his coffee mug. The news made him forget all about his wet hands. He slung the dish towel over his shoulder and quickly grabbed the remote to see whether other channels were also discussing this development. None were.

With a groan, Benedict returned to CNN, increased the volume and dropped the remote onto the leather armchair next to him. They'll return to the story soon enough, he assured himself, and walked back into the kitchen. His phone rang just then and he picked up on the first ring.

"Did you see the news?" asked Olga, their fight seemingly forgotten.

"Just caught the tail end of it on CNN. That was unexpected."

"Are you being sarcastic?"

"No. I really am surprised."

"Are you okay?"

"I didn't think he'd off himself. Poor Jennie. She doesn't deserve this."

"Does it change our plans?"

"I don't think so. Although I'd rather leave the country today instead of waiting until Friday. Come with, won't you?"

There was a long pause on the other end of the line.

"Please?" Benedict prompted gently.

"I'll meet you at Grand Central and decide there."

Benedict sighed with relief. "Right. By the information booth in the middle? In an hour?"

"See you there."

Benedict headed to the third floor of his townhouse, taking two steps at a time. In his bedroom, he took a small suitcase out of the closet and checked its contents. It was nearly fully packed, and he decided it only required the addition of toiletries, a pair of socks, and a pair of cuff links.

After quickly showering and changing, he went downstairs and scanned his suitcase and himself for tracking devices with a hand-held wand, silently cursing his paranoia, but not willing to take a chance. Satisfied that he wasn't a walking beacon, he armed the state-of-the-art alarm system he'd recently installed and left the house.

⸻ ◉ ⸻

"Benedict," Olga said, her hands in the back pockets of her jeans. Benedict turned around, a wide grin on his face.

He took a step forward, but she took a step back. He gave her her space, his happiness undiminished. The important thing was that she'd come. They'd have plenty of time to sort out their differences when they were traveling, their disagreements attenuated by the luxury their new wealth afforded them.

He took in the skinny jeans, slouchy brown boots and an oversized t-shirt that made up her outfit. "Will you be traveling as Olga Mueller or as Daisy Fenton today?"

"As neither." Benedict's face fell. Olga hurried on with her explanation. "I see no reason to run away. We've done nothing wrong."

"The use of forged passports? The extortion of five million dollars from Peter? The…"

"Okay, yes. If you're going to worry about technicalities, then we're up a creek without a paddle. But in the grand scheme of things, we've played a spotlessly clean game."

Benedict smiled with some astonishment. "I continue to be equally amused and appalled by your remarkably cavalier attitude to breaking the law. What do you say to taking this conversation to one of the bars here?"

"Sure, why not."

They walked to Michael Jordan's The Steak House and asked to be seated at a table in a deserted corner. Olga picked up the menu and Benedict noticed that she wasn't wearing her engagement ring. He bit the inside of his cheek to avoid commenting.

They ordered a bottle of red wine and fries. Then Olga continued her train of thought. "We made sure that everybody had access to absolutely everything, and it was their choice to review it or not. You've given Kress Rubinoff an attractive way out. And Correx came begging to buy more stock of its own volition—a textbook demonstration that drinking one's own Kool-Aid is dangerous."

"Still. If Peter left a note, who knows what it says? I think leaving now is the more prudent course to take." He poured wine for both of them but didn't drink any. "I didn't think Peter was that fragile."

"His entire life was going up in smoke. And who knows how Jennie took the news. Maybe she packed up the kids and left. He had a close-knit family. If that were taken away from him…"

Benedict pushed his hand through his hair, his anguish palpable. "I gave him a heads up. A chance to make a deal with the Feds, dump his Sliema shares and reimburse his investors, something."

"Look, we're hurting quite a few people. Do you think Martin Kress and his partners will be happy tomorrow? Or the Correx people? Just remember two things. Our goal is right, and everybody had choices. This has been nothing more than an elaborate decision tree. At every point, Gardiner, Correx, and Kress Rubinoff chose the option that would maximize their profits. Not the right thing to do."

"So you'll sleep well tonight?"

"No."

"You will if you drink copious amounts of the champagne that the flight attendant will serve you in first class."

"Nice try!" Olga smiled. "But I don't want to leave. I've known for the last four months how I want to spend tomorrow morning, and I intend to adhere to my plan. I will to get up at 6, pick up two copies of the *New York Times*, and take them to the 'foundation's' office. Mary and I will drink our coffee, read the article, and coo over how awesome a writer our Anne Blakely is. Then we'll switch on the TV and watch Hoffmeyer take credit for every ounce of our work and it'll still feel great."

"William read the final version of the article and positively glows with pride whenever Claire is mentioned." Benedict said.

"Thank you for introducing me to them."

"And what about me?"

Olga didn't meet Benedict's gaze. "If it weren't for you, I'd still be stuck at Kress Rubinoff. Or maybe they would have fired me by now, who knows." She looked up and smiled. "And, of course, I wouldn't be feeling smug about doing cool and righteous things or petrified about not knowing what I'm going to do next."

"Shall I tell you what your real problem is?"

"You're doing a great job irritating me with your diagnoses."

"You don't see any danger or excitement in your future. You're an addict, and you don't know where your next high is going to come from. I'm not being critical. It takes one to know one."

Olga didn't reply so Benedict went on. "You have twenty-five million dollars less taxes. I'd say this disqualifies you from feeling sorry for yourself."

"Money doesn't buy happiness. Oh, God, I *am* the oracle of triteness," said Olga, rolling her eyes at her cliché.

"Money does, however, buy you plane tickets and false

passports. And other such things that one might need to up the fear and excitement quotient in life."

"Are you suggesting I join the Foreign Legion?"

"No, I'm suggesting you join me on a trip to Moscow. I have it on good authority that a certain somebody has a comprehensive collection of artifacts looted from Iraq. Real ones. Don't know how or whether we can repatriate this collection, but wouldn't it be fun to try?"

"No."

"Admit it," Benedict said. "You loved every moment of the chase."

"I didn't sign up for eight months of mystery theatre. I agreed to help you because lives were at stake. And now I won't be going anywhere with you. I need to sort out my life first."

"I see you took the first step in sorting it." He looked at her ring finger.

"I don't think it would be wise to have that conversation again." Olga said, frowning.

Benedict leaned down and unzipped one of the pockets on his carry-on. Straightening, he pushed the Asprey's bag toward Olga's plate. "Please take it this time."

Olga played with the rope handle of the bag for a few seconds, trying to make up her mind. "I hate dealing with people like you," she said, looking up at him. "Why can't you just be a jerk all the time? Why do you have to show flashes of thoughtfulness?"

"I promise to reform on that front."

"In that case, I'll take these as a memento of your last unreformed gesture."

He touched Olga's hand. "If I promise to bring espresso and croissants, may I join you tomorrow morning?"

"No. Besides, you'll be halfway around the world by then."

"I want to be where you are," he said quietly, looking so intensely at her that she blushed and turned away.

"I can't afford to take a chance on you," Olga said eventually. "I don't think I can hold your interest for very long, and I'm not a big fan of heartbreak." She stood and picked up her handbag, then leaned over and kissed Benedict's cheek. "Have a safe flight, wherever you're going."

Epilogue
August 30

G reg Banting walked into the newly-renovated lab on York Avenue on Manhattan's Upper East Side and his eyes welled up. It was a beautiful space with top of the line equipment, from centrifuges to incubators, to PCR machines. Glassware, sorted by kind and size, gleamed in its designated cupboards. Everywhere, chrome shone spotlessly. There were individual stations for ten scientists, each equipped with a full set of digital pipettes, timers, and other miscellaneous items that lab personnel were likely to fight over if made communal.

He ran his hand along the sleek black counter and shook his head. If he were told two months ago that he'd be back in the saddle, running a lab in New York, he would have laughed at the preposterousness of the suggestion. Yet here he was, about to host a celebration of the inauguration of JMV Labs, a nonprofit pharmaceutical research group dedicated to studying possible interventions for obesity and cancer.

"Greg, the caterers are here." Mary Olsson popped her head into the lab, then stood back to admit a parade of uniformed servers carrying platters of canapés, cheeses and antipasti, large vases filled with fresh flowers, and many bottles of champagne, wine, and soft drinks.

Olga came in right behind the caterers and her jaw dropped. "This is nice! And a view of the East River, too. Sure beats the lab I did my Ph.D. in."

"You, me, and 99.9% of the graduate student population," said Greg, smiling and coming over to shake her hand. "The only thing I dread is the first drop of corrosive acid to inevitably drip on the counter and singe it. That first mark will really hurt."

"I hear you. Maybe we should have gone with second-hand stuff to reduce your stress level."

"No, thank you. I believe in starting with a clean slate so I know exactly what's been done and how it got screwed up."

"Before I forget, Benedict executed the agreement giving JMV Labs the right to practice the technology covered by Sliema's patent portfolio. It was also recorded in the Patent Office about a week ago, just for formality's sake. You can now go forth and do your thing without fear of infringement."

"Hello, hello!" Claire called out as she, William, and Benedict walked in. "So this is what a lab looks like. Show me around, Olga. Tell me exactly what we've spent millions on in here."

"It would be my pleasure. Would you like to join our tour?" she asked, including William and Benedict in the invitation.

"No, thank you." William shook his head. "We'll read all

about it in Claire's next journalistic triumph."

When Olga and Claire were out of the others' earshot, Claire said, "Benedict is trying to convince us to help him rescue some stolen Iraqi antiquities from Russia. We are trying to convince him that he's not serious. Given recent history, my money is on Benedict. More important, who are you and what have you done with Olga Mueller?" Olga was wearing a sundress with a neckline that left very little to the imagination, four-inch stiletto sandals, makeup, and red nail lacquer. "Why the transformation from lab rat to sex kitten?"

"Just following in your footsteps. I want to know what it feels like to turn heads occasionally."

"Right. This wouldn't have anything to do with you and Benedict being in the same room for the first time in over two months, would it?"

"Benedict who?"

"Pull the other one. It's got bells on."

Olga changed the subject. "Kress Rubinoff has dissolved."

"I hadn't heard that. When?"

"Officially, only two days ago."

"What happens to everyone?"

"Most will go into Jack Rubinoff's new firm. I wonder how long it'll be before it turns into yet another Kress Rubinoff." Only twenty-seven associates had taken advantage of the fund Olga had set up to provide stipends to those wishing to practice public interest law or move to underrepresented areas.

As their tour was nearing its end, Claire said, "It's fascinating to watch the ripple effects from what we've done. One just never knows what the pattern will look like, does one."

"I agree."

"Going through men's wallets is fascinating, too."

"Excuse me?" Olga's eyes opened wide in astonishment.

"What can I say? I'm a journalist, trained to investigate. I sometimes cannot help going through a house guest's belongings while he's in the shower."

———— ⊲⟨◉⟩⊳ ————

The scientists who made up the original Sliema Pharmaceuticals group slowly trickled in with their families, including Margaret Drewry and her husband. When everyone had a glass in hand, Benedict jumped onto a bench.

"This is a bittersweet day for me," he began when he had his audience's attention. "I'm thrilled to know that a lot of good science will be done here. But I'd give anything to have my brother with us today. By naming the lab after him, we will keep his memory alive, so that the work done here will be guided by the principles and ethics he consistently adhered to in his research.

"I know that you're essentially starting from scratch and that there will be no commercial product for years to come, but rest assured that funding for this lab is secure. Our goal is not to chase publications or grant money or venture capital. It is to solve certain medical problems, preferably without creating new ones. But when, not if, you create a good and useful product, we'll show the pharmaceutical companies that it's possible to make a commercially successful product ethically.

"So join me in raising a glass to Jon's memory and to JMV Labs' future."

Benedict got down and found Olga, following her to the microscopy room. "You look beautiful. The dress really suits."

"Thank you."

"How have you been?"

"Oh, great. Fine. You?" Olga asked, fidgeting with her hair.

"Couldn't be better."

"I forgot to congratulate you! It's Dr. Vickers now, isn't it?"

"Yes, thanks. I went off to a summer house on the shores of a fjord in Norway. The lack of a television or of cell phone reception forced me to bang out the dissertation in one very painful stretch. Did Claire tell you?"

"Yes, she kept me informed of your triumphs."

"Such as they are. Is this how our conversations are going to go from now on? A whole lot of polite nothingness?"

Olga shrugged. "I'm changing—I'm learning to develop a new conversational style. One where I don't ambush people with all my questions from the get-go."

"What would you have me change about myself?" Benedict asked.

"That's a loaded question and I'm not going to answer it."

"Why not? I'd try to change for you. I'd do just about anything for you," he said, then grinned, "I fleeced the partnership of your law firm for you, didn't I?"

"You did, and I never thanked you."

"It's not too late. I can think of several ways for you

to thank me that will be pleasurable for both of us." He watched with satisfaction the instant flush his words produced. "Goodness me, but you do blush easily, don't you."

"Shut up, Benedict. It doesn't mean anything."

"Surely something can break down the walls you've erected around yourself!"

"May I please see your wallet?" Olga asked, causing cracks to appear in Benedict's composure. "That thing in your back pocket," she prompted, "the thing you use to carry money, credit cards, ID."

Benedict pulled out the item requested and handed it to her. She opened it and reviewed its contents systematically.

"If you tell me what you're looking for, I may be able to help," he offered.

"I don't know what I'm looking for. Oh!" Olga snapped her head up and shot him a disbelieving glance, then looked again at the clear compartment hiding behind a leather credit card holder. She pulled a photograph of herself out. "This is the headshot from my bio page at Kress Rubinoff."

Benedict cleared his throat. "So it appears to be, yes."

"They took this down the day I quit."

"I printed it in November."

"Why?"

"What kind of a silly question is that?" Benedict bridled. "Why do you think?" Olga smiled and put the photograph back where she found it, placed the wallet on the smooth surface of the lab bench, and gave it a gentle shove.

Benedict's brow creased as a question occurred to him. "Hang on, how did you know to look for it?"

"That is entirely immaterial to the issue we're discussing."

"I disagree. I told no one about it."

"Some of us might be a touch more curious than others."

"Claire went through my wallet, didn't she?"

"I can neither confirm nor deny the allegation."

"Bugger that! What else has she gotten into?"

Olga sighed. "We seem to be at an impasse."

"What do you want to hear? That I kept your photograph because knowing I wouldn't see you for months was hard to bear? Or that I was gutted when you told me about Brian? Or the biggest of all clichés, that I love you? Why does it need to be spelled out? Surely you knew."

"How would I know?"

"As I said earlier, I thought we had an understanding. I was wrong and for that I apologize." Benedict's tone assumed its old glacial tone, but Olga wasn't fazed by it.

"Besides, you said something unforgivably rude to me. Something that hurt me deeply," she said.

Benedict had a good memory, but it was failing to come up with anything that offensive.

"You said I was ordinary," Olga explained.

Benedict burst into laughter.

"There's nothing worse than that." Her voice contained an unmistakable quiver.

Benedict stopped laughing and chose his words carefully. "You couldn't be ordinary if you tried," he said. "There's not much you can't do, but being ordinary is the one thing that is truly outside the range of your capabilities." Olga looked up at him, trying to gauge whether he was making fun of her.

Benedict had had enough. "Right," he said and strode the three steps that separated them. He lifted Olga's chin and kissed her. After a momentary hesitation, she put her arms around his neck and kissed him back.

"I'm mulishly steadfast in how I feel about people, you know." Benedict ran a strand of her hair through his fingers.

"I know. And I know that life with you will never be boring."

THE END

Acknowledgments

I am very grateful to the many readers of POISON PILL drafts, including members of the NaNo and Algonkian writing groups. Their combined wisdom has plugged tens of plot holes, made the characters more human, and fixed many, many verb tenses.

R. Judson Scaggs was kind enough to share his encyclopedic knowledge of corporate law and some of the war stories from his years as a corporate litigator in Delaware. Whatever errors of law are still present, they are entirely my own.

Both Margaret McGhee and Jehan Aslam Patterson pointed out significant plot-destroying errors in earlier drafts and suggested ways to fix them. Thank you both.

My father, Dr. Moshe Granovsky, did a yeoman's job reading draft after draft after draft, and his comments were invaluable to plot and character development.

This list would be woefully incomplete without the thanks due to my editor, Jane Cavolina. Not only did she provide guidance and a master class in writing, but she was also a great cheerleader along the way.

I also couldn't ask for a more dedicated or talented graphic artist to design the cover than Christine Van Bree, who worked tirelessly to capture the essence of POISON PILL in a single picture.

And finally, I am truly thankful for all those who remain my friends despite months of hearing me lament about writing and publishing. It will be different with the sequel. Promise.

To paraphrase Hillary Clinton, it takes a village to raise a novel.

CPSIA information can be obtained at www.ICGtesting.com
Printed in the USA
LVOW101926151112

307521LV00001B/109/P